**His desire**

His lips trailed down her neck. "I want to take ~~~
Reaching around, he grabbed her ass and pulled her closer so she could feel his desire for her.

Jesse's mouth returned to hers as he palmed her breast. She moaned and arched her body into him. Breaking the hungry kiss, he took several deep breaths to slow his racing pulse, then he held her hand to lead her up the stairs. Kate was finally going to be his.

Only, she didn't move. Instead, she slowly shook her head and breathlessly whispered, "No. I can't do this, Jesse. I can't just do sex."

"What if it's not just sex, Kate? What if it's more?"

Her eyes looked hopeful. "Is it?"

Running his fingers through his hair with frustration, he answered, "Hell, I don't know." What the fuck was wrong with him? He knew it meant something. Why couldn't he admit it?

"Then I can't do this."

Jesse looked in her eyes and saw a fire blazing. One that he'd ignited. There was no denying she wanted him. "I want you to look me in the eye and tell me you don't want me."

Again, she hesitated. "It doesn't matter."

Furious, he raised his eyebrows. "Hell yeah it matters. Tell me you don't want me, Kate."

Her body trembled either from lust or nervousness or both. "I don't want you, Jesse." She quickly looked away.

"Liar."

*"Trust me, this is a book you should be one-clicking!"*
*- The Book Gurus*

# PRAISE FOR THE NOVELS
# OF SHEILA KELL

## HIS DESIRE

"This book is filled with plenty of twists, off the charts chemistry and will leave you on the edge of your seat while reading it."

—Escape Reality with Books

"★☆★☆★ 5-Edge of your seat, Lust filled, Emotional-Stars ★☆★☆★"

—BookwormBetties

## HIS CHOICE

"Sheila Kell has created a stand alone entry that will have readers wanting more!"

—InD'tale Magazine

"Sheila Kell is a great author. She writes a great story with fantastic characters that draw you in and make you feel for the characters and what they are going through."

—Steamy Book Momma

# HIS RETURN

Hamilton Investigation & Security
HIS Series, Book One
*Jesse & Kate*

*Sheila Kell*

Cunningham
Books

*To my mother, Jannice Kay Hollis*
*You always believed in me*

# Acknowledgments

In the debut publication of HIS DESIRE and this updated version, I was amazed at the individuals and professionals who came to my aid, no matter the question or situation. I've made wonderful friends and business relationships I look forward to enjoying for life.

I want to extend a thank you to Kim Engstrom and Mary Salinas for naming the dogs and Lee Harper for helping me remember Baltimore and finding the right location for the story. In addition, I extend a sincere thank you to my sister, Dawn Stanton Tohill, for all of her wonderful ideas and encouragement.

Becky Johnson of Hot Tree Editing has been a miracle worker, and this updated version goes to prove how well an author and editor can work together to create a wonderful story. I am blessed for knowing her.

The day I met Eric Battershell was one of the brightest of my life. I had been toying with working with a photographer and mentioned to him what I was seeking. Within hours he'd found perfect photos for the first two book covers. I am excited that all of the HIS novels will display his brilliant work.

Thank you, Clarise Tan of CT Cover Creations, for stepping in at the last minute after I'd driven everyone crazy on my design ideas for this novel. You captured the idea I had been unable to express.

I, of course, would be remiss if I did not give a shout out to my PA, now author, Lucii Grubb, for keeping me in line. I've said it before, but it's true – you are a gem.

To the ladies without who this wouldn't have been published – my critique partners and friends – KJ Resseguie, Christine Ardigo, Sharon Gibbs and Stacy Nelson, this story would have been completely different and completely boring. I love you, ladies.

And, finally, to those friends and family who supported and believed in me before the book was published, you have my upmost thanks.

# One

THE WOLF WHISTLE didn't surprise FBI Special Agent Kate Ross on her approach to the bench outside the federal building. She shook her head and rolled her eyes at her partner, FBI Special Agent AJ Hamilton. He couldn't go a moment without flirting. He'd done so with her when they'd first been assigned together. She smiled thinking of the bemused look he'd had on his face when she'd pinned him to the floor in response. Now seven months later, they were good friends.

Kate raised her brows and shook her head at him in amusement. "Seriously, AJ, you're going to get a slap or a lawsuit one of these days."

He grinned back and shrugged. "Nah. I'm all charm, Kate. Didn't you know that by now?"

She watched on in disbelief as his wink appeared to have placed a little pep in the leggy redhead's step as she continued on her way, tossing an encouraging smile over her shoulder. Kate expected AJ to jump up and follow the woman, but his butt remained glued to the bench, sandwich in hand.

Smiling, Kate plopped down beside him, finally having a

SHEILA KELL

chance to eat lunch. Although at the late hour, it could've been called an early dinner. They'd spent the day wrapping up a murder case of an elderly couple who had unfortunately been in the wrong place at the wrong time.

She removed the plastic container lid on her Cobb salad and chuckled at AJ's peanut butter sandwich. For a twenty-five-year-old man, he still hung on to his childhood favorites.

"Date of the month?" Kate poured ranch dressing on her salad, silently cursing when she splashed a drop on her dark slacks.

"Month?" AJ laughed. "Try week. I may love women, but I need to be able to hold an intelligent conversation with them." He tore off a large bite of his sandwich.

Wiping, hopelessly at the white stain, she couldn't help teasing him. "When are you going to start eating adult food? Maybe that's why she kept walk—"

"You're charging the wrong kid with murder," a deep, masculine voice came from behind.

Kate tensed, chucked her fork in the container and stood with her partner. Even though she hadn't eaten all day, the thought of food no longer appealed to her. Jesse, AJ's older brother, walked around the bench and stopped in front of them.

He looked at his brother and gave a quick nod. "AJ."

He turned his gaze to her. "Hello, Agent Ross. It's good to see you again." Jesse's patronizing voice, the thin-lipped smile and hardened expression, assured her that he meant nothing of the sort as he stretched his hand out in greeting.

"Mr. Hamilton." Kate tried to ignore the tingling feeling as his large hand swallowed hers in a strong handshake. *Please let*

2

*the goose bumps be from the chilly breeze and not from his touch.*

Holding her hand longer than necessary, he tilted his head ever so slightly. "Haven't I told you to call me Jesse?"

She drew in a deep breath, flattened her mouth and fought not to sigh heavily. She'd also told him to call her Kate. Neither seemed inclined to display that much familiarity.

Not waiting for an answer, he released her hand and cleared his throat. "You're charging the kid with a murder he didn't commit. Samuel's innocent."

Arresting teenagers such as Samuel, who they'd arrested earlier for the double homicide, always broke her heart. But this was a tough case. And his father, a sitting judge, had hired Hamilton Investigation & Security, HIS, to clear him as soon as he became a suspect.

Jesse Hamilton, a former FBI agent himself, co-owned HIS with most of his brothers, and because of his relationship with the FBI deputy director, he'd been granted access to the investigation from the beginning. For the last month, he'd questioned everything AJ and Kate had done, and any evidence they'd collected, going out of his way to annoy the hell out of her in the process.

"We've been over this before. All of our evidence points to him," Kate stated. She didn't state it was only circumstantial evidence. Jesse knew that. As did the powers that be when they'd ignored her request for further investigation.

"Jesse, Kate's right. Samuel is our killer." AJ dropped onto the bench, wiped a hand down his face, then looked at his brother. "Besides, we've been told to close the case."

Jesse crossed his arms over his broad chest, his expression a mask of stone, his hard eyes narrowed. "And you're happy with that? I thought better of you, AJ."

3

Kate sat, prepared to watch these two devastatingly handsome men go at it yet again. She got to observe their dynamics of play out almost daily, and even though they were easily recognized as brothers, they couldn't be more different. However, she preferred AJ's fun-loving, flirtatious nature, to Jesse's serious, aggravating personality any day of the week.

"Of course I'm not. Neither is Kate. But we have our orders."

"You know you're wrong, AJ. Hell—" Jesse pointed at Kate. "I bet even Agent Ross knows you're wrong on this one," he said in a sarcasm-drenched tone.

Kate stiffened and fisted her hands so tightly her nails bit into her palms. "What the hell's that supposed to mean?" She failed to keep the bitterness from her voice.

AJ jumped up, closed in on his brother, pointing his index finger at him. "Watch it, Jesse."

Kate didn't need AJ standing up for her. She'd already shown she would not let herself be put down by this egotistical prick. She could handle *Mr. Hamilton*. She opened her mouth to speak, but he held up a hand, effectively silencing her.

"I have a witness."

Now that grabbed her attention. "A witness to what exactly?"

He shot her an incredulous look, and a sensation of unease dropped in the pit of her stomach.

"A witness to the murder. Someone *you* overlooked." His voice dripped with disdain.

The jab of the accusation hit its mark. She spoke with as reasonable a voice as she could manage, "A witness *you* just so happened to find."

He released a long, audible breath, which she interpreted as a heavy, frustrated sigh, at her. "Yes, Agent Ross. Why is that so hard to believe? I've been investigating crime far longer than you've been. I know what I'm doing. Hell, that's what *I* stands for in HIS."

The man sorely tested her patience.

"Let's go inside and talk about this. Calmly." AJ had tried to play peacemaker between the two of them many times but had ended up acting more like a referee.

"Oh, I'm calm." Jesse's lips twitched. "And I took the initiative for you, Agent Ross, and brought in both the witness and the correct suspect."

Kate wondered if she could get away with shooting him. Nothing major, just a toe. Enough to let him know how much he irritated her. While she was relieved they would get a chance at another possible suspect and potentially righting a wrong, his arrogance rankled her.

On their walk through the park back to the government building, AJ asked Jesse about his daughter. AJ was proud of Reagan, his five-year-old niece. Like any loving uncle, he bragged about how smart and beautiful she was.

Kate could picture AJ on the floor playing a children's board game with the little girl. She'd yet to meet any of his family, except Jesse. She was curious what the other brothers were like, but if they were like Jesse, she didn't need to meet them.

Always the gentleman, AJ held the door open for her. They walked past their desks and entered an interrogation room with a beat-up metal table and four uncomfortable chairs. Her partner humbled her when he sidled his chair beside hers in a show of loyalty. She wanted to tell him not to bother, for Jesse would find a way to anger her no matter how close he sat, but she allowed him to feel needed.

Jesse walked them through his evidence without rubbing in the fact he'd found the alleged killer, and not the FBI. His treating her as an equal to AJ throughout the discussion surprised her. How long would it take for him to turn into an ass again? An ass with her. She caught Jesse's gaze and found herself momentarily mesmerized by golden-brown eyes he'd yet to harden.

Once Jesse finished, Kate's gut churned with anger, and she wanted to blast her superiors. They never should have ordered her and AJ to stop investigating. Had the two of them spent a little more time on this case, they could have found this witness and brought in the correct murder suspect.

"The kid says he was hired by the Facilitator." Jesse picked up his paperwork, and tapped it on the table to straighten the edges.

Kate and AJ looked at each other. *The infamous hit-man.*

The Facilitator murder case—actually cases—was one of their dead-end investigations. He mocked the FBI by leaving his business card at each crime scene—"Facilitator for Hire."

Disbelief at the young man's statement made Kate wrinkle her nose before she caught the action and swiftly assumed her professional face. "You mean a hit-man asked a kid to do his job? I don't believe that for a minute."

"Maybe he's branching out." Jesse shrugged. "Most likely the kid is lying. I'll leave that to you."

AJ nodded and kept his focus on his brother. "We'll take care of it. Thanks for this, Jesse."

"I remember the constraints you have. I believe if you had more time, you would've found the real killer."

Her jaw dropped at the compliment. At least she took it as a compliment for them even though he'd spoken directly to his brother and said, "you."

"As you can imagine, Samuel's attorney is on his way to the DA with this information in order to get the charges dropped."

Kate tensed and suppressed the growl rising from her throat. "What? We haven't talked to this witness or suspect yet."

He closed his briefcase, then frowned in exasperation. "But *I* did."

And there was the Jesse she'd come to know. "And the DA's just going to take your word for it?"

He stood, scowled and leaned over to address her. "Yes, Agent Ross. He'll take my word for it."

A single shot would make her point.

———————

KATE walked into the bar and stopped to let her eyes adjust to the surprisingly bright lights. She scanned the room automatically and heaved a sigh of relief when she saw her friends Josh and Mary at a corner table.

Making her way to the table through the leftover happy hour drunks attempting to block her path, she barely avoided someone spilling a drink on her. "Rylee's not here yet?" she asked, sliding into a seat.

Josh shook his head and stood. "You need a beer, Kate?"

"Sure, that'll be great."

Josh refused to allow women to go the bar for drinks. He

called it manners but Kate knew it had something to do with the female bartender. Smiling at her friend, and once blind date that hadn't worked out, as he weaved his way to the bar, Kate turned to Mary.

"I'm glad you could make it tonight," Mary said with true pleasure in her voice.

"Me too." Kate's frustrating day flashed before her, and she shoved it away. She would enjoy the evening with her friends.

"I'm sorry to have to tell you, but Mark called me, asking me to help him get back together with you."

*The bastard.* Wasn't it bad enough she'd given him a part of herself for a year and he'd betrayed her? They'd been in a relationship, which he'd crushed. No way did she want that again. "What? Seriously? He can't possibly think I'll forgive him after all the lying and cheating?"

Mary grimaced. "Believe me, I called him a few choice words and reminded him he was with you only for the money your parents left you."

Kate chuckled. Mary had been her best friend since they'd grabbed for the same book in the library in their freshman year of college. Mary was her shy, reserved friend, who changed into a tiger when it came time to stand up for her friends. If only she'd be that way for herself. "And what did he say to that?"

"He said." She paused and bit her lower lip.

"It's okay. I know. Because of my problem, I was lucky he wanted to be with me. Something like that?"

Mary nodded, closely observing Kate's reaction. "Yeah, something like that."

"Why didn't I realize it sooner? I can't have children so no man is going to be serious about me unless he's after my money."

Mary reached over and covered Kate's hand. "That's not true. There's someone out there for you. Just be patient."

Josh returned, bringing the conversation to a halt. "Rylee's here."

Rylee Hawkins could always be counted on to dress in the current trend. That night she wore tight jeans and a faded T-shirt. Her light auburn hair dropped just below her shoulders. As a natural beauty, she could have easily joined her sister as a successful international model. Instead, she'd chosen law enforcement.

She carried herself with confidence as she walked through what could be described as nothing other than a gauntlet, with man after man trying his luck. She shook her head each time and continued toward the table.

Dropping in the chair beside Kate, she shook her head. "Good grief. I didn't think I'd make it over here. Damn drunken men."

The sudden loud sounds emanating from the band, as they sound checked their equipment, drowned out any reply she could've made. When they'd apparently tuned them successfully and they didn't need to shout to be heard, Josh beat her to the punch.

"You're just in time," Josh said. "Let me grab you something before they start playing."

The frustration that had lined Rylee's face vanished. "Thanks, Josh." She reached for her purse.

Waving away her action of getting money to pay, he winked and then returned to the bar.

The noise level increased as patrons continued to arrive. Although it was a Tuesday night, a crowd packed the Bayfront enjoying the band and drink specials. Kate searched the room for anyone she knew. Her gaze passed over a tall man with a woman plastered to his body. She stopped and turned back to him. *Dammit.* Jesse Hamilton. The only man to make her seethe one minute and lust after him the next. The last man she wanted to see.

He stood there devilishly handsome, dressed casually in a pair of jeans and a blue polo that emphasized the muscular body his business suit had been hiding. *Holy crap.* She tried to turn away, but was held transfixed by the sex appeal emanating from him in those little things she loved, like the shadow of a beard and mussed-up hair. He appeared to be enjoying himself. Was he actually smiling? He looked nothing like the man she'd been dealing with since they'd met.

He caught her watching him. His smile widened in approval, and he winked at her. Actually winked. To her annoyance, heat creeped up her cheeks. *Damn him.*

Thankfully the lights began to dim, but not before she turned to avoid his knowing gaze. "How was Vegas, Rylee?"

Rylee's jaw tightened and she closed her eyes, then released a long, deep breath. Her eyes snapped opened and she seemed as if she would speak, but then she shrugged as if to dismiss the question. "Fine."

Kate studied her. It wasn't like Rylee to avoid a question. Before she had an opportunity to ask more, and she knew there was more, Josh returned with a question.

"Who's the tall guy at the bar who keeps looking at Kate?"

Kate couldn't resist and glanced over her shoulder at Jesse.

"That's Jesse Hamilton. Kate's partner's brother." Rylee smiled playfully. "He and Kate are *perfect* for each other." She laughed and held her beer bottle up in a toast to Kate. Rylee knew how volatile their relationship happened to be and was enjoying this a bit too much.

Kate shook her head. "Not even close." She and Jesse? No way. She took a long draw of her beer. Sure his eyes had done something that flipped in her stomach. But? No!

"Kate, you should go for it. It's been awhile since you got any."

She almost spewed her beer across the table. It may have been *awhile*, but she refused to have this conversation with Josh.

Rylee leaned over. "You should go for it. Jesse's hot."

Her friends meant well, but this had to be the most awkward conversation to have. "He's already with someone."

Josh picked up his beer. "You're hotter than she is and he doesn't look like he's into her. Well, we can find someone else. What about that guy in the yellow shirt? He may have long blond hair, but he's built and smiling this way."

She glared at Josh until he realized it was time to stop talking, but he kept his mischievous grin when he turned to other conversation.

After several sets of the band playing, Kate glanced at her watch and noticed the early morning hour. Bidding her friends good night, she left, avoiding a final glance at Jesse.

Outside, she rubbed the chill from her arms. Even in early fall when it remained warm, a cool, crisp breeze blew off the Bay.

Her phone beeped. She removed it from her handbag,

entered her password for messages and heard her sister Ariana's voice.

"Hi, Kate. Give me a call tomorrow. We've got a lot to catch up on. By the way, I booked our spa trip, and you are *not* getting out of it this time."

She smiled. Before she could delete the message, a knife-wielding bum, whose stench should have forewarned her to his presence, confronted her.

"Give me your purse, bitch," he hissed, pointing a knife at her stomach.

*Oh fuck no!* She kicked the guy in the crotch, his weapon falling with a clatter. He grabbed himself and fell to his knees with a high-pitched sound emanating from his throat.

Keeping her eyes on the man, she reached down to pick up the knife with her left hand, and he lunged. She tightened her right hand into a fist and came up with an uppercut to his chin. He staggered back. She tossed the knife behind her, out of his reach, and ignoring the explosive pain in her right hand, grabbed his arm, twisted it behind his back, and then slammed his body against the wall.

The bar door opened. A hand came from behind, clutched her arm and tossed her aside before she could react.

*What the fuck?* When did bums start having backup?

She moved toward the new threat only to stop short at the sight of Jesse, now holding the bum's arm.

"What is *wrong* with you? I don't need your interference."

"Well, hell. Here I thought I was being of service protecting a lady," he drawled.

"As you saw, I had everything under control."

Jesse looked at the bum, then released him. "What the hell, Lucas?"

Her mugger turned and looked at Jesse. His eyes widened and his shoulders dropped in a sign of defeat. "Shit, Jesse. I just wanted her purse. You know I wouldn't hurt her."

"Get the hell out of here, and I don't want to hear of you bothering her or any other lady again."

Lucas nodded, then ran down the street, not looking back.

Even in her heels, she could catch him. She stepped around Jesse to chase the criminal but only took two steps before a strong hand clamped firmly on her bare arm halted her.

"No, sweetheart. Let him go."

She rounded on Jesse. After a long pause, during which she fought for self-control, she demanded, "Let go. That dirtbag held me at knifepoint."

"I'll let go if you don't run after him. He's harmless."

Too far away for her to catch, she saw no reason to prolong her time with Jesse. She raised her hands, palms out, in an "I-give-up" gesture. "Okay. I won't chase him, but you'd best hope he doesn't hurt anyone, or I'll put your ass in jail. I don't care who you know."

He chuckled and released her. "What the hell are you doing walking by yourself?" He crossed his arms over his chest. The muscles rippling under his shirt quickened her pulse.

Ignoring his question, she backed away, turned on her heels and took long, purposeful strides down the sidewalk away from him.

He caught up to her, his powerful body moving beside her with an easy grace. "You didn't answer me."

She stopped and whirled to face him. "Look, Mr. Hamilton, you've done your chivalrous act of the day, so you can leave me alone." Kate had no idea why he was bothering her, especially since he didn't like her.

He cracked a lopsided smile. His alluring eyes contained a sensuous flame that almost turned her insides to mush. "Let's start over. It's good to see you again, Kate." He reached out his hand for a handshake.

Kate considered spinning and hurrying away, wishing she could outrace the carnal thoughts of Jesse faster than she could him.

Instead, she controlled her physical reaction to him and her traitorous thoughts of his touch. "Okay. Hello, Jesse. I walk alone because I can take care of myself. Good night." With a brief forced smile, she walked away.

His full and masculine laugh sent warm shivers floating down her spine.

"Go away, Jesse." She groaned when he appeared beside her.

He stuffed his hands in the front pockets of his jeans. "It's not safe for a beautiful woman to walk home alone."

She stumbled over a loose cobblestone. Did he say beautiful?

With impressive reflexes he caught her. "How much did you have to drink?"

Embarrassed, she steadied herself, her face feeling impossibly hot. "We're not going to have sex," she blurted, scarcely aware of her own voice. *Where had that come from?* She almost snorted out loud. It came from her mouth that couldn't always control itself. How she'd kept it in check when undercover, she had no idea because when it came to any other time, the words expelled

14

themselves through her mouth before she fully formed them in her mind, and sometimes they were better left unsaid, or at least said more tactfully. Like when she'd told the worker at the drivers' license bureau she was in a hurry and it was taking too long. Funny how the computer broke after that and it took twice as long.

"Sweetheart, I don't recall asking. But now that you mention it," he said, an easy smile playing at the corners of his mouth.

It took her a minute to regain her senses, wishing she'd not allowed her mouth to run away from her. It was so unlike her, but after their confrontation that morning, the wink at the bar, and Jesse unnecessarily coming to her aid, he'd thrown her for a loop. "Let me go," she pleaded.

His thumb caressed her skin before releasing her arms.

She had to get to her apartment. Something was obviously wrong with her. Maybe she had too much to drink. She quickened her pace down the sidewalk, and he moved with her like a protective shadow. If he thought she couldn't handle herself, he would be wrong, so wrong. He might not think her a strong investigator, but she excelled at kicking ass.

"Do you walk home by yourself often?"

She refused to get into a conversation. After her mouth had already run away with itself there was no telling what she'd say.

Arriving at her doorstep, Kate pulled her keys from her purse and turned to him. She kept all inflection from her voice. "Jesse, thank you. Good night."

He reached a hand toward her. His fingers lightly traced a line across her cheekbone to her lips. A shudder of pleasure raced through her before she froze, not wanting to stop what she knew would come next.

He leaned close and brushed his lips lightly against hers. "Good night, Kate."

The clinking of her keys hitting the doorstep startled her.

Pulling back, Jesse grinned, reached down and picked up her keys, offering them to her.

Fumbling to insert the key in the lock, Kate took a deep breath to steady her hands. With one last look at Jesse, she entered and closed the door behind her, she leaned against it, then reached up to touch her lips that were still warm from his kiss. Closing her eyes, a strange inner excitement like a million butterflies skittering around inside her stomach and over each muscle filled her.

Something about Jesse aroused her, and it had done so from the first instance she had looked into those gorgeous golden-brown eyes a month ago. It rocked her to the core deeper than any other man had. The man was maddening, but she couldn't deny she wanted him.

A LARGE sinister smile slowly spread across the Facilitator's face while observing the interaction from a darkened doorway across the street. The purpose for the night's trip had been to quietly take out the target, but this unexpected change of events screamed for a more inventive plan.

He slid from his hiding place and moved silently down the street, keeping to the shadows, pulling out his cell phone. "I need you to drive in the morning."

Yes, tomorrow his revenge would finally begin.

# *Two*

JESSE STOOD OUTSIDE Kate's door until the click of the deadbolt sounded. What had just happened? He'd kissed her, just a light peck, but a kiss nonetheless. He'd been damn lucky she hadn't slugged him.

A visceral need pounded in him to bust down her door, throw her over his shoulder and take her to bed for days. He doubted the caveman thing would work on her. Frustrated, Jesse adjusted the growing bulge in his jeans. How could she get him this excited so quickly?

His interest had stirred at their introduction a month ago, but he had a rule against mixing business with pleasure. She'd been his only challenge to that rule. He'd thought if he kept her angry, kept the venom in her eyes alive, that it would diminish his desire for her and prevent him from wanting to throw her to the ground, pushing himself deep inside her, riding out waves of ecstasy.

It had backfired. He wanted her even more when her cheeks flushed, her eyes smoldering in fury and her temper flared. Arguing with her was an aphrodisiac.

A shiver of want ran through him as he imagined his hands and lips all over her tight body. His erection jerked, straining against his zipper. He considered knocking, then shook his head and walked away. No, if she answered the door, she might shoot him after he'd stolen the kiss.

He'd pissed her off again tonight. Yeah, she could've handled Lucas, but Jesse couldn't help himself. He wouldn't let another woman get hurt around him, FBI agent or not.

Walking the few blocks to AJ's house, Jesse planned to crash there for the night. Since his brother knew he'd be there, he hoped he wouldn't find a naked woman partially covered in whipped cream on the kitchen table with AJ opening a jar of cherries again.

When he finally made it to his brother's guest room, Jesse still sported a hard-on. He needed a cold shower, but knew that only one person would truly satisfy him—Kate.

He'd been drawn to her with an unexplainable deep need. He had to have her and get her out of his system before he lost his sanity. The beginning of a smile tipped the corners of his mouth. Their case was over so he didn't have to break his rule of mixing business with pleasure. With the little he'd come to know about her, she wasn't the normal type of woman Jesse was used to dealing with so he had his work cut out for him if he wanted her in his bed anytime soon. Challenge accepted.

---

KATE had a dire need for caffeine. Her sleep had been interrupted by sensual thoughts of Jesse and that kiss. She chastised herself for entertaining any thoughts of him further.

Giving her one little kiss didn't make up for the way he'd treated her since they'd met. That decided, she strode out in the brisk morning air.

She stepped into the short line at Morning Grind, her favorite coffee house, and briefly spoke with her friend Nolan who'd just finished his morning run. When Kate reached the front of the line, she ordered a cappuccino with an extra shot of espresso. She considered a third shot, but decided she wanted to be awake not wired.

As she waited, she took a deep breath and inhaled the heavenly scent of coffee beans. The relaxing atmosphere of the café was wonderful. She wished she could take the time to settle down in a cozy corner with a book, her dog curled at her feet and coffee for the day, but she had a hit man to catch.

At least she wouldn't have to deal with Jesse any longer. Their case was closed, and she since knew to never accept an invitation from AJ to any of his family affairs.

She picked up her coffee from the barista and left a tip for the smiling worker. "Thank you."

Turning, a striking woman, who looked vaguely familiar, blocked her exit. Although nothing warranted it, an immediate impression of a unnerving woman flashed in her mind.

Kate's cell phone rang.

"Excuse me." She scooted around the woman.

Once on the sidewalk she reached in her purse for her phone.

"How was your night out?" Ariana asked before she had an opportunity to speak.

Kate took a cautious sip of her coffee, her thoughts drifting to Jesse. She really had to get a grip. She didn't even like the man.

Maybe Josh was right. She needed to get laid.

"As usual, we had a good time." She continued sipping carefully, waiting for the caffeine to kick in. "I got your message. Is something wrong?"

"No. I just have some paperwork for you to sign."

At the age of four, Kate had been orphaned and survived a bullet wound meant to kill her along with her parents. The Rosses had fostered her while she'd recovered. When she'd turned six, they'd officially adopted her and raised her as their own daughter. She couldn't have asked for better parents. Kate had decided she would be an FBI agent early in life. Jay and Kelly Ross, her adoptive parents, never pushed her to work at Ross Communication, as they'd understood her need to join the bureau. They respected her decision and supported her wholeheartedly.

Jay and Kelly had perished in a car accident the past year. Much to Kate's dismay, they'd split their fortune evenly between Ariana and Kate, and they were both millionaires. Their inheritance included co-ownership of Ross Communication, a multi-million-dollar radio conglomerate Ariana managed.

"You really should be more involved in this, Kate. This is your legacy now, too. Leave the FBI. You've caught your parents' murderer."

"Ariana," she turned to walk toward her car, "you know the company's important to me, and I have been thinking about it. When I decide anything, I'll let you know."

The long pause worried her.

"How did your interview with that Richard guy—Robert... no, Richard go?"

Kate frowned. "Ariana, I'm sorry, but I can't talk about it. I shouldn't have said anything to begin with." Kate had made a mistake telling her sister where she'd had to go upon canceling their lunch, but it'd been the third time and Kate had wanted to explain so Ariana didn't think she was just being blown off.

Richard Freeman was one of many men she and AJ had questioned as a suspect on the Facilitator case. A little over two years ago, Richard had been charged with the murder of three men, but the charges were later dropped. Kate had reviewed his case and found that Jesse had been the lead FBI agent. It had been his last case.

She had to admit, at the interview last week Richard had given her the creeps the way he'd stared at her with his beady eyes, but he'd alibied out for the murders. He couldn't be the Facilitator.

They had more potential suspects.

A heavy sigh traveled through the line. "I understand. Are we still set for the spa?"

Jesse strolled around the corner, a phone pressed to his ear, and she felt her treacherous heart skip a beat. "Ariana, I've gotta go."

Too late, he'd seen her. Panic set in. What should she do? Why was she acting this way? It had just been a little kiss. It didn't mean anything, and she was a grown adult.

"No, Kate. You aren't going to back out of our spa day again."

A brief shiver rippled through her. Her pulse skittered alarmingly as Jesse's lips curved into that sexy smile she remembered from the previous evening.

Even though she'd told herself she didn't want to impress him, she became self-conscious about her appearance. Wanting to get an early start, she'd rushed to get ready. Now she wished she'd taken more time with her appearance. At least put on makeup.

Jesse studied her, his gaze intent, as if he was searing her into his memory. The thrilling current moving through her irritated her. This was not happening. Not with *him*.

She made a quick, involuntary appraisal of his features. She didn't want to tear her attention away from this impressive man. He carried himself with a commanding air of self-confidence. His massive chest perfectly filled the charcoal suit, white shirt and crimson striped tie.

Locked in his gaze, she forgot about her phone call with her sister.

Jesse finished up his phone call with, "I love you, too."

Kate froze at his words, dread seeping into her gut. Knowing the caller could be anyone, a sister, a niece... a girlfriend... she swallowed her confusion and the rush of anger—if it was the latter—that threatened to hurry to the surface. Instead, she brushed off his words and raised her chin with a cool stare in his direction.

---

JESSE couldn't stop staring into her beautiful blue-green eyes. The need to taste her still had him on edge. Imagining what she hid under her plain black suit, which had hinted through the tight jeans from the club, made him want to step forward, clasp her body tightly to his and find the closest place to strip her down.

He felt the invisible web of attraction building between them. Her flushed skin and parted lips, damp from her tongue darting out to moisten them, were positive signs she was as affected by him as he was with her.

Jesse disconnected his call and stopped in front of her, his fingers itching to reach up and push back the hair that escaped her ponytail, then use it to pull her head back while he devoured her mouth. Certainly she would slap him if he acted on the impulse.

Her expression of desire exploded into heated anger. He would not be deterred from having her, even though the mission was trouble with a capital T. "Good morning, Kate."

"Good morning, Mr. Hamilton." She forced a bleak, tight-lipped smile.

Chuckling, he teased, "So, we're back to Mr. Hamilton." He hadn't missed her obvious examination and approval. She couldn't completely hide it, even with her civil politeness. There was definitely something between them. Something that had to be resolved. In the bedroom.

"On your way to the office?" He kept his voice calm and his gaze steady. He had to break through the invisible barrier she'd erected between them.

Kate nodded. "Yes." She surprised him by asking, "You?"

"I'm meeting with someone at the coffee shop."

She nodded and sipped her coffee.

A glint over her shoulder caught his eye. *Fuck.*

Tires screeched and adrenaline surged through Jesse's veins. He grabbed Kate's arms, pulled her to the ground and drew his weapon as the car neared and gunfire erupted.

"ARE you all right?" Jesse was covering Kate.

*Son of a bitch! He'd done it again!* Untangling herself from him, she automatically reached for her weapon. A searing pain engulfed her hand, but she ignored it, knowing he'd already slowed her reaction time by interfering. "Damn it, Jesse! Get off me."

"It's too late, sweetheart. They're long gone." He replaced his weapon in the holster under his suit jacket. "I would've thought you'd be grateful for my pulling you out of harm's way. A drive-by shooting isn't a great way to start the day."

Closing her eyes, she took a moment to accept what had happened. "You're right."

He quickly raked a gaze over her body when his expression changed to one of concern. "You're bleeding."

Drive-by shootings didn't happen in Fells Point. Not in this safe neighborhood. No gangs. No problems except beggars from time to time.

Since the car came from behind, she wouldn't have seen it until it was too late. As much as it needled her, she had to say it, "Thank you." Great. Now she owed the asshole her life.

Nolan jogged up to them from the direction of the coffee house. "I've got 911 on the phone. Do you need an ambulance?"

"No, Nolan. I'm fine." Warm, wet clothing told her where her coffee had landed. But it was the sharp painful throbbing that drew her attention. Kate held her hand, one in the other, and blood ran over both from the gunshot wound to her right hand. *Oh God!* Her firing hand. How badly was it injured? She tried to wiggle her fingers and cried out in pain. *Nooo! I have to be able to shoot.*

The woman from the coffee house strolled up to them. "Oh, Jesse. I saw it all. Oh my God, you're bleeding. Here, let me see."

Kate rolled her eyes at the melodrama. Now she remembered where she'd seen the woman. She'd been the one at the bar with Jesse. Was that who he'd been speaking with on the phone? The person he was meeting this morning?

"It's nothing, Elizabeth." He shook off the woman's hands. "Kate, let me take a look at your hand."

Before she could deny him, he reached for her wrist and held it firmly. She flinched as he touched her wound.

He looked at her, pity in his eyes.

Nolan knelt beside them, handing Jesse a small towel. "It's a little sweaty, but it's better than nothing."

"Kate, I'm going to tie this around the wound until I get you to the emergency room."

"Jesse, I can drive you to the ER, and she can ride in the ambulance." Elizabeth glared at her.

Jesse kept his focus on Kate. "You look like you're about to pass out on me."

She hated that he was right. Her light-headedness and fuzzy vision were a precursor to unconsciousness. The red-hot pain in her hand didn't help.

"Nolan, I think I've ruined your towel." Her words slurred. Nolan looked at her with concern. He and Jesse put their heads together, but she couldn't make out what they said.

"I won't pass out, and I don't need to go to the emergency room with you, Jesse. I can drive myself." Why did those stupid words pop out of her mouth? The man brought out the worst in her even when she needed him.

He reached down to help her stand. Hesitantly, she placed her left hand in his and he pulled her to her feet. She gasped and collapsed into his arms as her left ankle gave way. Jesse winced when he grabbed her to keep her from falling, and that was when she saw the blood soaking the left sleeve of his jacket.

"I think you've just proven you're not okay to drive. It won't be so bad riding with me. I don't bite. At least not while I'm driving." He chuckled.

How could he be joking? They'd both been shot. Didn't he hurt also?

The wail of sirens screamed in the air.

"Since it appears your carriage has arrived, you won't have to ride with me after all."

She couldn't fight it any longer. The last thing she remembered was falling into a black hole and hearing Jesse cursing.

# *Three*

AJ ENTERED THE hospital recovery waiting room and spotted Jesse pacing. Scanning the room, AJ quickly honed in on the only other occupant, a bombshell in a red business suit with incredibly long legs. She looked up at him then, with a disappointed look in her ocean blue eyes, returned her attention to her laptop. *Damn, she's hot.*

"It's about fucking time you got here," Jesse growled.

AJ turned to his brother. The bombshell would have to wait.

"Hey, Jesse. How's the arm?" He held his breath for a moment when his gaze landed on his brother's bandaged arm. *Thank God the bullet had only grazed him.*

Jesse grunted. "What are you doing to catch this bastard?"

His brother's surliness amused AJ. Jesse always had to be in control, which meant he'd probably refused pain medication so that he could stay alert.

"Thought you might need this." He handed Jesse a clean white shirt he'd found in the back of his SUV.

Disregarding the other room occupant, his brother changed out of his bloodied shirt. AJ frowned when he turned away in an attempt to hide the wince of pain and the trembling hands buttoning the shirt.

"I spoke with the nurse on the way in. She said Kate should be awake soon," he informed Jesse.

She'd been his partner for less than a year, but he liked her. He didn't know why, but he felt a different bond with Kate than most women. It wasn't sexual. It was more familial. He trusted her to have his back.

"Has BPD come by?"

Jesse shook his head. "No. I told the officer at the scene she was FBI, but he just shrugged and said someone would be here. I didn't argue because I wanted to get Kate here."

"What the hell happened out there?" AJ had been at home when he'd received the call that both his brother and his partner had been shot. Once he'd been assured neither had life threatening injuries, he'd rushed to the crime scene and argued with his boss to lead the investigation. Afterward, he couldn't get to the hospital fast enough. Hell, he'd even parked in a tow-away zone. He didn't care if they towed his car. He had the urgent need to see his brother.

Rubbing his hand over his face in what appeared to be an agonizing gesture, his big brother cleared his throat. "I was talking with Kate when a car raced toward us. I pushed her to the ground, but it was too late." He paused. "The driver was Ed Wright."

AJ nodded, took his phone from his pocket and called in for an APB to be placed on Ed.

With what sounded like a touch of distress in his voice, Jesse spoke, "It's her right hand, AJ."

The distress in his brother's voice had his curiosity piqued.

He'd heard it before when one of their brothers had been hurt. But Kate? They didn't even get along. Then it hit him. *Shit.* Jesse had to know this was nothing like his wife.

"Don't worry. Dr. Harris is supposedly the best orthopedic surgeon on staff."

"This wasn't a gang shooting. Ed's a petty criminal, but he's not a gang member."

"Jesse, the question is, were you or Kate the target. Anyone you can think of offhand who wants you dead?"

He shrugged. "There's a long list of people who want me dead. What about Kate? Any threats against her?"

"Not that I'm aware of, but after what happened with her first partner, she'll keep that to herself if she can."

Tension crept up AJ's shoulders and neck. He could've lost two people he cared about today. Now, he had a shooter to find who apparently had his sights set on one of them. AJ had to protect them, but as stubborn as they were, it'd be a battle to get either to agree to any type or protection because they'd insist they could take care of themselves.

Kate wouldn't have a choice. She'd get a detail whether she wanted it or not. Jesse, on the other hand, would elude any detail he was assigned. The only solution was to call his brothers. Jesse would be angry with him, but at least he'd be alive.

AJ slapped Jesse on the shoulder. "Let's get some coffee while we wait."

---

KATE opened her gritty eyes to an unfamiliar room. She reached up to rub them only to find an IV in one hand and a large bandage on the other. The memory rushed back to her. She'd been shot this morning. Her hand. Thank goodness she was at the hospital.

How did she get here? The last thing she remembered was…. *Oh God.* She was mortified. She'd actually passed out in front of Jesse.

"Kate, you're finally awake."

She turned her head, relieved to find her sister sitting in the chair near her. Ariana put the word beautiful to shame. Any time she tossed her long, silky dark hair over her shoulder, men's heads turned. If only Ariana would stop working so hard and take notice.

With a dry mouth, she croaked, "Water."

Her sister poured a cup of ice water and handed it to her. "Let me get the nurse." She left Kate alone.

Lifting her right arm, Kate looked at the large bandage on her hand. Her heart raced, thumping against her ribs, as if it were about to explode in her chest. How bad was it? Would this end her career as a field agent? She loved her job.

Before panic fully sunk its teeth in deep, Ariana returned with a nurse and a handsome, compact man who walked with a spring in his step and his eyes on Ariana's rear.

"Kate, I got lucky. This is Dr. Harris. He conducted the surgery on your hand."

The man smiled widely, his perfect teeth strikingly white against his tanned face. "Hello, Ms. Ross, I'm Dr. Harris, an orthopedic surgeon on staff at the hospital."

She nodded as her only form of greeting. "How bad is it?"

He cleared his throat. "You were extremely lucky. The bullet went through the webbing between your thumb and index finger, so no bones were broken. There is some potential nerve damage. It's hard to say at this point if you'll regain full strength in your hand." He gestured to her ankle. "The ankle should be fine. You only lightly sprained it. The swelling has already subsided."

Dread crept into Kate's belly. "But there's a chance my hand will be like it was before?"

"It's too early to say for sure, but I have complete faith."

She forced a smile while Dr. Harris examined her hand and instructed her how to care for it. All thoughts of possibly leaving the FBI for Ross Communication as she and Ariana had been discussing, vanished. She wouldn't quit until she caught the shooter. The son of a bitch would pay.

"From what I understand from your sister, you'll leave with or without my permission so I may as well get the paperwork signed so it's all in order."

Could anyone out-negotiate her sister?

He smiled at Ariana and left the room, and the nurse who'd patiently waited stepped closer. "Ms. Ross, there are two police officers waiting outside to see you. I was told to let them know the moment you were awake."

Kate closed her eyes. They were not going to be pleased when they found out she was FBI, and her boss would take the case from the Baltimore PD. "You can let them in."

Two uniformed officers entered the room and almost fought over who would hold the door open for Ariana as she exited the room. "Ms. Ross? I'm Officer Nathan Miller, and this is Sergeant Arthur Watson."

Officer Miller, in his young twenties, average height, lean and sporting a crew cut, looked to be the gung-ho officer hoping to make a difference. Sergeant Watson, much shorter and with a paunch and some serious hair loss, had to be riding it out until retirement, which should be soon.

"We need a few minutes of your time to discuss the incident this morning."

"You should know that I'm an FBI agent." She looked for her purse to get her badge.

Her statement didn't faze Officer Miller. He did at least have the decency to ask about her hand before he jumped into another question. "Did you see the car?"

"I'm sorry, I really didn't see anything. The car came from behind me, and it was out of sight before I recovered."

*Shit.* She'd be put on medical leave. She hoped AJ would get to lead the investigation. At least if he ran it, he'd share information with her and get her involved.

Officer Miller didn't take the hint the interview was over and asked more questions until Sergeant Watson dragged him from the room.

After the officers left, Ariana returned. "The nurse said there are two men waiting for you and one is an FBI agent. I think I saw them earlier." Ariana tossed something on the bed. "They've stepped out, but said they'd be right back to see if you're awake."

Only one was an FBI agent? She hoped that was AJ. Was Jesse the other man waiting? He'd saved her, but she didn't want to see him. Some unexplained, irrational emotion told her to run from him. Still. Icy fear twisted around her heart. They may not get along well, and she'd contemplated shooting him herself, but she didn't like the idea that someone could've killed him. "Was… was the other," she attempted to ask, then gulped, "was he okay?"

Waving her hand and looking around the room as if looking for a specific object, Ariana responded, "He seemed fine. He was walking around."

With anesthesia leaving her system and new drugs entering, Kate's hands shook and she felt weak. "Ariana, we're leaving." AJ would be at her door at some point so she wasn't waiting here.

"I expected that is why the doctor is completing the paperwork. These are for you." She gestured to workout clothes on the bed. "We can't allow you to escape gorgeous men in a hospital gown, now, can we?"

Dizziness assailed her as she stood. She reached to grab the bed and cried out in pain. Kate couldn't believe she was acting like such a coward. *Damn him!* She chuckled. That was probably the pain medication, but it was funny. She was running from him in her sister's running shoes.

Ariana drove her home, and they avoided speaking about her injury and Ross Communication. Instead, she'd learned her sister was dating a banker. It was time her sister found a good man who wasn't after her fortune and Ross Communication.

Ariana did her standard perusal of Kate's apartment. "You know you can live at the house in Chevy Chase. It's yours too. You don't have to live in this small apartment."

"I like this place. It has character." She was able to live off her FBI pay and the small legacy from her biological parents, so her Ross inheritance collected interest and could be passed along to other heirs.

Ariana frowned. "I'll never understand how you can leave what you had for something so small and without a housekeeper or cook."

"We've been over this before. I like this. You make it sound terrible, but it's a nice place in a nice area." Even though they didn't agree, Kate saw no need to take half of what was Ariana's birthright. Her birth parents had left her a tidy sum. No, she couldn't afford the mansion like she'd grown up in, but she didn't want it. She wanted what she had.

"They left you that money and half of the house and business because they loved you. Kate, you're an heiress. You shouldn't be living like this." Ariana waved her hand around.

Kate changed the subject back to the banker. After assuring her sister for the fifth time she would be fine, she convinced Ariana to leave her alone.

Being alone wouldn't last for long. A team from the FBI would appear to question her, give her hell for leaving the hospital, and AJ would certainly be one of them. She'd take whatever grief he dished out to her because it had been worth leaving to avoid Jesse.

Although she'd said, "Thank you," to the man for saving her, she probably needed to say it again since she couldn't guarantee she'd sounded sincere since she'd been upset with him and injured, but she didn't want to see Jesse again. Maybe she could thank him through AJ. No, that was cowardly. She would have to face the man who kissed one woman yet told another he loved them, and thank him. Even if it wasn't another woman, AJ had told enough stories for her to know Jesse was a player. She didn't want to be attracted to him because she couldn't handle more rejection, like he'd be apt to do once he tired of her.

Showing her appreciation. It was the right thing to do. She began to hate that she always tried to do the right thing.

---

*HOW dare she sneak out of the hospital?* Jesse had waited, worried, guilt riding him because he'd failed. He should've moved faster. He should've been more aware of his surroundings. All of his focus had been on Kate, and that wasn't like him.

He parallel parked on Thames Street, then saw her in the park, a couple of blocks from her apartment. Sunlight glinted off auburn streaks in her brown hair, loosely flying around her face. He took a moment to drink in the beauty of her body, the one he'd had to pretend not to notice every damn day they'd work together the month prior. She didn't know, but he'd seen her workout at the FBI gym, and the thought of those long, toned legs almost had him forgetting why he was there.

It suddenly occurred to him that in the workout clothing she wore, she didn't have a weapon at her waist. *Dammit.* Someone might be trying to kill her, yet she stood outside without protection. What FBI agent would do that? He wanted to turn her over his knee. What the hell was wrong with her?

Jesse exited the car and walked toward the park.

She stiffened when she saw him, reached down, put a leash on a Dalmatian and then led the dog out of the park.

Intercepting her, he reached down to allow the dog to sniff his hand. "Who's this beautiful dog?" Petting the dog, he hoped to calm himself. He didn't want to immediately incense Kate, not like he'd intentionally done in the past.

He watched her luscious lips as she responded. *Damn!* He needed to pay more attention to his surroundings than on her. Didn't he learn anything from this morning?

"Her name is Dottie, and she's ready to go inside," Kate responded flatly.

She didn't want to talk with him. Well, she had another thing coming. He wasn't letting her off that easy. "What are you doing out here without a weapon?"

The subtle narrowing of her eyes preceded her answer. "How I take care of myself is none of *your* business. Now, I'm going inside. Good-bye, Mr. Hamilton."

So much for not spiking her temper right away. "I'm afraid it's not going to be that easy for you, Kate. AJ will be here shortly. We have questions for you."

"AJ I understand, but you don't need to be here." Pink crept into her cheeks, and she appeared more adorable than ever. "But, I did want to thank you again for saving me."

"You're welcome. How's your hand?" *Stupid.* He should've asked her about it first.

"It's fine." She waved her bandaged hand around. "How's your arm?"

A smile split his face at her concern. "It's fine."

The conversation lulled and Kate nodded, then turned and limped off toward her apartment. He silently walked beside her, wanting to carry her and take care of her.

At her doorway, Jesse spotted AJ with FBI Special Agent Trent McKenzie, *God's gift to women*, walking toward them. The last thing Jesse wanted was for Trent to be around Kate. Why the hell had his brother brought him?

"The bad thing about Fells Point is the parking. I can never get close to where I want to go. We don't all have your luck at parking, Jesse, and find front row parking everywhere." Trent turned to Kate; his boldly handsome face smiled warmly down at her. "Hello, doll. It's good to see you again."

Jesse gritted his teeth when she didn't slap him for calling her *doll*. So what, Trent called most women *doll*? Jesse didn't want him calling Kate that. Had he and Kate been together before? He did go out of his way to flirt with her at the field office. Were they together now? Unexpected jealously surged through him.

She flashed Trent the smile she'd held back from Jesse. "Hey, Trent. This is Dottie. I hope you don't mind dogs because she's a love bug."

"It's not a problem with me. I love animals." He reached down to pet Dottie.

The dog growled at him, and Jesse couldn't help but laugh. She had taste.

"Dottie!" Kate tugged the leash, pulling her pet closer to her. "I'm sorry, Trent. She's never done that before."

He shrugged, unfazed by Dottie's actions. "No problem."

When Jesse caught Trent watching Kate's rear as her dog led them into the apartment, Jesse envisioned wringing his neck.

They entered her apartment and Jesse immediately relaxed into a warm and welcoming environment, his eyes drifting from the off-white living room set with Mediterranean theme color accents decorating to a stone fireplace. Intrigued, and nosey, he approached and looked at the framed photos on the mantel. One was of Jay and Kelly Ross in winter gear on a rock in front of a rock canyon. The other was of a couple sitting on a beach. The breeze had been blowing through the woman's hair as the photo had been snapped. He turned. "Are these your parents?"

"Yes." His heart clenched at the pain in her gaze. Why did she affect him so strongly?

———————————— —

KATE sat in the chair to prevent Jesse from sitting close as Dottie curled up by the fireplace. Trent and AJ lounged on the couch while Jesse settled in the middle of the love seat. She attempted to look cool, calm and collected. She didn't want Jesse to know he affected her—his close physical proximity made her senses spin. In fact—"I don't mean this to sound wrong, but what's Jesse here for? Has Arthur hired HIS?"

He narrowed his eyes at her, and she fought back reciprocating.

"Calm down, Kate. Someone shot at one of you. I'd like to talk with you both," AJ answered.

Jesse knew more about what happened than she did. Maybe he could shed some light on it for her, which would make it easier for them to catch the shooter so she wouldn't fight it. For now. "I'm not going to be much help. I didn't see a thing."

AJ shook his head. "You know the drill, Kate. Let's walk back through it. Maybe something will return."

She nodded, even though she doubted she'd remember anything new. She walked them through the event, then looked at Jesse. When their gazes locked, warmth flooded her. Then she remembered his phone call this morning, his declaration of love to someone and turned away from him. She wished she had the nerve to ask him who he'd spoken to, but that would imply she cared, and she couldn't afford to care for a man who didn't settle for one woman.

"Kate, have you had any threats that you haven't told me about?" AJ scratched his chin that he hadn't stopped to shave this morning.

She shook her head. "No."

Trent leaned forward, putting his forearms on his thighs and clasped his hands, all business. "Kate, Jesse saw the driver—Ed Wright. This wasn't a gang shooting. One of you was the target."

No wonder they'd included Jesse. She looked at the bandage on his left arm and her stomach rolled over. Was it her fault he'd been shot? The thought brought out a surprising pounding of her heart. "Well, we can go through my case files, and we can go through what Jesse's been working on. I can—"

AJ raised his hand and stopped her midsentence. "We're well ahead of you. And we won't include you, Kate. You're out right now. Relax and spend some time with your sister. You always say you don't get to see her enough." He sheepishly grinned at her and then winked. "Maybe you'll finally introduce me."

She shook her head with a chuckle. She couldn't picture AJ and Ariana together. "AJ—"

"What about protection for Kate? If she's the target, you need to take care of her."

She should be pissed Jesse interrupted her, again. But, was that concern she heard in his voice? Couldn't be. "I don't need anyone to protect me. I can take care of myself." There was no need to waste other agents' time on her when there were criminals to catch. Her right hand may be useless, but she didn't think she'd have a problem with a weapon in her left hand. She wouldn't be accurate, but there were plenty of bullets in a clip.

"It doesn't matter what you want. We *are* assigning you a protective detail."

Kate's heart pounded against her chest. "No, AJ. As far as we're all aware, I have no connections to Ed Wright at all. The last thing I want is to pull an agent from where they're really needed." Ted had been enough for a lifetime. No one else.

The men stood.

AJ shrugged nonchalantly. "They'll still be there, whether you want it or not."

Kate ran her good hand through her hair. It was protocol, so he wasn't going to change his mind. It would only be a few days. She planned to go back to the office as soon as possible. She'd survive deskwork while she healed. They had too many cases to work for her to lie around like a princess. Her priority was her shooter. He needed to be removed from the streets.

"Okay, but no one stays in my apartment. They have to remain outside. No one steps in front of me."

AJ opened his mouth to speak.

"Otherwise I'll fight you on this, AJ."

Kate heard the weighty sigh escape AJ's lungs. "I'm sure you will anyway. No one in your apartment. I won't promise anything else."

"Promise you'll keep me updated?"

The glow of his boyish smile warmed the room. "That I will."

Kate ushered the men to the door, but it was too late when she realized Jesse had hung back.

Instead of following the men outside, he walked to the door, held it and then turned to her. "Would you like to watch an O's game with me tomorrow night?"

"I don't think that'd be a good idea. I heard you tell someone on the phone that you love them."

He nodded. "I did."

Okay, since she was too chicken to ask outright who it was, she needed to make herself clear. "I don't mess with men who are involved in another relationship."

He flashed an irresistibly devastating grin. "That's good to know. I don't mess with women who are involved in another relationship." He winked. "I'll be over at six o'clock with dinner, popcorn, and beer."

Jesse closed the door behind him before she could form a response. He could show up at six all he wanted. But she'd show him the door.

# *Four*

THE FACILITATOR SLAMMED his fist down on the desk in front of him. He hated failure. She'd survived.

This had been his first time using a drive-by shooting to murder someone. It had been thrilling watching people all over the street duck for cover. It had been a shame he hadn't been aiming at them.

*Dammit.* He should've been successful. How could he have foreseen that Jesse would be there to save her? The Facilitator had watched Kate for days and knew her morning routine by heart. He'd had her in his sights. She should be dead. Jesse should be mourning right now.

The Facilitator stood and walked from behind his large oak desk, crossed his office to the bar and poured himself another drink. He looked around the paneled room and couldn't summon the pride he'd once held. He'd worked hard to have a successful, legitimate business to keep one step ahead of the law, to be respected.

He'd make Jesse suffer just as he'd suffered. Jesse had ruined his life. If Jesse hadn't convinced that weasel he'd bought his bomb parts from to give him up, he'd never have been accused of murder. His wife never would've left.

The charges had been dropped when the state's witness disappeared. He'd made sure the weasel never resurfaced. But, it was too late. Jesse had convinced the Facilitator's wife that he was guilty of murder. Of course he'd done all they'd accused him of doing, but that shouldn't have mattered. His wife should've stood by him, no matter what. That was what a wife did. A wife didn't believe an FBI agent over her own husband, no matter what the evidence showed.

He returned to his desk and took a long drink, barely feeling the burning sensation as he swallowed the Scotch. He felt numb. Nothing mattered anymore except revenge.

His wife Mona had been the best thing that had ever happened to him. Now she was out of his life. Eighteen years and she'd walked away. All because of Jesse's accusation.

The Facilitator had tried to win her back. He'd brought her flowers, jewelry and asked her to dinner. She'd refused the gifts and wouldn't go anywhere with him.

He remembered his last encounter with her at her apartment.

"What are you doing here?" she'd demanded upon opening the door.

"I just wanted to see you, Mona. I miss you." He'd handed her the long-stemmed red roses, her favorite. "These are for you."

"Don't do this. You know I won't accept them. We're finished."

The chill in her voice struck him hard in the gut.

"Don't say that. There has to be a way. I love you. I need you in my life." She'd been his balance. Around her he hadn't been just a stone-cold killer. He'd been a loving husband and a successful businessman. He needed her to help him keep that balance. Without her, he feared he'd fade into the darkness and never return, living his life only for his hobby… his distraction… killing.

"You should've thought of that before you killed those people."

"The charges were dropped."

"Yes, but I believe you did it." Then she broke his heart when she whispered, "You scare me."

He felt the tightness in his chest. The last thing he wanted to do was to frighten her and push her away even more. He wanted her to love him like he loved her. She did once. She could again. He was sure of it. "Don't be scared of me. I'd never hurt you, Mona."

"What about the next time someone crosses you? Will you kill him also? Will I be married to a mass murderer? Or have you killed before and gotten away with it?"

He'd killed plenty of times and never been suspected. He wouldn't give up his hobby, not even for Mona; he was addicted to it. She didn't need to know he was still involved.

Mona didn't understand. She'd loved the lifestyle they'd lived. Did she really think it had all been gained legitimately? Everything he'd done, he'd done for her.

"I'm serious, don't come back here. I don't ever want to see you again." She'd shut the door in his face.

He'd stood on her doorstep for a few minutes thinking about his options. He could break down the door and make her see reason. That wouldn't work. She'd said she was scared of him.

He would find a way to make her love him again. He was confident she would come back to him. She just needed time.

After she'd left him, he'd thrown himself back into watching the life drain from someone with more effort than a hobby. It'd become his life to irritate the cops, the Facilitator had been born. He wanted the police to run in circles, fear for their city. It'd been a shame Jesse had left the FBI. He'd love to see Jesse work a case that would never be solved. Maybe he'd play games with his brother AJ.

He looked down at the divorce papers that had been delivered that morning. She was really going to leave him for good.

An animalistic growl formed in the back of his throat. It was all Jesse Hamilton's fault. It was Jesse Hamilton who'd charged him. Jesse Hamilton who'd told his wife and made her leave.

The Facilitator swept his arms across his desk and papers flew everywhere.

Jesse Hamilton would pay, and losing Kate Ross was a good place to start.

# Five

WITH HER LEFT hand, Kate tossed slacks and skirts across the room, frustrated at her attempt to dress without the use of her dominate hand. Her sister wasn't around to help her today. She searched her closet until she found a simple dress that had been banished to the back. Giving it a once over, reminded her of why it had been shoved there. It could be described as nothing more than a piece of blue sackcloth with holes for the right places so it could be labeled a garment. Pleased it hadn't been donated, she pulled it over her head and smiled at how much she loved her plain dress with no buttons or zippers.

After completing that torturous task, she towed her FBI protective detail to the Irish Pub for a late lunch with her friends. Even though happy hour wasn't for a couple of hours, people crowded the bar. Who could pass up a place holding the title of Best Daytime Bar?

Spotting Josh and Mary, Kate moved toward them. Her detail followed and claimed a table next to them.

Mary looked cheerful in a sundress with large multi-colored flowers, especially compared to Kate's sackcloth, but at least she didn't have to embarrass herself by asking an agent to help her dress. Noting Mary's large flower jewelry, a necklace, a bracelet, and earrings that would have looked gaudy on most people, reminded Kate she wore none, and of another task she didn't look forward to attempting.

A large bruise on Mary's face was the first thing Kate saw when she slid into a chair at the table. She opened her mouth to speak, saw Josh's subtle head shake, and closed it.

Anger twisted in her veins. The bruise ruined the cheerful effect of Mary's outfit.

Mary bowed her head. "He came by the apartment." She spoke in a soft voice that was barely audible over the noise in the restaurant. She brushed her shoulder-length, strawberry-blonde hair forward to hide the bruising before continuing, "I let him in."

"Why?" Her voice was surprisingly calm and soothing despite her rush of anger. "You should be calling 911 instead of letting him into your house. He's dangerous." Kate took a deep breath to keep calm.

If only Mary would stand up for herself, be strong, like she was for her friends. It was beyond frustrating knowing how Dan White, Mary's ex-fiancé, treated her. Dan became violent after Mary had moved in with him. She, Rylee and Josh had eventually convinced her to leave him, but she'd refused to call the police on him and wouldn't allow Kate or Rylee to interfere.

The waitress arrived to take their order, but Kate waved her away with a rueful smile.

"He was so apologetic. He said he just wanted to talk with me. I believed him. He's been so nice and caring lately. He told me that he still loved me and still wanted to marry me."

Josh's jaw tightened. He'd wanted to give Dan a taste of his own medicine but promised Mary he wouldn't touch him. When would his limit be reached? By the muscle tick in his jaw, Kate would say it would be soon.

"Why would you want to marry someone who hits you?" Rylee dropped into an empty chair.

Mary winced. "He apologized for hitting me in the past and promised it wouldn't happen again. I told him that I wouldn't marry him. He told me that I would be his wife. When I wouldn't let him kiss me, he hit me." She hurried to add, "It's nothing though. I should've just kissed him."

"It's nothing? You've got a bruised and swollen cheek, Mary. Why do you make excuses for him? I've told you before a leopard doesn't change its spots." Guilt flooded Kate as she witnessed tears form in Mary's eyes. *Why can't I remember that Mary is the victim before I open my mouth?* Mary had to understand that he wasn't going to go away unless she was more assertive. And a small stint in jail for Dan might be the solution.

Mary's lips trembled. "I know that, but I can't help it. Even though I don't love him anymore, I still care about him. I know he can change. It's just a matter of time."

"Mary, time isn't going to change him. When are you going to see that?" Rylee had an unusual softness in her voice that surprised Kate.

Josh broke his silence. He took Mary's hand in his. "Mary, he's no good for you, even as a friend. You don't deserve to be beaten."

Rylee leaned forward, her arms resting on the table. "We love you and are just looking after your well-being. He doesn't understand it's over, and one day he may not stop in time."

Kate chewed on her lower lip as she thought of the best way to phrase her thoughts and then spoke in a concerned voice. "Mary, Rylee's right. We love you. We only want the best for you and that's not Dan."

She didn't want to upset Mary any more than she already had, but she needed to get her to stop letting him into her apartment, and to also file charges. She knew that truly nothing she, or any of them said would change Mary's mind, but they always had a bit of hope. Mary believed the best in everyone. She truly believed Dan would change and be the man he used to be and wanted to help him.

*Enough.* "I'm going to talk with him again and remind him not to bother you. Maybe he'll listen this time."

The last time Kate reminded Dan of Mary's request to leave her alone, he'd laughed in her face. They'd been in a public place, so her options had been limited. She couldn't arrest him because Mary wouldn't press charges. And, she couldn't kick his ass because others were around. So she reminded him that she'd gladly take him to prison, then walked away.

"Kate, there's no need to talk to him. After he hit me, I told him to leave me alone. He left and said he wouldn't bother me anymore."

Mary's naivety about Dan concerned Kate. "Mary, your turning him away isn't enough to stop him."

Mary looked away and picked up a napkin to wipe the tears sliding down her face.

Josh must've sensed the unbearable pain and embarrassment

Kate felt emanating from Mary, but he reacted a bit faster. "So, Kate, I can't believe someone shot at you."

*Thank you, Josh, for changing the subject.* "And I wasn't even chasing a bad guy when it happened," Kate said in an attempt at levity, then she held up her bandaged hand. "Luckily, it was only my hand." She forced a chuckle to feign good humor in the situation.

"I've never known anyone shot in a drive-by. This is cool." Josh rubbed his hands together in excitement.

Josh, an attorney, worked around the clock trying to become the youngest partner at his firm. He'd surprised her when he'd taken the time to eat lunch out of the office today and worse, he'd shocked them when he'd actually removed his suit jacket, loosened his blue tie and unbuttoned the top button of his shirt. She knew he wouldn't step foot out of the pub without tightening up his appearance first.

"Josh, it's not cool. She could've been killed." Rylee was one of the first FBI agents to call her after the shooting and she'd vowed to help find the shooter.

"But I wasn't." Neither was Jesse. It was odd how she and Jesse's lives had been safe during the murder investigation, digging down in the slums of Baltimore, where danger lurked around every corner. Yet a drive-by shooting found them while walking down a street in the historic district of the city. Forces were either conspiring to bring them together or pull them apart. If it wasn't deadly, she'd blame AJ as payback for the headache they'd caused him, and they'd rightly deserve it. But now wasn't the time to think on something so heavy. Besides, it was more than likely a coincidence since they hadn't planned to be there.

The waitress returned and they ordered. The entire menu made Kate's mouth water, but she never deviated, wherever they ate, from Maryland crab. Her friends hid behind menus, and she knew they were laughing quietly as she ordered appetizer size of everything possible, crab soup, crab bisque, crab dip, requested they substitute crab into other dishes, then dinner size crab cakes plus a to-go box up front. When the waitress departed, the other three at the table had tears in their eyes and she thought they might fall out of their chairs. What the hell? She couldn't help it, she laughed right along with them.

Mary dabbed at the tears of humor in her eyes. "Do you get to be part of the investigation or are they making you take time off? I know you, and I'm guessing even if they put you out on medical, you'd still work the case."

"AJ's leading the investigation and is going to keep me in the loop while they make me stay home. I couldn't convince my boss otherwise."

"I wondered what Agents Brent and Keller were doing here. I take it they're your protective detail." Rylee gestured to the next table. The two agents gave her a barely noticeable nod.

"Yes," she said while shaking her head. "AJ did what I would've done had he been shot. But, I'd prefer they weren't here."

"No, Kate. You should have protection. We wouldn't want anything to happen to you." Mary looked at Kate's hand. "Well, anything else."

Kate loved her friends for not asking her if her injury would affect her future as an agent.

Josh cleared his throat. "What about the guy who was also

shot? Couldn't they have been after him?"

"Anything's possible."

The undeniable and dreadful facts of the shooting, and the wound on her hand were grim reminders Ed Wright had already made an attempt on her life, but they also could have been trying to kill Jesse. She wanted to believe it was just what it was, a drive-by shooting, and they'd been caught in the crossfire like many unfortunate, innocent victims in those crimes.

Josh looked around nervously. "Should you even be out? Shouldn't you be holed up somewhere? Like a safe house or something?"

Smiling, she recalled the look on the face of her guards when she'd told them they'd have to physically restrain her to keep her from having lunch with her friends. When they looked uneasy, she reminded them Rylee would be there, on duty. Luckily for her, their uncertainty, her promise to carry her weapon, and their inability to contact AJ, allowed her to keep from pushing her luck. They might've actually locked her in her room. She shivered at the thought.

Rylee chuckled and winked at Josh. "You watch too much TV."

"One good thing came of it. We'll have the pleasure of watching Kate try to eat with only her left hand."

Leave it to Josh to say something that made them all laugh.

Their food arrived, and they chatted about everything except her injury and Dan visiting Mary.

After they finished eating, Josh and Mary slipped away, leaving Kate and Rylee alone.

Kate glanced at Rylee, someone who had met Jesse while he'd

been aggravating her and AJ on the case, and cleared her throat. Maybe she was overreacting. She just needed someone to help her understand this craziness in relation to Jesse. She had a date with him. If one called it a date. *Crap, is it a date or not?*

"I know you can't go, but is tonight's game one of the ones you purchased? If so, I'll buy it from you. Well, you won't take my money so I'll buy another game tickets for you in place of them."

Perfect lead in to what she needed to ask. As for purchased, this wasn't one of the games she'd purchased in her mini-season package. Rylee went with her the majority of the time. When she couldn't go, Rylee or Josh typically took the seats. She wouldn't accept their money. "No. However, Jesse is coming over tonight to watch the ballgame."

Rylee smiled. "That's great. Isn't it?"

"I don't know." Kate exhaled a troubled sigh. "We don't get along all the time, and now he wants to spend time with me. He kissed me the other night, when we left the bar. It's confusing."

The mischievous smile and twinkle in Rylee's eyes preceded her friend's chuckle. "And?"

Kate shook her head. "And nothing. My problem is that I'm attracted to him." Attracted was an understatement. Her breath hitched as her body came alive with a sudden craving for the fevered sensations she'd yet to experience with him, except when he'd invaded her dreams and waking fantasies.

Swirling a cold French fry in ketchup on her plate, Rylee tilted her head. "How's that a problem?"

"You know I don't date casually. Well, Jesse doesn't do relationships."

Snapping her head up, eyes widened, "Doesn't? That doesn't mean *can't*."

"According to AJ, he's sworn off relationships. I'd be wasting my time." The call came to mind. "Do you think he's the type of guy to cheat?"

Rylee's lipped tightened into a thin line. "I don't see it with Jesse. And, just because he isn't in a relationship now, doesn't mean he won't consider one with you, no matter what his brother says. He's a widower. He had at least one solid relationship."

She sighed. "I don't know. I mean, he kissed me, then I heard him tell someone he loved them. Heck, he could have a girlfriend for all I know."

Her friend harrumphed. "Are you listening to yourself? You just told me AJ said he doesn't do relationships. That call could've been to anyone. And, if he kissed you and asked you out, that's good."

"And if he's seeing someone else?"

"I can't help you there. You'll just have to ask him about it, Kate."

"I know." She would never be *the other* woman. She sighed. "I guess I just don't want to like him—I mean really like him—and get attached and he move on to the next conquest. He stirs something inside me that I fear would break if that happened."

"Mark really fucked you up, didn't he?"

Kate shrugged, knowing the answer to be true. Even then, her intense attraction to him was hard for her to handle.

Why were men the way they were? Kate wondered if women would ever figure them out. Her experience had taught her they wanted sex, fast sports cars, hot young women, money and more sex. Yep, that about summed them up as far as she could tell.

Mark Strickland has assured her it was not a problem that she couldn't have children because he couldn't either. They'd adopt. Things had been going well until nine months later, when he was pushing a wedding even though she hadn't accepted his proposal. She'd found out he was only with her for her money until he and his hot young, pregnant woman—yep, she'd been on the receiving end of the other woman—could leave for Tahiti.

It really didn't matter. All men wanted a child of their own, no matter what they said, so she would be fooling herself to believe a guy who told her he loved her and that her inability to conceive didn't matter. Still, she'd at least try to find *the one* who would keep her from living an empty life.

"Not everyone is like Mark. From what I've heard about HIS, Jesse is doing well and doesn't need money. Plus, you know their family has never been exactly poor so he isn't after your money."

Kate sighed. Rylee was probably right. According to AJ, HIS was in high demand and had their pick of jobs, civilian or government. She hoped their next one wasn't beside her. She was struggling with her attraction as it was.

"Kate, the real question is what do you think of him?" Rylee smiled slyly. "Well, besides being attracted to him?"

Kate took a sip of iced tea to collect her thoughts then played with the condensation on the glass. She inspected the droplet of water on her finger. "He irritates me. I think he tries on purpose to get a rise out of me. I can barely recall not being angry with him. But there's just something about him. When he's not trying to provoke me, I like him."

"Find out what's going on then make your decision. If he's

single, let your guard down and go for it."

"I'll… try." She didn't know if she could do it—let her guard down enough that she could get trampled in the process.

Rylee chuckled. "I've got to go. By the way, I may be going undercover soon. I'll let you know." Rylee stood to leave.

"Are you going to tell me what happened in Vegas? I thought your team was taking a well-earned week vacation there after closing the case in Houston. Two days after you landed, you rushed home like the devil was on your heels."

"Nothing happened. At least, nothing worth discussing. I wasn't enjoying myself and decided to come home early. Besides, I wanted to see my sister. I'll see you later."

Kate waved. "I'll see you for our monthly dinner."

Rylee nodded and then sauntered away. Kate didn't believe her. *Nothing worth discussing, my ass.* Something serious happened, or Rylee wouldn't be so evasive.

She took another sip of her iced tea and saw an unwanted face make a beeline for her. Her protective detail jumped to their feet. Kate waved them off, but they still flanked her, not allowing the woman to get close. A chuckle almost bubbled out. She must look like a mob boss with muscle.

"May I help you? Elizabeth, isn't it?"

The woman sneered at her, not bothered by the two agents. "You can leave Jesse alone. He's mine."

So, he was in a relationship. *Fucking bastard.* "Is Jesse aware of this?"

She sneered at Kate, twisting her face in what Kate's technical descriptive term for was *crazy.* "Just know that I'll do anything, *anything* to ensure he's mine." Before Kate could reply, she watched Elizabeth all but glide away, her head held regally. She almost chuckled at the high school drama of it all.

For a second she considered canceling on Jesse, but her instincts told her not to. She had to find out what the hell was going on. Kate wasn't sure she could believe Elizabeth. She sighed, or maybe she just didn't want to believe her.

"Does she need following, Kate?" Agent Keller asked.

Although, she had run into the woman three times in a couple of days, her gut told her the woman was more nuisance than anything else. "No. It's fine," she responded, but told herself to keep an eye out for Elizabeth.

***

KATE twisted the antique ring on her finger, a ring that had been passed down her biological mother's family for generations. Why had she agreed to this? That was right, she hadn't. He'd dictated. She'd dressed in her Orioles' jersey and spent extra time to look presentable. Maybe better than presentable.

Watching a game together would be safe. She watched them all the time.

The knock on the door startled her. Well, it was now or never. She could do this. It was an O's game, and she'd be watching it anyway. Company made any game better.

She opened the door and her breath caught. "Hey," she finally managed to say, feeling like a love-struck teenager. When had things changed for her? How could she go from despising him to desiring him?

Jesse smiled, his gaze touching her, all of her. How did he do that? She had to stay strong. He belonged to someone else.

Maybe. Possibly. Hell, she was driving herself insane. She needed to ask him, but she realized she was scared of what the answer might be.

"I see you're an avid fan." He brushed past her on his way to her kitchen, holding two plastic bags in one hand and a six-pack of beer in the other. "I promised food, snacks and beer."

She closed the door. "I see you're an avid fan too." The man oozed sporty and sexy as hell in his Orioles' jersey and baseball cap, tight jeans and a five o'clock shadow. She was screwed.

"They're playing the Blue Jays tonight, so it should be a good game." He unloaded the bags then reached down to pet Dottie, who'd followed him, or the food, to the kitchen. "I brought hot dogs, so we can pretend we're at the stadium. And, of course," he paused and handed Dottie a dog chew, "I brought something for your girl."

Her dog ambled off with her treat while he made himself at home.

"Why are you doing this?" Kate blurted.

Jesse turned to her and drew his brows in. "Doing what?"

She cleared her throat and gestured to the spread he had on the kitchen counter. "This."

"You have to have food to watch the game, and I'm guessing it's hard for you to cook with only one hand." His lips split into a silly grin.

"No." She shook her head. "Not just the cooking. The rest of it. The kiss… inviting yourself over." *Doing things a boyfriend would do on a date.* Except he wasn't her boyfriend. And they weren't on a date.

Jesse walked to her and placed his hands on her waist.

She stiffened. The mere touch of his hands sent a warm shiver through her, which she fought to keep him from noticing.

"Because I want to get to know you, Kate. How's that for a reason?"

She narrowed her eyes. "But, you have a girlfriend."

His eyes flooded with surprise. "No, I don't."

"What about Elizabeth?" Kate didn't stand a chance against the exquisite Elizabeth. Not many women would.

"What about her?" He glanced up to the ceiling and shook his head before his eyes connected with her, amusement dancing in them. "Did she tell you we were together?"

All she could do was nod. She hated games, and after being hurt so badly, the last thing she wanted ever again was to be caught up in anything where she could end up being hurt. She'd barely recovered from Mark's betrayal.

His hands glided up to her shoulders. "Kate. I have *never* dated Elizabeth and never will. She has this screwed-up vision of us together, but it will never happen. I only put up with her because she's the sister of a close friend."

"Did you sleep with her then dump her?" Kate momentarily closed her eyes, realizing what she'd said. "I'm sorry. That's none of my business."

He dropped his hands and turned back to the counter, but not before she noticed his change in demeanor. "It's okay. No. I've never slept with her. Never wanted to."

She'd already gone this far. She had to know. She blamed it on the investigator in her, but she knew better. "But, I heard you on the phone tell someone you loved them."

He spun around and pulled out his cell phone. "I did. I do

love someone." After a couple of swipes and taps, he turned it to show her a picture of a little girl with his hair and eyes. "It was my daughter, Reagan. She'd stayed overnight at her aunt's house while I was granted a guys' night out to celebrate Samuel's release."

She had the good grace to blush and feel like an idiot. Embarrassment filled her chest, hating she'd thought the worse of him. Kate knew she'd been jealous, even if she hated to admit it to herself. She just wasn't sure what to do with that though. She smiled and looked at the image of his daughter. "She's adorable."

He put his phone away. "Come on. Let's get ready to watch some baseball."

***

"SO what made you want to become an FBI agent when you have a big family business?" A mouthful of popcorn was tossed into Jesse's mouth.

Kate relaxed against the sofa, and recited what she told people who asked that question. It bothered her a bit giving Jesse her canned lines, but she did it anyway. "My parents were murdered when I was four, and their killer was never brought to justice. The man who pulled the trigger had been murdered immediately after the shooting. But, the *real* killer gave the order from behind bars. I joined the FBI to ensure he paid for ordering it to happen."

She took a bite of her hotdog, chewed and swallowed before continuing, "Nick Mendoza had been convicted for embezzlement. He'd been caught red-handed, and there was nothing my parents, who were criminal defense attorneys, could do to win his case. He blamed them for his conviction and threatened the family. My parents went into hiding, but someone didn't keep the location quiet. It cost them their lives."

Jesse grabbed another handful of popcorn from the large bowl they shared. "And did he?"

"He paid."

Jesse took a sip of his beer.

Now that she knew he was available, she thought about what Rylee had said. Could she just go for it? She had to if she wanted to try, and according to the butterflies in her stomach, she did want to try. Reaching out first wasn't something she was practiced at doing. She wondered what he was thinking and realized she was like a teenager hoping for her first kiss, even though it wouldn't be her first kiss. She needed to just sit back and see what happened. She turned her attention back to the game. They'd enjoy themselves tonight.

"Yay!" They gave each other a high-five as the O's hit a home run.

"Looks like they might get rain." Kate took a sip of her beer. "I'm glad we aren't there."

"Fair weathered fan?" he joked.

Before she could respond, he jumped up from the couch.

"Bullshit!" He threw popcorn at the television. "That was clearly a ball!"

She giggled. Actually giggled. *What the hell?*

"Shit. I'll pick it up." Taking the bottle to the kitchen, he tossed it in the garbage can. "Want another one?" He held up his beer bottle.

"No. I'm not ready."

"Lightweight. This is an O's game. Lots of beer is required." He gave her a challenging look.

*Lightweight?* She enjoyed his banter, but she wouldn't rise to his bait. "Go ahead and grab me one. I'm almost done with this one." She'd switch them out and he'd never be the wiser.

"That's my girl."

*His girl?* Warmth flooded her and her body tingled. He may have said it jokingly, but…. Or, he may have said it to tell her he wanted to date. This dating stuff was too damn confusing.

He handed her a new drink, sat and tapped his bottle to hers. "Go O's."

She looked up when their hands touched in the popcorn bowl, and the smoldering flame in his eyes startled her.

Kate withdrew her tingling hand quickly and turned away. *So, he wants me. That's not in question. But, does he want more? How the hell do I ask that?* She knew asking him troubled her because she wasn't skilled in answering all the questions men could sometimes ask. She wouldn't be his bedmate and if he asked that, with as excited as her body was becoming being so near him, she might say yes, and that wouldn't do. She needed to level herself, which meant getting to know him as a person.

She needed to like the entire picture if she wanted something to work. She looked back at him. "Um, tell me about HIS. When did you start it? Why?"

Pride radiated from him and he appeared to sit taller. "Two years ago, Matt and Devon, my brothers, and I decided to form Hamilton Investigation & Security, or as you know us, HIS, where we put together our skills to solve the complex problems of our clients." He grinned. "Through any means necessary."

She rolled her eyes, ignoring how her insides turned to jelly at his smile.

He winked, and she almost melted on the spot. "As to why? We were tired of red tape, stupid orders, you name it, and we were through."

She waited for him to expound. When she realized he wasn't, she said, "Tell me about the role your brothers play. I know you were an Army Ranger and FBI agent, so you have excellent security and investigative skills."

He elbowed her playfully in the ribs. "Ah, Kate, was that a compliment?" he teased. "If so, you forgot that I'm an excellent marksman, too."

Was that joking and playfulness? From Jesse? Butterflies bounced against the wall of her stomach as his mouth curved into a silly grin. She liked this Jesse. A lot.

"But, seriously, as you said, I'm security and investigation, but since I'm the oldest, I get to be the boss." He took a swig of beer. "I didn't give them a choice."

With the exception of talking about Reagan, she hadn't seen him smile this much. She smiled at the thought that she hadn't seen him enjoy himself before tonight. It'd been with her that joy had grabbed him. If only... together they could—

"Matt is a former SEAL and leads our protection and security, and Devon is a former CIA agent and our computer forensic expert. Last year, Brad, Matt's twin, left the secret service and joined us. He does a little of everything so it was a nice balance. Well, except work with the computers. No one dares mess with Devon's computer setup."

Chagrined at her mind drifting off, she focused hard on the conversation. "What about the others?"

"You mean the rest of the men?"

Reaching for popcorn, she nodded. "AJ said your team is a strange mix."

"They are." He took a swig of beer before continuing, "They're a mixture of former military and former law enforcement—Navy SEALs, Army Rangers, Air Force Pararescues, FBI agents, DEA agents and deputy U.S. marshals. Their diversity works well to accomplish our missions."

Wow. She'd heard they had strong backgrounds, but Jesse didn't play around with the experience he required of his men. "What else, besides show up the FBI in a murder case, have you been hired for?" She felt like a reporter rushing out questions, building up to what she really wanted to know.

"You sure you want to hear all of this?"

She smiled and nodded. "Yeah."

"We've done a little of this and that—kidnapping investigation, international corporate security protection, witness protection and asset searches are just a few things. The majority of our clients are civilian, but we've also recently accepted a few government jobs. We prefer civilian work though."

He hadn't told her anything she hadn't already learned from AJ. He was going to make Kate ask. "I'm intrigued. Tell me more." Damn. She sounded awfully flirty. She turned from Jesse's questioning look.

"Well, when we started, we hired a few of our old pals with law enforcement or military backgrounds as our initial team. But business has grown so rapidly, we've expanded and added more men and two K-9 units. That has really come in handy for protective details."

"If it's a family business, and I'm assuming it is…."

He nodded, but his eyes narrowed a little, and he raised an eyebrow in question.

"Why isn't AJ part of it?"

Jesse took a deep breath, rubbed the back of his neck and loudly exhaled. "He's our baby brother. Unfortunately, we've always treated him that way. He thinks if he can prove himself, then we'll take him seriously."

Her eyes widened in disbelief. AJ not take care of himself? She wanted to laugh.

"Don't think it, Kate. We do take him seriously. It's some fucked-up thing in his mind. Anyhow, he thinks he belongs at the FBI and not with us so he can show us he's grown or something or other."

Was Jesse taking it personally that AJ wouldn't join HIS? She wanted to reach out to him. Comfort him.

He ruined the moment by looking back at the game on the television and saying, "I heard you went out today."

AJ had tattled on her. *Damn him.* "I did. I had lunch with friends."

"You know better than that, Kate. You shouldn't be out in the open, and you shouldn't put your friends at risk like that until we find the shooter."

So much for a relaxing time. "I can take care of myself, and my friends were protected.

Jesse closed his eyes and pinched the bridge of his nose. "Kate, someone may be trying to kill you. Don't make it easy on them.

Why do you think we're here instead of at the ball park?"

"Someone may be trying to kill you as well. Those bullets could have been meant for you just as easily as they were for me. You took a risk coming over here."

"I can take care of myself, Kate."

She tightened her left hand into a fist. She wanted to pound his chest until he listened. "I. Can. Too. So quit treating me like I'm some whimpering little girl. Injured or not, I'm a trained FBI agent. I know what I'm doing."

He reached over and his hand enclosed her fist, his thumb softly rubbing her white knuckles. "I know you can take care of yourself, Kate."

Funny, he never acted like it.

She felt the warmth of his hand, the comforting strokes. Relaxing her fist, she hoped he wouldn't let go.

"This guy is bold, and you shouldn't take any unnecessary risks."

They had been unable to locate the driver. Ed's brother said he'd left town and didn't know where he'd gone or when he'd return. Without the driver, they couldn't find out who the shooter was.

"I'm not going to live my life in fear and never leave my apartment. No one is going to do that to me. Especially not some asshole," she stated matter-of-factly.

He sighed. "Just don't do anything stupid."

Kate didn't reply or pull her hand from his. Did he really care about what happened to her? How would that change things?

Before she realized it, the baseball game ended and an awkward silence ensued.

Jesse lifted her hand to his lips and lightly kissed it then pulled her forward for a quick, light kiss on the lips, lingering longer than before. He slowly pulled back from her. "Thank you for having me over, Kate."

Swallowing, she hoped to catch her errant breath. The man drove her body wild with lust. After what seemed a long time, she was able to respond. "You're welcome."

She made the mistake of looking into those gorgeous eyes, and her pulse skipped, captivated by the heated desire she saw building in them and the question they posed.

Her uncertainty must've shown in her eyes because he surprised her when he shook his head and stood. "I had a great time. Good night, Kate."

"Good night, Jesse." She'd done the right thing. Otherwise, she'd hate herself in the morning. Besides, he didn't even try to get her into bed.

"Come lock the door behind me."

JESSE whistled on his walk to his SUV. He'd had a great time with Kate. Something about her called to him. Not just the thought of sex. And there were lots of thoughts of sex. Those thoughts were mostly of her soft, naked body beneath his as he took his time worshiping every inch of her, and then plunging his cock deep inside her.

Deep in thought, he almost missed the car idling near his SUV. As he came closer, the vehicle sped off. His pulse accelerated as a note on the windshield of his SUV grabbed his attention. Quickly scanning the area, he pulled out his phone and then jumped in the driver seat. His heart thudded against his ribs. Ignoring the honking of the car he cut off when he pulled away from the curb, he gunned the vehicle.

Working to calm his breathing, he all but screamed into the phone, "Get everybody to the girls. Now! There was a death threat waiting for me," when it was answered.

"Shouldn't we be protecting you then?" Devon asked.

The HIS emergency alert call rang on his phone. Before it interrupted his current conversation, he responded to Devon, "No, it's a threat against someone I love."

# Six

JESSE APPROACHED THE rear of his home where a room had been specially designed for HIS headquarters. His brothers and most of the team waited for him. Because of the importance of the meeting, AJ had joined them as both an FBI agent and a Hamilton.

The previous night, shaken by the note, Jesse had broken every driving law racing to Emily's house where Reagan had stayed while he and Kate had watched the ball game. All of the women he loved had been in one place and unprotected. His heart had pounded and his hands had shaken the entire drive, afraid the team would be too late. That he'd made the wrong choice, again. This time not staying when his daughter had asked.

Jesse had arrived to see his brothers, Ken and three team members at Emily's house. He'd uttered, "Thank God," when Ken had indicated the girls were secure. The brothers didn't play their leftover childhood game of rock-paper-scissors to find out who'd break the bad news to Emily. They'd left everything to Jesse.

Emily Hamilton, their baby sister, as all the men knew, was a handful. One would think growing up with five, actually six, overprotective brothers, she'd be some meek, mild woman who depended on her brothers to take care of her. Somehow they'd pushed her to become a strong-willed, independent woman who loved her brothers but didn't want them interfering in her life.

If it hadn't been for her daughter, Emily wouldn't have agreed to a team at her home. She'd refused to go to the safe house. She'd told them she trusted them to do their damn job and protect them where they lived.

That was what they would do.

Jesse cleared his throat, and the room quieted. All eyes turned to him. "As you know, someone recently tried to kill either myself or AJ's partner, Kate Ross."

The men nodded.

"You all should be aware of what happened last night. I received a note on my SUV that reads, *"Because of you, I lost someone I love. Now you're going to lose someone you love. Facilitator."*

Matt looked around the group. "Since the note isn't specific, we have to branch out in a couple of directions. Some of you will join the team watching Emily, Amber and Reagan."

Jamaal Lewis, a former deputy marshal, asked, "Are we to believe Emily has agreed to do everything you tell her to do?"

Jesse grimaced and rubbed the back of his neck. They knew his sister too well, and the fact she didn't like them taking over her life.

Some of the men chuckled lightly. He knew their fun was at his dealing with his sister and not at the situation.

"Okay. Okay." He waved his hands and his team immediately sobered. They took a bit of levity when they could, but they never lost sight of their tasks. "For now, Reagan will stay with her."

"Why isn't she staying with you?" Steve Smith, a former FBI agent, asked. "We can cover both houses."

His chest swelled with pride at how much his team loved his daughter, and he knew they'd never allow anything to happen to her. They treated her like their niece, and they spoiled her worse than he ever could.

Jesse stuffed his hands in his pockets, swallowed hard and hoped they believed his hunch. "Because we have someone else to protect. Someone who won't want us around. It's not someone I love, but it's a gut feeling I have that she's the actual target. FBI Special Agent Kate Ross."

After thinking through it all—receiving the note while on a date with Kate, and being shot while standing together on the street with her—Jesse realized there was some confusion, and that it had to be Kate the Facilitator thought he loved.

"What the fuck? She's not going to agree with you on this," AJ stated frankly.

Jesse heaved an exasperated sigh. How could he explain to her that he thought she was in danger even though the note said someone he loved? He had no doubt the note meant Kate. "Well, I'll have to find a way to convince her."

"She already has an FBI detail. She doesn't need HIS protection, too," AJ stated testily.

"Well, she's getting it."

"We're not hiring you in to consult on this one."

Jesse massaged his temples. "I never asked you to. This is

personal, AJ. We're going to handle it no matter what the FBI does."

Drawing the attention from his and AJ's standoff, Matt spoke up. "Okay, the women's protection is set. Let's get to the most important part. We need to find out who this guy calling himself Facilitator is, and stop him." He rubbed his leg.

Matt and Brad may be twins, carrying the trademark Hamilton dark hair and golden-brown eyes, but their problems set them apart from each other and the family. Those problems made Jesse worry about the challenges the Hamilton's have yet to face. And Matt's may be the most difficult.

AJ moved forward. "After Jesse called me last night, I made reviewing his old FBI cases a priority. I'll leave it to you to check his cases here."

"I'm already on it. I also have copies of his FBI cases," Devon said, glancing up from his laptop with the grin of a boy who'd snuck his first kiss under the bleachers.

"Dammit, Dev! I don't want to hear that," AJ insisted.

Jesse saw several of the team's chests shake as they tried to stifle their laughter. They liked AJ, but they enjoyed poking fun at him even more. Not only was he the youngest brother and not part of HIS, but also he had the unfortunate reality of being born on April first.

"Then don't listen." No one was sure what Devon's job had been when he'd been in the CIA, but there was nothing he couldn't find with a computer, and no one asked how he acquired things, as long as they were able to do their job. Devon ran his hand through his long, curly, jet-black hair stopping at the bump on his head and winced.

"Still hurt?" Jesse asked.

Devon shook his head. "No. It's fine." He had traveled to Vegas to purchase some equipment and returned with a large knot on his head and short-term memory loss. His entire trip was gone.

Jesse wanted to help his brother, but he couldn't take time to deal with this now, but it had to be addressed at some point. Something had to have happened.

"Okay, AJ. Tell us about this perp." He needed to find out whom they were up against. Time to remove the fucking threat to the women in his life.

"About two years ago, not long after you left the agency, this guy pops up. We only know who he is by the card with 'Facilitator for Hire' imprinted on it, which he leaves at his kills. He likes to kill in a variety of ways. A bullet between the eyes, broken neck, and strangulation... you get the picture. Our profile suggests he enjoys it, considers it art and that's why he leaves his card. It's his signature on his masterpiece. We're not sure what made him choose a drive-by shooting this last time. It was risky." AJ shook his head in disbelief. "Unfortunately, no one knows who he is. He's a ghost."

"Then how does he get hired if no one knows who he is?" Matt asked the obvious question.

Rubbing his hand along his jaw, AJ took a moment before responding. "You don't select him, he selects you. If you want someone killed, you quietly get the word out, and if he chooses you, he'll come to you. Not personally, of course. That would make it too easy for us. We've sent people undercover, putting out the word we want someone killed but haven't been contacted. It's a gut feeling, but I think he knows who we really are. Since no one will admit to hiring him, we don't know how he gets paid. We've looked through our suspect's finances and haven't found anything."

"Give me their names. If there's something there, I'll find it." Devon rubbed his hands together, always ready for a challenge.

AJ stared at his brother, then narrowed his eyes. "You'll pull the names if I don't give them to you, won't you?"

Feigning insult, Devon placed his hand on his chest. "Me?"

Shaking his head and finally expelling a resigned sigh, AJ said, "I'll go ahead and see what we can work out with HIS so I don't have to arrest you later."

Devon winked mischievously.

"What about the car and the note?" Ken asked.

"We found the car this morning. He'd left his calling card. No prints. The car had been wiped clean. Whoever this bastard is, he's careful," AJ said.

"How can you label a drive-by in Fells Point careful?" Jesse asked.

"Well now," AJ drawled, "I didn't say he was smart."

"I want Steve and Joe to comb through the files with Dev then follow up on any leads," Jesse directed. Joe Stone was a former FBI agent who'd worked with Jesse and was familiar with some of his old cases. Jesse hoped Joe's exposure to his cases would make the file-sifting move faster.

Looking around, Jesse continued his assignments. "Ken, keep a team on Emily's house and a team on Kate. Make sure Kate doesn't know your team is there until I contact her."

They'd been lucky the day Ken Patrick, Jesse's senior enlisted member of his Army Ranger team, had agreed to join HIS and lead the team in the field so the brothers could remain flexible. Jesse's life had been in Ken's hands more than once, so he trusted the man to protect anyone with his own life if necessary.

"The girls are secure. We'll head out right after this for Ms. Ross's protection. What do you want us to do about the FBI detail?" Ken spoke to Jesse, but his gaze slid to AJ.

AJ grinned at Jesse. "Yeah, Jesse, what are you going to do about the FBI detail?"

Jesse's eyes narrowed at his baby brother. "We'll have to cover their asses too, now, won't we?"

The room broke out into laughter. AJ glowered at everyone. "How quickly some of you forget where your training came from."

"Matt and Brad will stay inside with Emily and the girls. I'll stay inside with Kate," Jesse said quickly, not wanting a fight to spring out between AJ and the men on which agency was the best. Damn, he wanted Reagan with him, but if Kate was the real target, as he suspected, then it would be too dangerous to have his daughter beside him, and he had to protect the women he'd place in danger. It broke his heart, but it was best she stayed with his brothers for now.

AJ burst out laughing. He caught his breath, his hand holding his side. "You really think she's going to let you stay with her? You really don't know Kate."

Jesse knew she wasn't going to willingly let him stay with her. He hadn't worked out yet how he was going to manage it, but he would. She had to be protected, and he wasn't leaving that to the FBI. He didn't understand it, but he knew he had to be close to her and protect her.

AJ sobered. "What are you going to do, Jesse?"

"Don't worry about it. She'll agree."

A broad smile flashed across his brother's face. "I can't wait to see this."

Ignoring his statement, Jesse turned back to the men. "Team, we've always treated everyone we protected as if they were our own. Well this time they're ours. They're mine. Nothing happens to them. Protect them with your life."

The men nodded and a few *hoorahs* were heard as they grouped around Ken for orders.

"Why do you think it's Kate?" AJ asked, moving to stand beside Jesse.

He frowned. "Because we were together at the shooting then together when I received the note."

"Wait a second. Where were you when you got the note? You never said exactly."

"At her apartment."

"You got the note at her apartment? What the fuck were you doing there?" AJ moved closer to Jesse, his nostrils flaring and his face red.

"We had a date."

AJ froze. "A what?"

"A date. You know, it's where two people get together and do something fun. The night usually ends with a goodnight kiss."

His attempt at humor went unappreciated.

AJ surprised Jesse with a right hook, knocking him back a step. Their brothers stepped forward, but he waved them off. He rubbed his jaw and looked at AJ's scowling face. "What the fuck was that for?"

"Leave her the hell alone. She's not for you to use and toss aside. She's a good person who's been hurt too much."

*Who had hurt her?* "I don't use and toss women aside. They know what they're getting into with me. I'm upfront about it. And I don't plan to hurt Kate." Hurting Kate was the last thing he wanted to do. It made his insides churn just thinking about it.

"Why her? Why can't you find someone else?"

"I like her, AJ." Jesse knew he shouldn't chase her. She was the marrying kind, not the affair kind, and he wasn't getting married again. Yet, he couldn't walk away from her. Especially not now.

"No, you don't. You've been an ass to her this past month. I'm surprised she even let you in the door."

A smile split Jesse's face. "You know I can be lovable when I want to."

AJ growled and rubbed the swelling knuckles on his hand.

"She's a big girl, AJ. She can decide if she wants to see me or not." She was about to see a whole lot more of him whether she wanted to or not.

"You hurt her, and I'll kick your ass."

Jesse nodded. "Fair enough."

They stared at each other a minute longer and broke apart with an assumed truce.

"Dev, I'm counting on you to do that magic you do with computers and find out who this guy is before it's too late."

Devon smiled. "You can count on it, Jesse."

Matt and Brad left to protect their sister and nieces.

"Come on, AJ. You're going with me to explain to Kate that

she and Dottie are getting a temporary roommate."

AJ groaned. "What did I do to deserve this torture?"

Jesse laughed. "It's what you get for not joining HIS." One day he would convince AJ to join them. He'd sleep better knowing AJ was back with the family. Then they'd find Jake, their foster brother. It'd been close to four years since he'd left without word, and it wasn't getting any easier on them. AJ and Emily had taken it the hardest. But Jesse would pull this family back together.

AJ looked at his ringing phone. "Uh-oh. Speak of the devil. It's her detail. There's no telling what she's done now."

# Seven

THE WORRY OF ever regaining the full use of her hand and being a field agent again ate away at Kate's spirit. Although she'd gone into the FBI for personal reasons, she'd found it had been the right fit for her. Now, she may lose the ability to do something she loved.

Had her job as an FBI agent set a madman after her? She had to know.

She wanted to be out there, searching for the shooter.

Whether she or Jesse were the target, or if it were a random shooting, had thoughts racing through her mind, searching for an invisible finish line. Thinking he could be the target ignited a strange feeling inside her. She couldn't identify it, but it overtook her concern for herself. While they'd enjoyed their evening, she'd forgotten about the possible threat over one of them. Last night, after he'd left, fear for him, worst-case scenarios had flown through her mind, and almost ruined what had been a great evening.

She'd itched to call him and ensure he'd arrived home safely but had managed to hold back.

Kate had no idea what was next for them, if anything. He'd left without mentioning seeing her again. The thought left her feeling hollow. They'd had such a good time, and she wasn't sure she was willing for it to be their last.

Sighing, she didn't want to fool herself; it was better it happened now. While the crushing pain in her heart confused her, Kate had to put him from her mind. They'd never work. He came from a big family, and big families liked big families. She could never give him a big family so it was best to avoid him.

Enough. Sitting around bemoaning and hiding out wasn't Kate. She may not even be the target. Hanging out was because she'd received a serious dressing-down from AJ after leaving to have lunch with her friends. He may have been right, but she couldn't stay hidden and put her life on hold. It could take weeks, maybe even months to catch the perpetrator. She needed to go out again. She had something important to do.

She picked up her handbag and walked out the door. Agent Keller immediately put his cell phone to his ear, probably notifying AJ that she wasn't following his orders.

"I'm going to Ross Communication."

Agent Brent cleared his throat. "Kate, you know that you really should stay inside."

She nodded. "Yeah, I should. But, I'm not and neither would you?"

His lips tightened and he slowly nodded.

The agents quickly moved into action to protect their departing assignment.

WHEN Kate strolled into the Ross Communication building, a sweet poignant feeling wound around her heart. She loved the lobby with its brightly shining hardwood floors, large two-tier crystal chandelier on the two-story high ceiling, and the beautiful oak railing staircase she remembered racing up and down as a kid. The added cosmetic details her mother had incorporated made it the most spectacular office-building lobby she'd ever seen.

The agents refused to wait in the lobby but agreed to remain as invisible as possible.

Smiling, she approached the receptionist. "Hello, Grace. How are you?"

"Hi, Kate. It's good to see you." Grace flashed her bright, Welcome-to-Ross smile. "I'm good. How're things with you? Ariana told us about the shooting. Are you all right?"

Kate waved her injured hand. "I'm fine. I'll be back in business in no time."

"Well, I hope they catch the criminal soon. We don't need more killers clogging up the streets." Grace shuddered.

Changing the subject, Kate steered to a safer topic. "How are the kids?" The staff at Ross liked that she took an interest in their personal lives, even though she didn't work in the offices. Ariana knew employees' names but nothing about them.

"Dawn's growing like a weed. She outgrows her jeans before she even has a chance to wear them a second time. Thankfully, her sister is right behind her and takes her hand-me-downs." She raised her eyebrows at the agents but asked no questions. "Ariana's in her office, but she's with someone right now."

Kate nodded. "I'll just visit with some of the staff on my way to see her. There's no need to announce me."

She enjoyed her visits with the staff. They were good people who had devoted themselves to the success of the business. She couldn't thank them enough.

"Go on up. Everyone will be glad to see you. I hope your hand heals soon."

She thanked Grace, then took the stairs to the third floor and the executive offices. Her first stop was Lee Genovese, the Executive Vice President, and Ariana's right-hand man. He was a middle-aged man, of average height with thinning black hair and beautiful olive skin. She could always count on him to lighten the mood in a room. He was intelligent and the most impressive man she knew.

She entered his office, and smiled brightly when he didn't notice his territory had been invaded. "Hi, Lee."

A large smile stretched across his face. "Kate, it's been too long. What've you been up to? Besides getting shot at."

She mentally shook her head. Did Ariana send out a company memo about it? "Just catching criminals."

"When are you coming to work here? We'd love to have you run things with Ariana."

Lee could run Ross Communication much better then she could.

"I'm thinking about it." *More and more since I've been shot and may not have a choice.*

She chatted with him for a few minutes, laughing at his young daughter's escapades.

"Let me take some time to visit with others before I see Ariana." They stood. "I'll see you later."

"Bye, Kate. Don't be such a stranger."

She pondered on her visit with Lee. He'd been extremely curious about whether they had any leads on who had shot her. She hadn't realized her getting shot would affect everyone so deeply. The feeling of being embraced in love by a parent welled inside her. Lee had been like the uncle who cares and spoils.

Kate visited with the rest of the executive staff. They would be an enjoyable group of colleagues to work alongside, who excelled at what they did. She just didn't know if working alongside them would be enough for her. She sighed.

"Ariana's in a business meeting. Another station is making a pitch for her to purchase it. She'll be glad for the interruption." Tamara, Ariana's assistant, reached for the phone.

"Don't interrupt her if she's in an important meeting." It upset Kate when someone interrupted her during an interrogation. She wouldn't do that to her sister.

Tamara frowned. "Kate, you know her. If she doesn't want to break up her meeting, she won't. Besides, she wasn't looking forward to this meeting."

"Well, okay. Let her know I'm here." She moved to the elegant waiting area, admiring the two antique chairs that had been with the Rosses since they'd founded the company. The scent of the lilies in the large floral arrangement drifted to her, bringing back memories of Kelly Ross. No matter what time of the year, her mother had required the florist to have lilies in every bouquet at the office and at home.

A few minutes later, Ariana exited her office ushering an unhappy man out the door. Either he hadn't swayed her into the purchase of his station, or he had the worst pleased expression Kate had ever seen.

Ariana walked him to the elevator before she returned to Kate. "Thank you. I thought that man was going to cry when I told him I wasn't interested in his station."

"Ariana, you can be so mean," Kate teased.

"Mean has nothing to do with it." Ariana waved her hand. "It's about business. I'll read his proposal, but it had best be better than his pitch if he wants me to buy it."

If Kate came to work here, she'd leave these types of meetings to Ariana.

"Are we still on for the children's hospital?"

"Of course we are." Ariana turned toward her office. "Come on, let's take a minute."

They entered Ariana's spacious office, bypassing the sleek cherry-wood design desk, positioned prominently in the center of the room, to lounge in the seating area with a soft leather couch and two chairs.

Kate sat in a Queen Anne chair and declined an offer of a beverage.

Adjusting her skirt from a spot on the couch, Ariana took a sip of water. "How's the hand?"

"It's just sore." It still throbbed terribly, but she didn't want her sister to worry any more than she already did.

"I still can't believe you were shot. You're lucky you didn't get killed."

"I'm lucky Jesse saw the gun in time to knock me to the ground."

A curious expression formed on Ariana's face. "The guy you avoided at the hospital?"

"How'd you know?" Kate should've known her sister would

figure out her odd behavior in her rush to leave the hospital.

"He wore a hole in the carpet in the waiting room while you were in surgery. I thought he was going to strangle the nurse when she wouldn't let him back to see you in recovery." Ariana smiled. "By the way, your partner is gorgeous."

Kate ignored the mention of Jesse being anxious for her. "AJ's a great guy, but he's too young for you. Besides, he's a ladies' man and plays the field."

"Too bad. So tell me what's up before we leave." Ariana could always read Kate, knew when she had something to say or something to hide. She'd never been able to keep a secret from her.

A loud noise sounded sharply from outside the room, and Kate's heartrate doubled. Common sense told her it was a book hitting the ground, but her mind initially thought gunfire and she had moved to hit the ground.

Ariana raised her eyebrows. "Kate?"

Shaking, she reclaimed her seat as the floodgates opened and Kate told her everything. Her concern for her ability to do her job. The idea of working at Ross Communication. Catching her shooter. Her date with Jesse, and her subsequent decision to keep away from him.

Like any good sister, Ariana sat and listened.

---

KATE rode with her sister in the backseat of Agent Keller's car to Johns Hopkins' Children's Hospital. After a lengthy conversation, she and the agents came to an agreement that this would be her last outing until something more was known on her case or until AJ put more precautions in place. Had AJ been available, she might not have had this small win. She agreed on needing to be smarter, and would, but this was too important to her.

Jay and Kelly had raised her and Ariana to make time to participate, give something of themselves. She tried to make the agents understand that volunteering at the children's hospital uplifted her spirits and those of the children fighting for their lives.

They entered the hospital with the agents in tow and stopped in the lobby. It was then that she realized how she'd feel if the roles were reversed. A knot formed in her stomach. She'd do better for them after this.

Kate greeted the receptionist by name before they walked to the large stairwell on the east side of the lobby. They made their way to Nurse Debi's office. After knocking on the door, they entered to see a desk overflowing with paperwork. The nurse stood and hugged each of them.

"Hi, Ariana and Kate. It's good to see you both."

"Hi, Debi." The overpowering scent of potpourri assailed Kate's nose. She didn't dare comment on it being too strong and too much in such a small office because she knew Debi made it herself and took pride in her creation.

The nurse put her hands in her cat covered smock pockets. "I'm glad you're here. The children always enjoy your visits."

"Where would you like us today?" Ariana's business suit had been replaced with a pair of slacks and a silk blouse. Kate wished she could get her sister to wear jeans and a T-shirt.

"Is Jason still here or has he been discharged?" Kate's heart ached that when the kid was released; there was no home awaited Jason. His parents had passed in a home robbery after he'd been admitted. Even with an uncertain future, Jason fought his leukemia with gusto.

Debi's smile faded. "He's still with us but...."

Kate's heart sank and she reached to the wall to steady herself. Jason couldn't lose his battle. He should be living the normal life of a child. She looked forward to watching him play football.

"An infection has set in and his body isn't fighting it like we'd like to see." The nurse shook her head.

Swallowing past the lump in her throat, she called to her sister, "Ariana?"

"Well, let's get to it, shall we?" Ariana turned to the door.

"You know the way, so I don't need to escort you." Debi waved a handful of paperwork. "I do need to catch up on paperwork. Enjoy your time with the children and stop back by on your way out. I'd love to hear how it went."

They entered the remodeled playroom that their last donation had been earmarked for with one agent in front of them and one behind, and smiled. Each wall had been painted a primary color and had a large mural featuring children's favorite characters, like Mickey Mouse and Winnie the Pooh, painted on them. Different sized children's tables and chairs were scattered throughout the room. The toy bins were overflowing with toys and books. Kate's joy almost burst out of her.

Ariana scanned the room. "It looks like we have a full house today."

"Look at Seth. Last time we were here, he was bedridden. It's good to see him up and about." Seth, at six years old, had been at the hospital for months. He was a precocious and lovable little boy.

"I'm headed to the train table with the boys. I'll leave you to play with Seth." Ariana walked away.

Seeing her sister like this reminded Kate of their parents' ability to help Ariana relax and let go. She'd been a girly-girl growing up, but every time they visited, she went straight for the boy toys as she'd done with their father.

Kate made her way around the playroom. She stepped around the Lego tower being built by two children and ruffled their hair as she passed. Children at the coloring tables looked up, smiled and waved at her, knowing she'd color with them before she went on individual room visits. Her left-hand colored pictures were bound to be interesting.

Seth jumped up from the building blocks he played with, ran to her and hugged her tightly. "Kate, you've come back. Just like you said you would."

She laughed at his exuberance. "I missed you. I had to come back and visit." She looked him over, noticing the positive change in him.

"Did you see that I'm playing? I don't have to stay in the bed no more. Doc Boyd says I'm getting better." He displayed a big grin on his face. "What happened to your hand? Did you get hurt? Doc Boyd can fix it for you."

She broke into a wide, open smile, happiness slipping in her every pore. "I'm so glad to hear you're getting better. Are you ready to play? I can't do much, but I'm willing to try." Telling him how she'd obtained the injury would start an entire conversation she didn't wish to have with a child.

He grabbed her good hand. "Come on. I know just what we'll do."

---

PLAYING with the children had worn Kate out, but it was time for her and Ariana to begin their individual room visits.

"I'd like to visit Jason first." Kate looked at her sister, unable to hide the pain in her eyes. She knew not every child survived leukemia, but she wanted Jason to be one of the survivors. He meant too much to her.

She received no argument from her sister. Ariana knew how close Kate had become with the boy.

Hesitating at his partially open door, a commotion down the hallway got her attention. A gunshot rang out. Immediately, she shoved Ariana in the room. "Lock it and call security." Then she moved swiftly down the hall.

A man attempted to pull a child out of a room where a nurse lay bleeding and unconscious on the floor.

Agent Brent pointed his weapon at the man. "FBI. Drop it."

She tapped Agent Keller, who stood between Kate and the room, on the shoulder. "I've got this."

"No. We're leaving. Brent can handle it."

"No," she said firmly, "We're getting closer. I can diffuse this. It's a child we're talking about, not my enemy."

He nodded but didn't move from his position, only moved closer, still behind the other agent.

Kate spoke around both men to the man holding the gun. "William, let him go. You know you aren't supposed to be here. Billy is staying."

"Stay out of this. He's my son, and he's leaving with me."

"That's not going to happen today, William. The court says he stays and you're not allowed to visit. He has to be treated."

On a previous visit, a concerned nurse had advised her of the court order and William's insistence he take his son home. Unfortunately, the boy's father felt "beating the devil out of him" was all he needed.

He pointed the weapon at his struggling son. "Move or I shoot him."

Tears streamed down Billy's face and he stilled.

She dropped her voice and spoke softly. "We can't let you out of here with him, William."

"Drop your guns and move. I'll shoot him if you don't let us pass."

Billy's eyes widened, and his small body trembled.

She told the agents to put their weapons away and leave the room. They refused, so she pushed her way in front of them. "Don't fight me in front of the child," she seethed under her breath knowing she was breaking protocol, but not caring if it helped Billy.

"Look, William, you don't have to do this. Hand me the gun, and we'll call it a day."

"I said *move*. I'm not leaving without him." He tightened his grip on his son's arm.

Billy cried out in pain and fear.

*Shit!* She slowly advanced toward them, inch by inch, hoping it went unnoticed as did the screech of shoes hurrying down the hallway and police radios crackling. "William, hand me the gun."

His hand shook. "Don't come any closer."

Stopping an arm's length away from them, Kate reached out her hand midway between them and kept her voice soft and calm. "Hand it here, William. You don't really want to hurt him."

His eyes searched the room resting on the two federal agents behind Kate. He swallowed hard and lowered the weapon. Kate reached out and removed it from his grasp.

"Now let Billy go."

He looked at his son. "He's my son. He belongs with me," he said in a broken voice.

"I understand this is hard for you, but Billy belongs here right now. So, let him go."

William complied then stepped toward her, his face a mask of threatening energy. He moved, ever so slightly, but enough that Kate saw the projection of his plan to attack.

She angled her body to his, pulled her bent arm forward and then shoved it backward until her elbow connected with his ribs before the agents rushed him.

Without regard to anything else, including the pain in her hand, Kate grasped Billy and hurried from the room. "It's okay, Billy."

Hustling down the hall to a new room, Kate's heart broke at the sobs coming from the child. She pushed off everyone, all of her focus on the little boy until his favorite nurse arrived.

After dealing with the police, she and Ariana were beyond exhausted, but they wouldn't deny the time with the kids. Besides, she had to see Jason and this was her last outing, so she planned to make the most of it. AJ was going to have a fit when he heard what had happened. She'd be lucky not to be chained to a chair in her apartment.

With lockdown lifted, she and Ariana arrived at his door. Smiling at the thought of seeing him again, she knocked.

"Yeah?"

They entered the room.

"Ariana! Kate! Kate, I heard you fought Billy's dad."

Jason, reclined back against the pillows, waited for each of them to go to the bed so he could reach over and hug them. Kate smiled inwardly at the excitement written on his face and held on tight when it was her turn. She couldn't let go because she needed to give him her strength to fight his current infection.

"I'd hoped you'd come by today," he said in her shoulder.

"We're glad to see you. I hear you've been good for the doctors and nurses." Reluctantly, she released him.

"They mean well." Jason, at twelve, acted like a young adult. He'd missed a great deal of a regular childhood due to his leukemia. "Are you going to tell me what happened?" The boy almost bounced off the bed with curiosity.

"No," Kate said firmly.

"So, tell us. What's been happening?" Ariana asked.

He frowned. "They're keeping me in bed most of the time and won't let me go play. They haven't told me, but I know that I'm not getting better." The boy's serious tone held too much resolve, as if he'd accepted his fate.

Tears formed in Kate's eyes, and she blinked rapidly to keep them at bay. She had to be strong for him. "I'm sure it won't be long that you'll be back out there playing." God, she hoped so.

"I have to. I have to be strong to be a quarterback. I want to be ready for next season." He picked up the worn football lying next to him in bed.

Her heart ached. "I bet you'll beat out all the other boys for the position." If he got out of here, Kate would hire a trainer to help him become the best quarterback his school had ever seen.

Being a young boy, he asked again about the incident with William. This time she told him a little about it, only what she imagined was being shared. After they played down her part in the excitement, she asked what he wanted to do, play a game or read.

"I'm reading a wizard, and it's so long. Will you read me a few chapters, please?"

She nodded and smiled, knowing that "so long" to a twelve-year-old could probably be read in a few hours. "We'd love to read to you."

Kate and Ariana took turns reading chapters out loud.

"I think that one professor is really bad," Jason told them after a big interaction in the story.

She raised an eyebrow. "Really?"

"Yeah, and, I think it would be cool to be able to change into a cat. Actually, I'd rather be a dog."

And so the conversation went until Jason tired. He stopped Kate at the end of a chapter. "That's enough. I'll read the rest later."

She closed the book and set it on his nightstand. "It's a good book. If you like this type of story, there are plenty more like it."

"I like that a good wizard will beat a bad one."

Kate laughed, already knowing how the book ended. "I think he just might."

"I know you visit other kids while you're here, so it's okay if you have to leave."

He was such a polite and respectful child. His parents had done a wonderful job raising him. What would happen to him now? It'd been four months and no relatives had come forward.

"I think I'll do just that. I miss some of the other kids, too." Ariana gave him a hug. "Good-bye, Jason. You keep fighting." She left the room.

"What about you, Kate?"

She reached for his hand and smiled. "I can stay with you as long as you want."

# *Eight*

A THUNDERSTORM DARKENED the sky. The fat raindrops pounding on the windshield hadn't eased up since they'd left Ross Communication, after returning from visiting the children. The headlights had little effect breaking through the blackness that accompanied the heavy rainfall. It was a reprieve to see a streak of lightning flash across the star hidden sky, highlighting the skyline. Even though expected, the loud clap of thunder that immediately followed startled her. She thought of how nervous Dottie got during storms.

After Agent Brent parked, she didn't wait for her protective detail. Getting to Dottie took priority. She opened her car door, popped her umbrella and raced to her apartment, arriving on her doorstep with wet shoes and pants legs.

A muffled, deep male voice sounded from her apartment, and she automatically reached for the missing weapon on her hip. Pain shot through her hand from the contact with her side. Before she could remove the weapon from her purse, Joy laughed and Kate relaxed. It must be Doug, Joy's boyfriend, visiting.

Kate quietly stepped inside and scanned the room for the

visitor, catching sight of two handsome men. She locked gazes with Jesse and awareness zipped through her, tingling down her spine. So lost in his eyes, she didn't notice AJ at first.

He cleared his throat and heat crept up her neck. If he didn't have good news, she might slap that knowing smirk off his face.

Dottie wasn't cowering from the storm. She sat in her usual spot by the door waiting for her, the dog's tail rapidly thumping on the floor. Kate set her purse on the small table and petted the excited pup, scratching her behind the ears.

"Hey, my Dottie-Girl. Were you a good girl today?"

The men were dressed casually, in jeans and T-shirts, and Jesse showed off his well-defined biceps. She fought to keep from reaching out to touch him. The craving flowed through her every nerve ending and settled low in her belly. This man was testing her no casual sex rule without realizing it.

He looked her over seductively and an electrifying shudder reverberated through her.

Or, maybe he did realize it.

Joy hopped up from the couch where she'd been sitting a little too close to AJ. "I hope it's okay, but I let them in so they wouldn't have to wait for you in the rain. AJ showed me his badge, and they assured me it would be okay," she rushed to nervously explain.

Taking a deep breath helped Kate keep her temper in check. No, it wasn't okay, but Joy didn't need to see her explode. Once her dogsitter left, the men would get a big piece of her mind.

Fixing a smile on her face, she tried to ease the girl's nerves. "It's okay, Joy. Hello, AJ. Jesse." She nodded at each man. Her gaze locked with Jesse's again, a strange flutter appearing in her chest.

"Well, Dottie's been fed, and we got her walk in before the rain started. I'll see you tomorrow."

"Thanks, Joy." Kate noticed she didn't have an umbrella or rain jacket and the rain still fell from the sky in heavy droplets. "Why don't you take my umbrella? It's right outside the door." She'd forgotten dropping it in her haste to grab a weapon.

Joy smiled, a look of relief covering her face. "That'd be great. Thanks." She petted Dottie and departed with a glance and smiled at AJ.

Kate locked the door then rounded on the men who were now standing. Dottie felt her agitation and whined. She reached down to soothe her, hoping to also calm herself. She knew that she had manufactured the anger to cover for her intense draw to Jesse.

Before she could speak, AJ put his hands up, palms turned to her. "Now, Kate, don't be mad at Joy."

She almost laughed out loud at how she'd put him on the defensive. He didn't deserve it, but it was kind of fun to see him squirm. "Mad? Why should I be mad, Special Agent Alexander *Joshua* Hamilton.

He cringed at what she hoped was the use of his full name. "Well." He paused and looked at Jesse for help and found none. "We do have something. Let's sit down and talk about it." He gestured to the couch.

A knock sounded on the door, and she turned and opened it to Agent Keller. "I'm fine."

He nodded at AJ, a nervous look in his eyes. She imagined part of that was for his taking so damn long to follow her. "Agent Brent and I'll be outside."

"Christ, Kate. You didn't even check to see who it was before you opened the door," Jesse said.

She didn't want the old Jesse, the one who had scrutinized her work and always found fault, around her. Sighing heavily, she glanced at him. "What are you doing here, Jesse?"

"Don't you want to take off your wet shoes and pants and get comfortable?"

She kicked off her shoes with eyes narrowed at him. "I'm changing, because I want to. It'll only take a couple of minutes."

Walking up the stairs, Dottie at her heels, she heard, "Need an extra hand?"

She pretended she hadn't heard Jesse or when AJ cursed at him… or when a flush swept through her at the thought.

Exhausted, but intrigued to find out what AJ knew, she rushed. Dottie led the way downstairs once she was changed. "Okay, what's this all about? Did you figure out who the shooter is and who he's after?" She sat in the chair, needing to focus on what AJ had to say.

"Yes and no." AJ sat, fidgeting.

AJ didn't fidget. Something had happened that she wouldn't like. "Are you going to elaborate?"

She glanced at Jesse. AJ straddled a thin line keeping Jesse involved in this investigation, even if he was a possible target.

As if reading her mind, AJ spoke, "Kate, this may involve both you and Jesse."

They'd already guessed that it was either one of them. "Wait, you said both."

"Jesse and I don't agree on whether the note refers to you or someone else." He glanced at his brother.

Her eyes narrowed. "Note? What note? Have you been holding out on me, AJ?" She thought she could trust him to keep her in the loop.

His jaw tightened, and he gave her a tight-lipped smile. "When Jesse left from your um… date, he found a note on his SUV."

Jesse finding a note after leaving her apartment bothered her. They'd followed him, or they'd watched her apartment. Either scenario wasn't good. "Okay, you've got my attention."

Her partner handed her a copy of the note.

She read and furrowed her eyebrows. "What does this have to do with me?" Her heart pounded. An image of Jesse's daughter flashed through her mind. The little girl he was so proud of was in danger. Reagan. That was whom he loved.

"I think it has nothing to do with you, but Jesse on the other hand has a different theory."

She turned to Jesse, who'd stayed curiously quiet. He appeared calm for someone who had a psycho after one of his loved ones. "What are you doing to protect Reagan? Why aren't you with her?"

"The women I love, my daughter, my sister and my niece, are protected. It's you I'm worried about."

The look on her face must've expressed her confusion and disbelief. "Why are you worried about me? It's obvious it's you the Facilitator is mad at. He must've followed you here."

Jesse leaned forward, put his arms on his thighs and clasped his hands together. "I think the note means you, Kate."

Her laughter was abrupt. Strange and disquieting thoughts began to race through her mind. Surely she'd heard him wrong.

SHEILA KELL

"Me? But, you don't love me. We barely know each other. Why do you think it's me he's after instead of one of your family?"

"It's the shooting. Something bothered me, and I finally figured it out. That was your daily route; anyone who watched you would know you'd be there. Me? It was coincidental that I was there. This is a cold-blooded killer who is careful. He wouldn't have just been on the street with the hope that I was there. No, he was after *you*."

Kate shuddered, a sliver of foreboding crawling up her spine. What he'd said made perfect sense. Still, the killer could've been following him. She turned to AJ who shrugged.

"That part bothered me, too."

Looking between the two men, she wavered, trying to comprehend and analyze. "So, what? What you're saying is they didn't follow Jesse and that I'm the target because someone thinks he loves me? How could they think that?"

Jesse wiped his hand across his forehead, then turned to her. "I think it started when we left the bar. Someone saw us and targeted you because of it."

Could it really be her? That was madness, pure and simple.

"Actually, you're getting HIS protection."

Her gaze jerked in Jesse's direction. Disbelief at the craziness of the whole situation filtered through her. The connection was too circumstantial. The note had let them know she wasn't the target. She wondered why they were struggling to understand that. "Seriously? This note proves I'm not the target. Even the FBI agrees." She threw AJ a pointed look. "Jesse doesn't love me. We mean nothing to each other, so honestly, I don't need any men following me around." A smile, one caught between amused and bemused play on her lips.

Jesse stiffened as though she'd struck him.

Confusion seeped into her thoughts at what the man must think of her. She controlled her instinctive reaction to physically reach out to reassure him, not wanting to offend him. "Look, Jesse," her voice softened, "I'm sorry to hear this psycho is after someone you love, but you two"—she pointed her index finger back and forth between them—"need to leave me out of this. I want this shooter caught because he hit me, but I don't want, or need, protection since no one is after me. It's obvious they are following Jesse not me." She'd been collateral damage. In the wrong place at the wrong time. "Honestly, HIS is best off being where they're needed."

"Kate, I may not agree that you're the target, but I trust Jesse. It's a long shot, but it's quite possible the killer is misinformed about your relationship. You should take this protection." AJ paused. "Just in case."

"It doesn't matter what you want," Jesse growled, looking thoroughly irritated.

Kate didn't know whether to laugh or be incredulous. She stood, ready for the conversation to be over. "Unless you can tell me who the shooter is, then this conversation is over, gentlemen." Damn overprotective, alpha men.

Jesse stood. "No, sweetheart." His face broke into a wide grin.

Butterflies fluttered away in her stomach at the challenging gleam that appeared in his eyes.

"This conversation is far from over."

WHEN angry, Kate tensed her body, squinted her eyes, and clenched her fists, making her even more desirable. She'd changed into a pair of slacks, accentuating her tight, firm ass. Jesse wanted to reach out and grab it, massage it, and squeeze it as he pulled her close to him, in his lap.

His desire for her had become a threat to her life and all-consuming to his. To properly protect her, he had to distance himself. He couldn't get personally involved. For the first time in his career, he didn't think it possible. Every time they neared each other, a jolt of lust like he'd never felt before seared through his body, and his fingers ached to reach out and touch her.

Yeah, he desired her, but he didn't love Kate, not like the Facilitator thought. But, Jesse liked her more than he should. He could've called in a favor and had the FBI protective detail remain with her, but he trusted his men more. No matter what she said, Jesse would damn well be staying.

He pointed to the chair she'd vacated. "Sit. We still have plenty to discuss."

She narrowed her eyes, probably cycling through possible retorts.

He didn't need to argue with her. He needed her to listen so he repeated, his request with his voice as pleasant as possible, "Kate, please sit. We need to discuss this."

Releasing an exasperated sigh, she reluctantly dropped into the chair. More like huffed and plopped, but he'd take it.

He sat and glanced at AJ, who appeared ready to referee again.

"I believe you're still in danger, whether you agree or not."

AJ hastily stood. "I'm leaving."

*Fucking pussy.* Jesse couldn't believe he was already bailing.

"You two can hash this out. Kate, if you want the FBI detail, I'll fight for it, but I know how you are about someone protecting you. HIS is the best there is, and I trust them."

"There's no need to have the agents here, AJ. Thank you for understanding how I feel about it."

He nodded to Jesse and turned to the door.

Jesse quickly deciphered the uncomfortable look that moved swiftly over her face when she realized they'd be alone. He didn't like that look. He didn't like it at all.

Standing, Jesse quickly moved toward his brother. "I'll lock up behind you."

"Uh oh," AJ warned.

She narrowed her eyes. "I'm quite capable of locking my own door."

He chuckled at the color creeping onto her cheeks as her arousing temper began to flare. "I'm aware of that." He brushed past her with his brother.

"Good-bye, Kate."

"Good-bye, AJ." She remained instead of following them to the door.

Before exiting, his brother turned to him and kept his voice low. "Treat her right, Jesse."

"I can't believe you said that," he responded incredulously.

"Yeah, well, just do it. Good-bye."

"'Bye." He locked the door behind the brother he wished he could watch over better.

Finally alone, Jesse took in the sight of her, stopping at her injured hand. A wound she had because of him.

She looked none too happy, and he would be on the wrong end of any anger.

"Kate, I don't want to argue with you. This is too important, and we need to discuss it like grown adults."

"There's really nothing to discuss. I don't know how you came to your conclusion, but you're wrong."

He stepped toward her and she stepped back. That hurt. Last night they'd shared some good moments. He'd thought they were moving forward. Obviously, she didn't want what he did. But he wasn't quite sure exactly what he wanted.

"I don't think I'm wrong, Kate. Maybe he thinks we're dating and things are more involved than they are." He had to convince her that she needed his protection.

She dropped into the chair with a deflated mien. "No. I don't believe it's me he's after. You really need to be with Reagan."

That was the second time she'd worried about his daughter, and he'd heard real concern in her voice both times. She hadn't even met Reagan, and yet, she wanted to ensure her protection from the psycho. A chunk of ice broke off his frozen heart. "My brothers are with her. She's in great hands."

He perched on the edge of the couch. "Kate, you can agree or not, but I'm going to ensure you're protected." Squirming a little with discomfort, he needed to discuss the real reason she didn't want someone protecting her. He cleared his throat. "Kate, I know about your first partner." Agent Marshall had stepped in front of a bullet meant for her; it had caught him in the throat. How would he assure her that no one else was going to die protecting her? He didn't want anyone to, but it was the oath they took. It could happen. "I know your worry, but it's not necessary with us."

"Okay, *if* and I do mean *if* I agree to this, promise me that one, your daughter is truly safer with others than with you."

A twinge struck his heart. He wanted to be with Reagan, but his gut told him that he needed to be here. And, she was safe, maybe not safer because no one would keep her safer than her father, but her uncles wouldn't allow anything to happen to her. He could live with that.

"Two," she continued, "that no one will try to confine me. I promise I won't be dumb and make life difficult, but I need room to breathe." She inhaled deeply and released it in a sigh. "And three, that as soon as we come up with any scrap of evidence indicating that I'm in fact not the target, the detail stops. The last thing you or your men need is to waste time or resources on me."

No matter what she said, she was worth every single resource he had and more. "I'll take those into consideration."

"Jesse, do you purposely try to piss me off?"

He chuckled. "No, but I like you when you're angry at me." He winked and before she could argue, he stood. "Deal. Now, I'm hungry. How about you? Let's take our minds off this and make some dinner." He moved to the kitchen leaving her to process what he'd said.

She joined him and didn't say a word about his still being there as they prepared penne with meat sauce together like a couple who had been with each other for years. It reminded him of the intimate times with his wife. If only he had gone into the store with her. He mentally shook his head. He had to wash away those thoughts. He needed to focus on Kate's safety.

They chatted during dinner over safe topics like the Orioles' and the upcoming Ravens' season. They avoided any mention of her safety or HIS.

As they'd cleared the dishes, he remembered what he'd brought her. "Come into the living room with me." Jesse clasped her good hand and gave it a tug. "If you're going to protect yourself, you're going to need this."

She opened the box. When she looked at the gift, pleasure washed over her face and her eyes sparkled.

*Is that how she looks when she comes?* Damn his raging libido. That was not how he should be thinking.

"It's a left-handed holster." *Like she doesn't know that.* He stopped himself from rolling his eyes. "I thought you might have easier access than digging in your purse."

"Jesse, this is so thoughtful. You didn't have to do this, but thank you."

He cleared his throat. "You're welcome. Maybe we can go to the range some time and let you practice shooting left-handed."

Stroking the holster, she smiled softly. "I'd like that."

The movement of her hands aroused him more than he already had been. *Fuck!* He needed to do something or he'd end up grabbing her and doing what he'd said he shouldn't do. "Why don't we sit and watch a movie?"

She arched a brow. "We need to talk about your men first."

"There is no discussion. They stay. Now, let's see what's on TV." He lounged on the couch and patted the seat beside him. "Come on."

Steam radiated off her and he had to admit, he enjoyed her struggle. He grinned when she sat in the chair. Stretching out his legs, he crossed them as he picked up the remote.

At least she hadn't tossed him out yet. Patience.

KATE yawned at the end of the movie. "It's time I turned in." She stood and stretched her arms above her head, inadvertently pushing her breasts out.

Jesse's mouth watered. "Okay, let's turn in."

She froze. "Um, Jesse. I'm not going to sleep with you."

"So you've told me." He grinned. "I guess now's as good a time as any to tell you that until the Facilitator is captured, where you go, I go." He waited for her reaction.

You?" Her voice pitched and she swallowed hard.

"Yes, me. And, I'm staying here. With you." Before she could respond, he added, "My bag is already in the guest room."

She spoke slowly and softly, "I'm safe in my apartment. I don't need you to stay. I'll walk you to the door. Good night, Jesse."

"Good night, Kate." He turned and headed to the stairs and the guest room, leaving her speechless and staring after him.

He settled in for the night and thought about his predicament. He had a psycho after someone he loved. He'd spoken with Reagan and his brothers earlier in the evening and had relaxed a little. His daughter would be kept safe.

His tension over Kate wasn't just because of a killer. The sexual tension between them couldn't be ignored. He knew he shouldn't, but he'd have her in his bed.

He told himself that he could still protect her and have amazing sex with her. He had to figure out what it would take to get her there.

HE hadn't been asleep long before the nightmare returned.

*Jen picked him up from work, and they were on their way to her parents' house where their two-month-old daughter was being looked after. He noticed they were low on gas and pulled into a gas station.*

*"I'll grab us some water. Do you want me to wait for you?" Her hand rested on the door handle, and she wiggled her eyebrows seductively.*

*Grinning, he shook his head. "Not this time. I'm ready to get home." He leaned over the seat and gave her a quick kiss, tugging lightly on her lower lip as they separated. "I love you."*

*She smiled. "I love you, too."*

*Jesse watched her walk away before he filled the gas tank. Her luscious ass was one of her best features, and he never missed a chance to watch it.*

*The tank was full, and he wondered what kept her. There was only one other car in the lot, so there shouldn't be a line. He smiled. Maybe she was waiting for him. Usually they went in the store together and played in the aisles. At least until he was so aroused they had to leave or risk arrest.*

*His stomach growled. The thought of homemade lasagna and then later the dessert that Jen served up in the bedroom was all it took for him to walk toward the store. Midway, his cell phone rang and he stopped to answer.*

*"Dev, what's up?"*

*"My security clearance came through. It's official. I'm CIA."*

*Devon made him feel like a proud papa, but he wished he knew what his brother would be doing. Even though his brother was a grown man, he still worried about him. "Congratulations! This is big. Sounds like it's time to get the boys together and celebrate."*

*Jesse heard a gunshot. His body went on instant alert and a sudden sinking sensation ran through him.*

*Frantic to get to her, he hastily dropped the phone in his pocket, pulled his weapon and ran toward the store. He reached for the door before his FBI training kicked in. It took everything he had not to rush into the store, to Jen. After several deep breaths, he calmed himself as much as he could.*

*He put the phone back to his ear hoping his brother was still on the line. "Dev, call 911."*

*"Already done. What's happening?"*

*Jesse peeked in the window and couldn't see her. He had to know. He couldn't wait for backup. His wife was in there.*

*"I can't wait. Just listen."*

*"Jesse!"*

*Ignoring protocol, he put his phone in his pocket and entered the store alone.*

*"FBI! Drop your weapon!"*

*Jen lay on the floor with a gunshot wound to her head. There was so much blood. Oh God. Oh God. Jen. He had to get to her. To help her. He couldn't lose her.*

*Losing himself for a minute, he dropped his gun and moved toward her before he remembered the situation and looked up. First, he had to get the fucker who had shot her,*

*He walked further into the store. The robber held his weapon on the clerk, turned to him with shaking hands and eyes wide, and with the look that told Jesse the man was strung out on drugs. He'd been in volatile situations before, but he'd never been this much on edge.*

*"You don't want to do this. Drop your weapon."*

*The blessed sound of sirens filled the air. He needed the backup.*

*He barely held on to his anger.*

*"I'm getting my money and getting outta here. There's nothing you can do about it."*

*The clerk pulled a shotgun from under the counter and pointed it at the robber. "You're not getting my money, asshole. I'll blow you away first."*

*"Put your weapon down. I have this situation in hand." Jesse didn't take his eyes off the robber and didn't need the clerk interfering. The situation was precarious enough. There were too many guns, and he needed this to end so he could get to Jen.*

*The robber looked around with panic in his eyes as police cars pulled into the parking lot. Jesse could see when the robber realized he wasn't getting out of there.*

*"Police! Drop your weapons!"*

*Jesse knew the drill. He set his weapon down, knelt and put his hands behind his head. "I'm FBI Special Agent Jesse Hamilton. My creds are in my jacket pocket."*

*"There's no need for that. Get up, Jesse," Officer Jeff Brandon, an old friend, said. "Shit. Is that?"*

*Jesse flew across the room and leaned over Jen. He touched her throat, searching for a pulse, hoping for a miracle. Nothing. His voice caught, no sound could come.*

*The room went out of focus as he held his wife's hand, tears filling his eyes. This couldn't be real. It couldn't have happened to them. To him and Reagan. Reagan. She'd grow up without her mother all because of some junkie.*

*He refused to release her hand when the paramedics arrived. She was gone. There was nothing they could do for her. He shouldn't have let her come in by herself. He should've gone in the store with her like he always did. He shouldn't have taken the phone call. He would've been with her. It was his job to protect her. His wife. The mother of his child.*

*His blood boiled. He'd never felt so much rage. Rage at himself. He'd failed.*

Jesse woke with a start, sucking air into his lungs, his heart pounding, grief bleeding from his body. He twisted to untangle himself from the sweaty sheets, then hopped from the bed and paced.

*Jen died because I made the wrong choice and wasn't there. I can't let the same thing happen to Kate. I have to protect her.*

# Nine

JESSE WALKED DOWN the stairs shirtless and with a morning shadow on his jaw. Kate was acutely aware of his tall, athletic physique. She gulped at the sight of a light sprinkling of black hair on his chest, followed by the line tapering down to his unbuttoned jeans. Her body warmed, her face flushed, and she jerked her head up before he caught her checking him out.

He grunted as he passed her on his way to the coffee pot. He filled the cup she'd left out for him, quickly drank and cursed at its heat.

Her chuckle earned her a glare. Obviously, he didn't handle mornings well. She wasn't a morning person herself, but that morning she had to be. She planned to send him packing. While she'd reluctantly agreed for HIS detail protection, there was no way she could handle Jesse 24/7.

Turning, he leaned back against the kitchen counter and took a cautious sip this time. "What's the plan for today? I won't even assume you'll do the smart thing and stay inside."

Dottie approached him, and he scratched the top of her head. *Traitor dog.* "Dot and I are going for our morning walk." Kate tried to keep her eyes level with his, but they kept slipping down to his chest.

He shook his head. "Didn't the drive-by teach you anything?"

"Yes. It taught me not to be near you on the sidewalk." She hadn't meant for the flippant remark to emerge, but it had and she wasn't sorry because it technically was true.

He sighed. "Kate, being out in the open—"

"Dottie needs to go and I, well, I need the fresh air also. I already feel cooped up."

Seeming to understand, he nodded. "Give me a minute to get dressed, and I'll go with you."

After returning from the park, Kate cooked breakfast while Jesse showered. When he was the nice Jesse, she liked being around him, but she couldn't let herself get too cozy with the situation. Affairs were not her style.

She wondered why she hadn't called AJ already. She'd picked up her phone several times, but hadn't made the call.

Her phone rang.

"Good morning, Mary."

She heard a heated conversation between Mary and Dan.

*Dammit.*

Kate rushed to the door then remembered Jesse. She raced up the stairs and banged on the bathroom door. "Jesse, I need your help. Right now!" She wouldn't let Dan hurt Mary and get away with it this time.

She put her cell phone back to her ear. "Mary, can you hear me?" She didn't receive a response and guessed Mary must have unknowingly voice-dialed her.

The shower shut off and Jesse opened the door with a towel

wrapped around his waist and a weapon in his hand. "What's wrong?"

Did he really take his weapon into the bathroom with him?

The image of his wet body burned in her mind. She felt a ripple of excitement, wanting to reach out and run her fingers through the damp curls on his chest. Damn. His hard body was a visual temptation that could break her resolve of not getting involved with him.

She mentally shook her head and deliberately shut out any awareness of him. She couldn't deal with her growing attraction to him.

"My friend Mary is being beaten and needs our help right now."

"Call 911 and let me throw on some clothes." He closed the door.

"No 911!" Kate didn't wait for a reply. Downstairs, she hurriedly clipped on her new holster.

Jesse approached her with damp hair. "Tell me what's happening while I put on my shoes. And why the hell aren't you calling 911?"

They left the apartment and were met by Ken and Danny, the HIS detail. "Follow us." Jesse didn't wait for a response.

Speeding to Mary's, Jesse asked, "Kate, why aren't you calling 911?"

She sighed, wishing she didn't have to share this "Mary won't allow it. I don't think she realizes she called me. I'm not sure how she's going to respond to our just showing up."

Kate seethed as she thought about all of the times Mary had called her after Dan had beaten her. She'd always made an excuse for him, blaming herself. One of the last times, she'd had to go to the hospital had convinced Mary to tell him to stay away, but it wasn't enough to get her to get a restraining order. Once she'd healed, she'd forgiven him, and he'd started turning up again.

Jesse cursed. "Tell me everything."

As they sped across town, Kate relayed Mary and Dan's history.

They arrived at her friend's, heard crashing, and entered without knocking. She scanned the room and saw Mary huddled in the corner.

Jesse had already pulled Dan off Josh. Kate wondered why he was there, but was also thankful because he probably saved Mary a lot of pain. She rushed to Mary. Kate looked her over, taking in the split lip. "Mary, are you hurt?"

Tears streamed down Mary's face. "No. Make him stop, Kate. He's hurting Josh."

She looked over to see Ken take Dan from Jesse.

"Who the fuck are you?" Dan struggled to free himself from their tight grasp.

"We're your worst nightmare, asshole." Disgust filled Jesse's voice. She'd never seen him this angry. She actually worried about Dan for a moment.

Mary pushed her way up and rushed to Josh. "Are you okay?"

With a swelling eye and bruising cheek, he looked at her as if she'd lost her mind. "No, I'm not okay." Then in a calm voice, he asked, "What about you?"

She sniffled and hugged him midsection. "I'll be fine."

Dan's face filled with rage as Kate stepped beside Jesse. "Bitch, you shouldn't interfere. You've stuck your nose into our business one too many times."

"Dan, she has asked you to leave her alone. She doesn't want you around her. This time, I get the pleasure of seeing you go to jail."

The bastard actually smirked. "Mary won't have me arrested. She loves me."

"First of all, she doesn't love you, and second, this time Josh will be the one pressing charges."

Mary grabbed Josh's arms. "No, Josh, don't do it. Let him go."

He jerked his arms from her grasp. "Are you crazy? He needs to go to jail for this. He hit you."

Through a stream of new tears, Mary looked into Josh's eyes. "Josh, leave it. I just want him gone."

Josh's face softened. "Mary, is this really what you want me to do? Just let him get away with this?" He lightly touched her split lip. "He deserves to be punished."

"Yes."

Kate couldn't believe what she was hearing. She didn't understand why Mary protected Dan. "Mary, both of you need to press charges. You can't let him keep getting away with this. Again."

"If I have him arrested, one day I'll have to appear before him in court and tell someone everything. They'll blame me because it's my fault. I don't want to do that, Kate. Surely you understand?" Mary wrapped her arms around her belly in a protective gesture.

Kate swallowed and took a moment before she answered. She'd never thought Mary let him get away with this for that reason. She didn't see her friend as a victim of abuse, but that was what she was. A victim enough that Dan had convinced her she deserved everything he did to her. That it was her fault. It made Kate want to kick his balls up to his throat.

"Mary, it's not your fault. You know we'd be with you in court. You don't have to do this alone."

Mary shook her head. "I don't want to do it, Kate. I just want to be free of him."

She looked at Josh who watched Mary closely. "Do we call the police?"

Shaking his head, his gaze didn't leave Mary. "No, Kate. I'm not going to press charges."

"What the fuck? You're going to let him get away with this? He beat a woman. He beat you." Jesse's nostrils flared.

Josh raked his fingers through his hair in frustration. "Mary wants him to be let go, so we let him go."

Jesse growled. "You may let him go, but we're not going to."

Dan's head snapped up and a look of fear appeared on his face. "What do you mean?"

Jesse nodded to the door. "Ken."

The first smile she'd seen on Ken's face appeared. "Let's go." He and Danny ushered Dan from the house.

Jesse looked around the room, his gaze stopping on Mary. "Do either of you need to go to the hospital?"

She shook her head. "I'm fine."

"I'll be okay. Nothing a bag of frozen peas won't fix." Due to the swelling, Josh's smile appeared lopsided.

Realizing they weren't acquainted, she introduced Jesse.

"I'm sorry we had to meet under these circumstances." Jesse shook Josh's hand.

He winced at Jesse's grip on his raw knuckles.

"Sorry, man."

Josh nodded.

"I'm thankful you came with Kate. Will Dan be okay?" Mary's concern had both men's jaws tightening.

"Don't worry about him. If he ever shows up here again, you call me." Jesse's voice brokered no argument.

"Okay," Mary responded weakly.

There'd be no call. Kate would talk to Josh about watching over her. He wouldn't mind doing it. She could count on him to call her or Jesse if Dan returned.

Jesse looked at Kate. "You ready?"

"Mary, do you need me?"

"She's got me, Kate." Josh moved closer to Mary's side.

---

JESSE and Kate rode home in tense silence. They arrived at her apartment, and she waited for him to unlock the door and checked inside. She felt like an idiot standing there waiting when she could check her apartment herself. He'd been helpful at Mary's, so she'd let him play the alpha male taking care of the damsel in distress, if that's what he really needed to do. For a few days.

"Thank you for being here today, Jesse."

She could see him reining in his anger with his jaw tight and his lips flat. Maybe he was imagining what Ken was doing with Dan like she was. Although she wasn't sure she wanted to know.

Jesse surprised her by putting a hand on her shoulder, sending an involuntary shiver through her. "Kate, I told you where you go, I go. I would've been pissed had you tried to handle that on your own. I need you to believe me that there is a possible threat against you. You can't take any chances."

"I still don't believe you, but you're right. I can't take the chance."

His thumb rubbed her shoulder. Her sensitivity to his touch shocked her. "I'll not fight you, unless you're unreasonable."

He nodded, seemed to realize what he'd been doing, released her and stepped back. "First, you don't walk Dottie any longer. My men can do it. That is too much time out in the open."

She couldn't argue about opening herself up as a target so easily. But she wouldn't let just anyone take care of her dog. "I agree, but I'd rather have Joy walk her. She wouldn't mind the extra pay."

"That's fine."

"Jesse, I may be the target, but I'm not hiding in here."

He grinned. "From you, sweetheart, I'd expect no less."

# Ten

"IF YOU DON'T have anything planned for today, I'd like to see Reagan. It's Saturday so she's out of school." Jesse pushed his chair back from the dining table.

"Go and see Reagan. I'll be fine." Kate stood, picked up their lunch plates and walked to the kitchen to rinse them, feeling something akin to relief that she'd have some time away from him. The more she was alone with him, the stronger the pull.

"Kate, I'm not sure why you aren't getting this. Where you go, I go. So it stands to reason, where I go, you go. You're coming with me."

Startled at how close he'd approached, she spun around, tripped on his foot and fell against his chest. She inhaled sharply at the contact and reveled in the smell of the soap he'd used, mingled with his fresh male scent, then cursed her body for being turned-on by something as simple as his smell.

He reached for her waist. "Whoa. You okay?"

She nodded and attempted to step back, but his hands held her firmly in his loose embrace. She dropped her gaze, knowing if she peered into his sexy eyes, she'd lose herself and drown in a sea of golden-brown.

"Kate, look at me."

Warmth surged through Kate when her name rolled off his lips in his husky, challenging voice. When their gazes connected, the intense heat blazing in his eyes singed her. He drew her tight against him, and she found herself in dangerous territory. There was no mistaking his desire.

"Kate." He slowly lowered his head.

His cell phone rang. Jumping back, Kate bumped into the kitchen counter. Her body felt the roaring flame that had ignited inside her, touching her deep down.

Watching her attempt to separate herself from him, he circled her waist with his arm and pulled her close, refusing to allow her to slip by him.

He answered the phone and immediately, a smile tugged at his lips. "Hey, sweetheart."

With nowhere to go, she stood there awkwardly trying not to get closer to him. No man had affected her like this. She didn't think she could fight where their relationship would lead. *Relationship?* What the hell was she thinking? It was nothing but sexual desire, no matter what she wanted.

Jesse laughed. "We're coming to see you in a few minutes."

She snapped her head up to see his eyes sparkling with humor. "Yes, I'm bringing her with me."

His daughter knew about her? Did she know about the danger or did she think Kate was daddy's girlfriend? Five-year-olds were smart. She'd understand her daddy's work brought Kate there, not a chance she'd have a new mother.

"See you shortly. I love you, too."

He laid the phone on the counter. "Now, where were we?" he asked seductively.

She put her hand on his chest, felt the heat radiating between them. "We were almost doing something we aren't going to do."

He arched his eyebrows. "Oh, really?" The laughter in his voice caressed her senses. He was so appealing.

"Really. Now, let me by so I can get ready to leave." She pushed against his chest, surprised when he moved. She'd expected him to try to kiss her and felt a little disappointed he'd made no attempt.

ON the drive to Emily's house, Kate tried to break the tension by asking questions about Reagan, which Jesse happily answered. His love for his daughter shined brighter than the North Star when he spoke of her.

She looked forward to meeting Emily, who was the baby of the family and had doubled up on her college classes to finish early with a degree in accounting. It hadn't settled well with the brothers that she'd talked about moving away after she graduated.

The subject was quickly changed when she asked about the father of Emily's daughter. It was clearly a taboo subject. She realized she had to be careful in what she discussed with his sister. It did pique Kate's curiosity, though. The brothers didn't seem the type to let a man walk away from Emily and Amber.

A small brick house with about one-half of an acre of lush green lawn that extended to a wooded area came into view.

Kate did a quick scan of the surroundings. "I don't see your men."

"Trust me, they're there," he said as they exited the car.

She surveyed the area but couldn't find them.

Two men with visible holstered weapons on their sides walked out of the house and stood on the porch.

Jesse stepped up to meet them, but before he had an opportunity to speak, a squeal erupted, and he leaned down to catch the little girl launching herself at him. Reagan squeezed his neck with her small arms. She then pulled back and put both hands on his face, kissing him with a loud smack.

"Daddy, I missed you. Come see what I *drawed*." She noticed Kate and pointed at her. "Is this that lady you have to protect?"

With his daughter held tightly in his arms, Jesse turned to Kate. "Yes, pumpkin. Reagan, I'd like you to meet Miss Kate Ross. Kate, this is my daughter, Reagan."

Reagan smiled and the cutest tiny dimples appeared. "It's nice to meet you, Miss Kate." She turned back to her father. "Did I do it right, Daddy? Did I do good manners?"

He chuckled and kissed her cheek. "That was perfect, pumpkin." He kissed her cheek again.

"Did you want to come see what I *drawed*, Miss Kate?"

"I'd love to, Reagan."

"Give us a minute, and we'll be in there to see your beautiful pictures." He set Reagan down and shooed her back into the house.

She smiled up at her father. "Okay, Daddy, you have two minutes." She held up two fingers, holding down the rest with her other hand. "I'll be waiting."

Kate couldn't hold in the light laughter as she listened to Reagan give Jesse an order. She bet the little girl had all of the men twisted around her tiny finger.

He turned to her. "What?"

Shaking her head, she bit her lip to stop laughing.

"Kate, these are my brothers Brad and Matt."

Brad whistled. "Damn, Jesse. No wonder you chose to protect her and stuck us with the kids." He gave Kate an appraising look.

A beautiful woman approached, and Jesse pulled her into a tight hug. "Kate, this is my baby sister, Emily. Em, this is Kate Ross."

She wasn't what Kate had expected. She looked nothing like her brothers. She was petite, had shoulder-length blonde hair and baby blue eyes.

"Emily, it's nice to meet you." Kate extended her left hand.

Emily smiled and awkwardly shook it. "The same goes here." She gave Jesse a sly smile. "Come on in but keep it down. Amber's taking a much needed nap."

They followed Emily into the living room where Reagan had papers and crayons scattered on a white children's table in the center of the room. Jesse pulled out one of the tiny pink chairs and attempted to sit, garnering giggles from his daughter when he purposely fell to the floor.

"Silly, Daddy, you're too big for that chair."

"Silly, huh?" He moved to his daughter and tickled her.

A child's laughter, especially while being tickled, was one of the most uplifting sounds in the world. The contagiousness of it had Kate chuckling at Jesse's antics. She'd never expected him to be so playful, so carefree. He behaved like a different person. A father who made a fool of himself for his daughter.

When he stopped, Reagan talked between catching breaths,

"Again, Daddy."

He didn't disappoint her.

Kate's heart expanded as she watched the interaction between father and daughter. She'd had a great life with the Rosses but had always wondered what her life would've been like had her parents lived. Would her father have played with her like Jesse did with his daughter?

From the pale red couch, the twins returned their attention to the sports channel on the television.

Emily lightly touched her arm. "Come on. I was about to make Reagan a snack. This could go on for a while."

Brad turned and winked at Kate. "Don't forget us, Em. We need a snack, too. We're growing boys."

Their sister put her hands on her hips. "Well then, get your asses up and get something. You know where the kitchen is. And quit trying to flirt with your brother's girlfriend."

Did they really think she was Jesse's girlfriend? Surely, he'd explained the situation and her appearance. "Um, I'm not, um, Jesse's girlfriend."

The looks that passed between the twins and Emily told her they thought differently.

Kate frowned. "Really, he's just trying to protect me."

Brad stepped forward and wiggled his eyebrows playfully. "Well, then, how about we change out bodyguards?"

Not knowing how to respond, she looked to Jesse for help, but he was in deep conversation with Reagan.

Emily laughed. "I'm glad to see something has taken away your surliness, Brad, but you're wasting your breath. He's not even paying attention." She turned to Kate and motioned her to the kitchen.

"Emily reached into the refrigerator and pulled out a bag of grapes, a block of cheese and two apples. "Are you able to pull grapes off the stem?"

This one-handed thing annoyed Kate. "I think I can manage."

As they prepared a small three-sectioned princess plate for Reagan, ensuring nothing touched, along with a platter of snacks for the men, Kate's curiosity got the best of her. "What happened to Reagan's mother?"

Emily stilled. "Did Jesse not tell you?"

Kate shook her head. "I didn't ask him."

"I think you need to ask him." She grabbed the platter. "Now, let's bring this to my uninvited guests."

---

JESSE stood frozen outside the kitchen. He'd never discussed how his wife died with anyone outside his family, except to say it had been a robbery gone wrong. The raw guilt he felt couldn't be shared. And he didn't need people adding more blame to him because he should've been there to save her and not bullshitting with his brother. He should've known something had been wrong when she'd taken so long.

Kate would see him as a failure. If she knew about his culpability in his wife's death, she'd want him to leave because she couldn't depend on him. He wouldn't let that happen. She needed him, and he would be there. Without trying, she'd innocently turned him inside out.

Kate's eyes widened at his entry into the kitchen.

He forced a smile and reached for Reagan's plate. "Here, I'll take that."

Emily swatted playfully at his arm, and he grabbed it and acted wounded. "Of course, I do all the work, and you reap all the rewards."

He chuckled and went ahead of them into the living room. The twins both reached for the platter before Emily could set it down.

"Devon's here." Brad shoved an apple slice in his mouth.

A minute later, deep male laughter preceded his brother and two men entering the room. He watched Kate's reaction as he introduced Devon. Without being conceited, Jesse knew he and his brothers were considered handsome men. But, much to AJ's dismay, Devon was the most fawned over. Women said he had a sensual appeal about him. Whatever the hell that meant.

Jesse relaxed when she didn't react any differently than when she'd met his other brothers. Before he could introduce her to Joe and Steve, his niece commanded everyone's attention.

"Uncle Dev! Uncle Dev!" Reagan reached her arms up in the child signal to "pick me up."

Devon did just that and gave her a tight hug. "Hey, pip-squeak."

She pulled back and wrinkled her nose. "I'm not a pip-squeak. Aunt Em says I'm a big girl."

He tweaked her nose. "What's my *angel* been doing today? Have you been good for Aunt Em?"

He loved how great his brothers were with his daughter. They'd been his salvation after he'd lost Jen. None of them had known what to do with a two-month-old, but they'd been determined to give her all the love they had. Until he'd hired someone to help, Emily, as a teenager, had stepped forward and had taken charge. In no time, she'd insisted the men change diapers and burp Reagan.

"Of course I've been good. And I *drawed* today, Uncle Dev. I did a picture just for you." She squirmed in his arms. "Put me down so I can show you."

Devon chuckled and complied. He ruffled her hair. "Go get it so I can see your masterpiece."

"Hi, Mr. Joe and Mr. Steve." She waved and skipped off.

Six grown men stood transfixed by the little girl, broad smiles spread across their faces.

"She gets cuter every day," Devon commented.

Jesse stood taller, prouder. "She does. And more damn independent, too." She was at the I'll-do-it-myself stage and refused to allow Jesse to help her. It gave him mixed feelings. On one hand, he had pride in her new found independence. On the other hand, it disappointed him that she no longer needed him all of the time.

Jesse grabbed a chair and moved it beside Kate. He'd heard Brad flirting with her, whether to just fuck with him or not; he'd wanted to punch his brother in the face. His brothers would learn that she was off-limits to them. She was his and his alone. That possessive thought startled him.

Jesse nodded at Devon. "Got anything new?"

"Not much. We've gone through your cases and nothing stands out. We don't know how the Facilitator lost someone he loves so that's making it difficult. Did you incarcerate them? Kill them? Send to WitSec? Was it a relative? A spouse?"

Devon tossed a grape in his mouth and took a moment before continuing. "While we're digging into your FBI list, Joe and

Steve shortened the list of possible suspects."

Knowing there would be a second attack, but not knowing how or when, wore on the brothers. Without knowing whom to look for, the killer could walk right up to any of them, and it'd be too late.

"We can't keep them under lock and key forever." Matt looked up as Emily returned to the room and snorted. "Under as much constraint as we can."

"Amen." She put her hands on her hips. "I want to take Amber to the park."

"Em...." The guilt weighed on Jesse. Some psycho had possibly targeted her or Amber because of him. For something he'd inadvertently done. He'd keep them protected, even if it meant a temporary change in their world.

Emily cut him off. "I know. It's okay. I just want it to be over."

Devon looked at Jesse then nervously looked at Kate.

"Spit it out, Dev," he said, his voice unexpectedly harsh.

Devon cleared his throat. "We're still working on the other list."

Kate sat straighter. "What other list?"

"We're, um, checking out women I dated, to see if one of their significant others blame me for anything."

"You mean you sleep with married women?"

"Of course not. Not knowingly, anyway." The only way he'd ended up in bed with a married woman was if she'd lied to him. He strongly believed in fidelity.

Her gaze softened. "You're right. It makes sense to check them out, too."

She sounded like the FBI agent he'd worked beside. He

breathed a sigh of relief. He looked at her full lips and wanted to kiss them, to thank her for believing in him.

"We also checked out your ex, Kate. He says he was with you when most of the murders occurred," Devon added.

She nodded. "That's true. I got the call on more than one occasion when we were out."

"What about other men?" Jesse wasn't really sure he wanted to know about her past sex life.

Kate thought for a moment then shook her head. "No. There's no one I dated long enough to fit the profile. Besides, if it were, I can't imagine they'd have waited until I was with you. But, I'll think back through them."

For the next hour they discussed Jesse's cases. Five overlapped with Kate and AJ's investigation, but they couldn't pin down how any of them had lost a loved one because of Jesse.

He scanned the dossiers of the five men Devon's team had at the top of their list. Remembering them all, he cycled through their cases and didn't have anything to add.

Deep in thought, he mindlessly handed the files to Kate for review.

"AJ and I interviewed every one of them. They all had alibis and no changes in their financials."

Joe nodded. "Like Dev said, we're focusing on these five. We'll dig deep into their alibis. If they're false, we'll find out."

Jesse had faith in the FBI, but he knew HIS would get to the truth faster because their family's lives were at risk, plus they had no constraints. He reached over and covered Kate's hand with his. "Keep Kate and I updated. We're in this together."

The way her face lit up told him he'd finally said the right thing.

# Eleven

"DADDY, WHY CAN'T I go with you?" Reagan fought to keep her eyes open.

Jesse sat on the edge of the bed. She'd insisted that her uncles and Kate come in to tuck her in and say good night.

When she'd hugged Kate, she'd whispered, loud enough for everyone to hear, to remember girls' night. She'd told the men that boys weren't allowed on girls' night.

Yep. She had them wrapped around her little finger.

"Oh, pumpkin. I need you to stay here so I can do my job and protect Miss Kate." Jesse spoke in a soft, almost apologetic voice. The difficulty of the situation, his leaving his daughter's safety to someone else to protect her, left knots in Kate's stomach.

"How come Uncle Brad and Uncle Matt are protecting me and not you?"

Jesse looked sharply at Brad who shrugged. He brushed a dark curl from her face. "Don't you like staying with Aunt Em and Amber?"

She sighed. "Of course, I do, Daddy. It's not the same. I miss you."

"I miss you too, pumpkin. But we get to see each other on the phone every day, and you know you can call me anytime you want. How about I come over one day soon, and we'll do a daddy-daughter night?"

She perked up. "Can I paint your toes again?"

The twins chuckled. Jesse tossed a scowl their way. "Sure, pumpkin."

She giggled. "Remember when I painted up your leg."

"I do." He kissed her forehead.

That made everything better. "Okay. Night, Daddy." She turned over, hugged the worn teddy bear, and closed her eyes.

Jesse stood, looked at his daughter and smiled. "Are you ready to go, Kate?"

How could she allow this man to put his life at risk for her? What if it was Agent Marshall all over again? Jesse had a beautiful daughter. Kate knew what it felt like to lose your parents when you were young. "Sure, if you are," she mumbled, wondering how she could change his mind.

After they exited the bedroom, Jesse stopped Brad. "Did you tell her she was being protected and not just staying for a few days?"

"Hell no! You know how she is. She quickly put it together. She's too smart for her own damn good."

Jesse nodded. "Yeah, she is. I'd rather she hadn't known."

"So, painted toes? Any preferential color? Pink, maybe?" Matt joked.

"Probably that sissy pink," Brad joined in, grinning.

"Fuck you, both."

The twins chuckled but immediately quieted when Emily

chided them for being too loud with the girls sleeping. Watching these big, strong men being ruled by a five-year-old and a young, petite woman struck Kate as humorous.

"Take care of them." Jesse turned and led Kate outside where Ken, the HIS team leader, and Danny waited.

"Did our little girl finally drop off?" Danny asked. She noticed the "our" in his question. This family extended beyond just the Hamilton name. *Damn.*

Jesse nodded. "By now she has. She had a big afternoon." He looked around. "Aren't you changing out for the night?"

"The guys are waiting at Miss Ross's apartment."

"Ken, how many times must I tell you? Please call me Kate." He may have left the military, but the military hadn't left him. She'd never been called ma'am so much in her life.

Danny chuckled and stepped off the porch. "Good luck with that."

Curious at his statement, she looked to Jesse who shook his head. The group was full of stories they kept close to the vest. She had to know more about them.

———————————

DURING the drive to Kate's apartment, Jesse ached to reach over and take her hand, but something told him that she wouldn't accept it. She'd withdrawn after they'd left Emily's. He'd tried a few topics of conversation but had only received short answers from her. He had no idea what had happened. She'd seemed to enjoy herself. His family liked her.

The thought of a relationship made him shudder, but he'd seen how Reagan responded to her. It made him realize what he'd denied his daughter. A mother. A good mother. He considered the possibility of marrying again to give her one. He swore he'd never do it again, but he needed to consider it for her sake. Emily had been a positive influence in Reagan's life, but she would probably move away soon. She wanted to work for a big firm in New York and nothing he'd said so far had changed her mind.

Emily's leaving was putting an invisible pressure on him to find Reagan a mother. Kate fit into it somehow. He had no idea why she'd never married and had kids of her own. AJ had told him about an ex-boyfriend he thought she might marry. He'd never heard why the relationship ended, but Jesse didn't think it ended well since she held back part of herself. No doubt to keep from getting hurt again. But no sane man would walk away from Kate.

"You don't have to do girls' night if you don't want to." He prayed she'd want to do it because it would break Reagan's heart if she didn't. But, if he allowed them to get close, it would break Reagan's heart when they parted. Hell, he knew they weren't parting. Not anytime soon, not even after the threat on her life ended. He was already in too deep.

She smiled unsurely at him. "If it's okay with you, I'd like to go. But if you think it's better that I not so she doesn't misinterpret our relationship, I understand."

He planned to work on her understanding of their relationship. Once he figured out what the hell it was. "I'd like it if you went to her little party."

"If you'd rather be with her, protecting her, I understand."

"Kate."

"No. I said I wouldn't argue about having HIS protect me. And I won't. You could send one of your brothers in your place. Just not Brad. I'm not sure how serious he was today."

No way in hell would he fucking send Brad to personally protect her day and night. "I want to be with my daughter, Kate, but I truly believe you are the target. It's my fault that you're in this mess, and it's my responsibility to ensure you survive it. Besides, I trust my brothers with her life."

"Jesse, I'm having second thoughts about my possibly being the target. I'm worried it might be Reagan he means."

He didn't hesitate. "No. It's you."

She surprised him by not arguing. "You've done a great job raising her, Jesse. She's incredible."

Pleasure exploded in his chest at her praise. Her approval mattered more than he'd imagined it would.

"She's in that "talking all of the time" phase and driving me crazy with the why question."

Kate laughed. "I caught that. It's adorable, especially when she asks you to explain something uncomfortable."

He'd squirmed when Reagan had asked him where babies came from. He'd decide soon on how to pay back his brothers for putting her up to the question. Thankfully, Emily had rescued him, asking her to help make cookies. The idea of being a big girl and cooking overrode her curiosity. Knowing she wouldn't forget he hadn't answered had him squirming again, though.

There were so many questions she would have growing up that a woman should be the one to answer. He'd robbed her of that, still robbed her of it. He'd never had these thoughts before

HIS DESIRE

Kate. He didn't know what the woman had done to him.

"Jesse." She picked at a piece of imaginary lint on her jeans. "What happened to her mother?"

He grasped the steering wheel so tight he constricted blood flow to his knuckles, blanching them. He should tell her the entire story. *No.* He didn't want her censure. Wouldn't be able to stand it. "It was a gas station robbery gone bad. Some crackhead shot and killed her."

Kate sat quietly, looking at him as if searching for something. "I'm sorry." Her voice had an infinitely compassionate tone that made him feel things he didn't want to feel.

He swallowed around the lump in his throat.

After parking in front of her apartment and checking it, he made a beeline to the guest room. He had a lot to think about, and it all revolved around the two females in his life.

---

KATE cooked breakfast while Jesse showered. He'd been distant since she'd asked about his wife's death. *Stupid.* She should've forced AJ to tell her. Jesse's body language had told her there was more to the story. Would he ever trust her enough to tell her what he'd left out? Had he been there? Had he witnessed his wife die? Her heart plummeted to her stomach just thinking he'd endured that kind of pain.

The knock on the door startled her. With the fire under the pan of bacon, she wiped her hands on the apron and she rushed to answer the door, trusting Jesse's men wouldn't let anyone up that shouldn't be here.

The man she saw through the peephole started her heart

pounding. Dan stood on the threshold. Grabbing for her absent weapon came naturally. Wanting Jesse beside her came next. *Dammit.* She could take care of herself.

The solution was simple. Don't open the door to him. If he tried to break it down like he had Mary's, she'd shoot him. Playing games with him was over.

"Miss Ross, it's Ken. You can safely open the door. I have him under control."

She felt a strange numbed comfort, thankful for Jesse's team. She opened the door to Ken, who held Dan's right arm behind his back.

"Kate, I need your help. Would you call him off so we can talk?" Dan's pleasantness shocked Kate. What was he after? He usually called her *bitch,* not pleaded to her.

"What are you doing here, Dan?" How did he know where she lived? Had he followed her at some point? She couldn't believe he'd show up after all that had happened.

"I want you to help me get Mary back. She'll listen to you."

The man must be drunk to think she'd help him. She'd been the one to threaten him to stay away from Mary.

"Shut up," Ken growled. He turned to Kate. "I thought I'd bring him inside for Jesse to have another chat with him."

She stepped aside and Ken pushed Dan through the doorway. The last encounter flashed through her mind. Fury almost choked her.

"She'll marry me if you tell her to." He grimaced as Ken twisted his arm a bit higher.

"I'm not going to help you, Dan. You beat her. I've had to take her to the hospital before."

Jesse jogged down the stairs shirtless, with his weapon in his hand. "What the hell is going on?"

"You had an early morning visitor." Ken pushed Dan forward.

Jesse touched her arm and searched her eyes. "Are you all right? Did he hurt you?"

She bit her lip, touched by the concern he'd shown. "I'm fine. Ken had him before he knocked on the door."

A muscle in Jesse's jaw twitched as he shifted his attention to their visitor. "Why are you here?" Jesse advanced on him, putting himself between her and Dan.

"I just wanted to talk with her. She's Mary's friend. She can help me get Mary back."

"I'm going to tell you for the last time. Leave Kate and Mary alone. My men only gave you a warning last time. Next time they won't be so nice."

Dan cringed, fear emanating from him.

She wondered what had happened last time and could see a few fading bruises that she wondered if they had been part of his warning. He was an idiot to show up at her place.

Straightening, he tried to act like a badass, but failed miserably beside Jesse and Ken. "Okay, okay. I'll leave her alone. Just call your goon off."

"This is your last warning, asshole. You're lucky you didn't touch her or this would've ended a lot differently, and I wouldn't feel bad about it at all."

He nodded to Ken who escorted Dan from the apartment.

Jesse closed the door and turned to Kate. "Are you sure you're all right?"

The only response she could produce was a nod. Dan's presence had shaken her more than she'd expected.

His eyes examined her, critically not sexually. "Now, what about that breakfast you promised me?"

She jumped. "Oh no, I forgot about the bacon." She rushed into the kitchen before the repetitive, high-pitched beep rent the air. "I hope you like it extra crispy."

He threw his head back and let out a great peal of laughter.

Kate watched Jesse as he reached up to reset the smoke detectors still chuckling and warmth slid through her veins. She wanted this man. The cravings running amok in her body could no longer be denied.

# Twelve

HOW DID ANYONE use a computer mouse with his or her left hand? Kate locked her computer screen, frustrated at the difficulty of navigating without her dominant hand. A picture of her and Dottie in the park covered the screen. The fact that she couldn't walk her dog had become a major source of chagrin for her. But it kept her safe.

The more she thought about it, the more she worried about Reagan's safety. The killer had to have meant the cute little girl who had Jesse's heart. Maybe they could bring her here, so they protected her together. Kate had to do something to help.

What happened if he tried to kiss her again and Reagan caught them? Reaching up, she touched her lips that had tingled at the thought. How had her mind flipped to that?

Worrying about that would be a wasted emotion. He hadn't made a move on her recently, which told her he didn't really want her. She must've successfully portrayed that she didn't do casual sex.

She wasn't cut out for sex without emotional attachment. Although, attaching emotions had yet to work for her. Look at what happened with Mark. Maybe that was the way to keep from having her heart ripped out, she considered.

The man driving crazy thoughts in her head walked down the stairs, stashing his weapon in a holster. His gray sports jacket slung over his shoulder. And damned if he didn't wear the black T-shirt that hugged the abs she remembered wet and glistening from the shower. The man epitomized sexy.

"About ready?"

She'd won the argument over eating lunch out, but she'd compromised on sitting inside instead of out on the patio. It would've been smarter not to leave the apartment, but she couldn't stay cooped up any longer. Especially alone with Jesse.

She glanced down at her pink blouse and white jeans. "I just need to put on my shoes."

"Yeah?" His question confused her. "Okay." He looked at her. "You've got company."

Dammit, she needed an earpiece from him so she could listen to his team. She hated not being in the know.

"It's your sister."

Even though he knew who it was, he still pushed her behind him before opening the door.

Ire at him for hiding her behind him abated when she saw her sister's frown. "Hi, Ariana. This is a surprise."

Kate watched Jesse's reaction as he assessed Ariana. Most men fell in love with her at first sight, especially when she wore a power suit.

After introducing them, she relaxed when his expression didn't alter. Could he be immune to her beauty?

She nudged him out of the way so her sister could enter.

Ariana's gaze drifted from her sister to Jesse and then to his weapon. "What's going on, Kate?"

Not wanting to worry her sister needlessly, she hadn't told her about what had happened since they'd last seen each other.

"Last time I saw you, you had an FBI team in tow. Now, I get interrogated by two Neanderthals before I can see you, and you have a man with a gun in your apartment." She waved her hand toward Jesse. "What are you hiding?"

"Let's sit." Kate led them to the living room. "It's just a precaution." She had to convince her sister she was safe, or Ariana would hire another security firm to protect her. Then Kate wouldn't be able to move without tripping over men with guns. Oh, and the testosterone from that many alpha males would push her over the edge she was already teetering on.

Ariana nodded, concern edged her face. "Explain."

"Well, Jesse thinks I may be a target for a psychopath trying to get back at him." Kate shook her head. "It's a long story, and it doesn't necessarily make sense, but Jesse and his men will be here for a few days. Just in case."

"Whatever's needed," Jesse interjected with a grunt.

"Is this an inventive way to get out of going to the spa?"

She didn't look at Jesse for approval. "Of course we're still going. Now, what's going on?"

"I have more paperwork for you to sign. We missed these the other day."

Ariana worked twelve hours a day, every day, like their father had. Kate worried about her sister burning out. She needed to do something to help her. Maybe taking half the burden at Ross Communication was the answer. She had to make a decision about her future soon. Stay in the FBI or take up her place at the office. While on leave, she had time to help her sister, as her sister had always helped her.

It was a blessing growing up with Ariana. She'd had the patience to deal with a younger sister, an adopted one at that. Kate remembered one time she'd played in their mom's makeup and spilled her favorite powder all over the floor. She'd been so scared, but then Ariana had taken the blame. Kate had wanted to confess, but her sister told her it was already done so let it go. Ariana had told Kate, that's what big sister's do.

Kate smiled. "I'm glad you came by. Do you want to come to lunch with us?"

Ariana looked at Jesse for a moment then turned back to Kate with a worried frown. "Is it safe for you to go outside?"

"I've got plenty of protection. I'll be fine. Besides, we're only going across the street."

Ariana thought for a moment. "No, thanks. I won't keep you long."

Jesse strolled from the living room to the front door with confidence and opened it for Joy and Dottie. Kate completed introductions before Jesse asked, "You expecting a delivery?"

She shook her head. "No."

A knock sounded and Kate didn't move.

Jesse opened the door to Ken and a young man.

"Kate Ross?" The man nervously rocked back and forth on his feet.

Jesse crossed his arms over his chest, trying to intimidate the visitor. "Who are you?"

"I'm here to deliver this." The man waved a box of chocolate.

He pointed at Ken. "He opened it though. I promise it was still wrapped like it was supposed to when I brought it here."

Ken nodded to Jesse. "We confirmed it."

The deliveryman clucked his tongue. "He even called the people who bought the gift. My boss won't be happy."

Having heard enough, she stood and walked toward them. "I'm Kate Ross."

Looking past her, his nervous smile faltered at seeing Ariana. Typical.

"Um, here." He shoved the box at Kate and bolted.

She examined the note. "Get well and get back to work. You're missed."

"Ooh, chocolate. Who's it from?" Ariana stood.

"From the agents at work. I'm betting Rylee put them up to it." The men wouldn't have thought to send her chocolate on their own.

"Well, don't mind me. Go ahead and dig in," Ariana said.

"I'll wait. Do you want one?"

Shaking her head, Ariana chuckled. "No."

Silly question. Her sister never ate sweets. Kate couldn't understand why someone would deprive them self of such decadence just to remain thin.

"Joy, do you want some?"

Her dog sitter's face brightened, and she jumped from the floor where she sat brushing Dottie. "Would I? Chocolate is one of my food groups."

Smiling, Kate remembered her college days when she'd lived off caffeine and junk food, specifically chocolate. After Joy took one, she sat the box on the kitchen counter out of her dog's reach.

"Let's get these papers signed, so I can get back to the office," Ariana said, pushing the pen in Kate's hand.

She signed the paperwork with an illegible signature and congratulated her sister on the new station acquisition. It wouldn't take long for her to turn around the struggling station. She had the magic touch.

After Ariana left, Kate looked at the chocolate again. The men at work were so thoughtful. They even remembered her favorite flavor—milk chocolate with almonds.

"Joy, have more of these." She'd have hers after they returned. It would be the perfect dessert.

"Thanks, Kate." She picked up another chocolate and popped it in her mouth. "Mmm. Excellent."

"Have as many as you want. I planned to give you half anyway, so I won't eat the entire box myself."

Jesse cleared his throat. "Does this mean you're ready to go?"

The HIS team met them and led the way to the restaurant.

The waitress rushed to their table, deposited silverware and glasses of water, took their order, then rushed away.

"I think you should bring Reagan here to protect her, or you should be there with her."

He set down his glass of water. "Why's that?"

"I've been thinking. I'm concerned that she's the real target and you're wasting your time with me."

He raised his brows and smiled. "There's no way I'm wasting time with you, sweetheart. But, trust me, she's protected. And, if you are the target, which I still think you are, I'm not bringing her into the line of fire."

"I'd understand if you felt the need to be with her." She

folded her napkin in her lap, refusing to meet his eyes so he wouldn't see her confused emotions. Having the same conversation with him didn't diminish what floated in her mind. Her concern for his daughter was real.

"I'm staying. Learn to deal with it."

Deal with his being close all of the time? Easier said than done.

The food arrived, and Jesse asked, "What's that alluring scent you're wearing?"

Her jaw almost dropped to the table, but she took the request in stride. "Light Blue by Dolce & Gabbana." She swallowed, needing to turn the conversation light. "Tell me more about your brothers."

He did and she enjoyed getting to know more of who he was as a whole.

They finished their meals and left the restaurant. Crossing the street to her apartment, she saw Nolan wave from the next block. A whining Dottie met them at the door to her apartment.

"Joy? We're back."

She didn't receive a response.

Kate walked into the kitchen and grinned at the large dent Joy had made in the chocolate.

"Joy?"

Worried, she followed an anxious Dottie down the hallway. At the first floor bathroom, she saw Joy on the floor. Unconscious.

---

KATE couldn't accept the dull ache of foreboding so she focused on the large picture of a forest landscape on the wall opposite the uncomfortable cloth-covered wooden chair she sat in. If the picture had been placed there to create a serene environment where pain and suffering were prominent, it failed. Only good news could lift the spirits of anyone in the emergency room waiting area.

The bitterness and cold of the coffee went unnoticed as she took a sip.

Jesse sat beside her. He took her coffee from her and held her hand, flooding her with comfort.

In the half-full room, she witnessed a family huddled together. It sounded like their son had been in a horrific car crash, having to be cut out of his car with the Jaws of Life. A mother with her daughter, the little girl told Kate they waiting to see if her father would survive, sobbed, hugging the child tight after the doctor delivered what Kate hoped was good news.

Impatient, Jesse stood, told her to wait and went in search of a doctor.

An elderly woman waiting for her husband's test results took the empty chair as an invitation to move next to Kate. The woman tried to strike up a conversation. All Kate could think about was Joy.

They'd rushed her to the emergency room with an idea of what had been wrong with her. She'd been unresponsive with evidence she'd been vomiting. Poison.

Jesse appeared before her and helped her to her feet. After walking her to a private area, he spoke. "She didn't make it, Kate. We were right. She was poisoned."

The room swam around her, and bile rose in her throat. Joy was dead. Gut-wrenching pain shot to her stomach. "There must be some mistake," Kate said hoarsely, her throat burning. She wanted it to be a mistake.

Jesse drew her into his arms and held her tight. "Kate, the last thing she ate was the chocolate. They obviously weren't from your fellow agents."

A stab of guilt rushed to her heart. She'd given them to Joy.

He pulled back, looked into her eyes with a gaze filled with compassion.

Swallowing the sob that rose in her throat, she was unable to hide the tears sliding down her face.

Jesse gently brushed away tears off her cheek. "Kate, now will you believe me?"

Instead of the I-told-you-so voice she'd expected, he spoke softly, his voice full of emotion, his eyes pleading with hers.

Kate felt icy fingers of dread crawling down her spine and seeping into every pore. She replied in a low, tormented voice, "Yes, I believe you."

"I called AJ."

"Thank you," she all but whispered. She relaxed, sinking into his cushioning embrace. Joy died because someone tried to kill Kate. *Oh God.*

Jesse left her to her thoughts on the ride home. Joy's death was an awakening experience that left her reeling. The Facilitator would have to deal with her wrath. He'd best hope she didn't find him first. She fantasized about how she would make him pay.

She replayed in her head every interview and every lead she and AJ had in the Facilitator case. There had to be something they'd missed. Or was it someone they hadn't suspected?

Lost in thought, Kate hadn't realized how long their ride had been or where they were until, in the middle of what seemed to be nowhere, Jesse pulled into a hidden driveway. He stopped in front of a gate, punching in a code on a hidden keypad.

Driving through a wooded area, Jesse remained silent as they arrived at a clearing where a two-story rustic-looking house stood. Drawn to the magnificent wood planks decorated with freshly painted white shutters and trim, Kate imagined snow on the roof and smoke drifting out of the chimney in what would make an excellent holiday greeting card picture.

"Where are we?" Several trucks and SUVs were parked in front of the house. She didn't feel like dealing with people.

"HIS headquarters. Emily and the girls will be here, so you won't be bored while we meet."

Kate ignored that he planned to exclude her for the moment and entered the headquarters. It had to be someone's home. The entryway, open to the second floor, led into a massive living room where about a dozen or so large men stood, some in jeans, some in black cargo pants. All armed.

Turning back to Jesse, her pulse skipped at the tenderness shown in his eyes. Putting her trust in him, she nodded, and he placed his hand behind the small of her back, guiding her closer to the group. The men stopped talking and turned their way.

"For those of you who haven't met her, this is Kate Ross."

She heard the familiar squeal as Reagan raced into the room with Emily on her heels, carrying a squirming Amber.

Jesse picked his daughter up, threw her in the air and then hugged her.

Devon completed the introductions with the men she hadn't

met—Rob, Jamaal, Mike and Les. She was told Nef and Kevin were outside. She wondered which had been the ones at Emily's she couldn't find.

She didn't know why, but after seeing Ken and Danny, she'd expected a military-looking group, not a mix of bad boy, clean cut and military men. Plus one cowboy. Jesse had called them a hodgepodge group of men, and she believed it.

The moment AJ arrived, the ribbing between them began. She wanted to stand up for her partner, but even though he looked incensed, she could see the underlying fun he was having.

"Men, settle down." Seriousness engulfed the room. "Let's do this."

The men filed down a hallway to what Kate guessed was their war room. She tossed Jesse a questioning gaze.

What preceded his answer shocked her. He lightly brushed his lips over hers. "We have to meet. I'm leaving you here. You'll be safe, Kate." He handed his daughter over to her.

It felt natural taking the child from him, feeling small arms wrap around her neck. "I want to be involved in this, should be involved." This was her fight, too. She'd just lost her friend. She wouldn't be left out.

"Kate, let us handle this. This is what we do."

Irritation surged through her and she tried to suppress it since she held his daughter. "Excuse me, what do you think I do for a living?"

Rubbing his hand on the back of his neck in frustration, he hesitated before responding, "I want you to stay with the girls. I promise that I'll share everything with you later."

He knew she wouldn't argue with him in front of Reagan. And if he didn't share everything, Kate would get it out of AJ.

She wouldn't let them hide her in a corner like a delicate porcelain doll. She was a trained FBI agent, dammit. Even injured, she could handle this.

Knowing it best for now, Kate reluctantly nodded in agreement.

"I have to go or poor AJ won't want to share with us anymore." He grinned and brushed a kiss on Reagan's cheek. "Be good for Miss Kate."

"I will, Daddy."

He followed the path the men took.

Emily smiled and Reagan looked confused. Kate was confused too. Jesse had kissed her in front of his daughter, and she hadn't stopped him. Was it a sympathy kiss? He'd held her hand at the ER out of sympathy. Or was it something else?

She bounced the girl in her arms. "How about you help me explore, Reagan?" Kate wanted to keep the little girl busy to avoid any questions about the kiss, plus she wanted to see more of this beautiful place.

Reagan stared at her for a moment, squirming to be released. "Let me show you my room."

Her room? This was Jesse's house? The man continued to surprise her.

---

WALKING toward the room he'd sectioned off as headquarters, Jesse thought about how to keep Kate alive.

He entered and the room quieted.

Matt stepped forward. "It's time we moved her to the safe house."

"She refuses to go."

"Then kidnap her ass and drag her there. It's too hard to protect her where she lives. A delivery of chocolate for fuck's sake! And we let it through. That girl's death is on us.

The men nodded with solemn looks on their faces. They'd never lost anyone before.

Frustrated, Jesse ran a hand through his hair. "You did everything right. You confirmed the delivery with the fucking florist who, by the way, was found dead not long ago.

"She needs to be where no one knows where she is until we solve this."

His brother wasn't telling him anything he didn't already know. "No. We have to make it work."

Maybe after Joy's death, she'd be more careful and listen to him. Stay inside.

"This was too close of a call. The FBI is kicking itself for pulling back. They want her in one of our safe houses," AJ said.

Jesse grunted. "That won't work either."

"Yeah, I figured that, and her boss knew if he ordered her that she'd turn in her badge. So, she'll have an FBI detail again. Don't let your men shoot them."

Over chuckling from the group, Jesse said, "I'd worry more about her shooting them." More men around were bound to piss her off.

AJ smiled. "We're not scared of her."

"What's the plan, boss?" Ken asked.

He smiled, reminding himself to introduce Kate to their bomb-sniffing dogs, Bomber and Daisy, if Reagan hadn't already.

"We need to find him before he finds another way to get to Kate." He looked at the twins. "You keep protecting Emily and the girls just in case he changes his mind."

"We never planned to leave Em. Not until that bastard is caught." Brad's surliness had returned. He'd been like that ever since he'd left the secret service. Of course, he hadn't left in the best of circumstances.

Jesse nodded. "Okay, AJ, what do you have?"

KATE held a photo of five boys who all looked similar, a blonde-headed girl and one boy with light olive skin. They surrounded an attractive man Kate knew was U.S. Senator Blake Hamilton.

"That's the family."

Startled, Kate jumped at Emily's statement.

Kate knew so little about Jesse's family. So far, with the exception of his talking about Reagan, she'd had to pry information from him, and he'd changed the subject most of the time. She ached with the need to know more about his life.

Kate pointed to the boy who looked nothing like the rest of the family. "Who's this?"

A sadness and grief encompassed Emily's face. "Jake Cavanaugh, our foster brother. That was taken not long after he joined our family."

It was the first time she'd heard his name. "When do I get to meet him?"

"You won't." Before Kate could respond, Emily added, "We'd best check on the girls again before Amber gets into everything."

AJ stepped into the room. "How are you holding up, Kate? Ready to come with me? We've got the safe house ready."

She wouldn't go into hiding with the FBI. Her parents went into hiding, and it didn't work. Too many people would know she was there. Someone might open their mouth and then she'd be dead, like her mom and dad. Better to stay and face the problem and resolve it. "Why aren't you at the meeting?"

AJ shook his head and chuckled. "It's breaking up. They're helping each other put on their big girl panties."

Kate tilted her head. "What's with you and them?"

The men shuffled into the room, saving AJ from answering. As they were leaving, they nodded her way.

"What's going on?" she asked Jesse, who approached with his brothers, serious looks on their faces. Had they learned something new? Something that didn't bode well for them? "We're getting ready to leave. Are you sure you won't go to a safe house either with us or the FBI?"

Kate glared at him. "Jesse Hamilton, if you ask me that again, I'm going to show you that I can kick your ass even with this injury."

His brother Brad slapped him on the shoulder. "You've finally met your match."

Devon shook his head with a twinkle in his eyes. "She's definitely a keeper."

Pulling her close to his side in a possessive gesture, Jesse's eyes danced merrily as he dropped his gaze to her. "Don't I know it," Jesse said in a low voice.

His words filled her heart, tossing heady elation flowing from her fingers to her toes. Thankfully he'd rendered her speechless so she didn't blurt out, "What the hell?"

# *Thirteen*

THE NEWS OF the girl dying reached the Facilitator. Kate had been lucky. Twice.

Now, Jesse would have her protected better than the President. Oh, he'd watched Jesse's men handle visitors to her apartment. In his disguise as an old man, he'd walked up and down the street, occasionally sitting on a bench smoking a cigar. HIS men had studied him the first day, but now give him a cursory glance.

He'd been close to them in the dog park. Kate had even said hello when she'd passed him. His hand had itched to reach into his jacket, grab his gun out and pull the trigger. But, he'd refused to risk going to jail, so he'd held back. He'd find another way. There was always a way.

Jesse had to spread out his team to cover everyone, so they were weaker. It had been telling that he chose to protect Kate himself instead of his daughter. The Facilitator was right about Jesse's feelings for her.

The Facilitator had expected them to go to a safe house. He'd anticipated they'd return to collect Kate's things, so he took this chance. From across the street from her, he'd be able to keep an eye and ear on them. No matter where they hid her, he'd find her. She'd never get away from him.

"Are you sure you only need the apartment for a month?" the young leasing agent asked.

"Yes. I'm just visiting family. It's crowded and a hotel room for a month is a bit costly. I appreciate you giving up your apartment for me."

"I'm practically staying with my girlfriend, so this works for me. Here's the key, Mr. Smith. It's been a pleasure doing business with you."

After the man left, the Facilitator unloaded his gear and pointed the high-powered listening device and camera toward Kate's apartment. He would fine-tune it when Kate and Jesse returned so he'd hear everything they said. Hear their plan to try to defeat him.

He was a patient man. He would refuse any new jobs until this mission was accomplished. It was too important for him to get distracted. Jesse had been tenacious trying to implicate him in the murders. He'd be just as tenacious ensuring this job was done correctly. He wanted to be able to celebrate his success for many years to come.

"Are we still doing this?" a man asked as he entered the room. "Do you still need me?"

"Is there a problem?"

The man shook his head and smiled. "Not at all. I want to participate in the fun. That's all."

"You're lucky. I do need your help this time. This plan won't fail. We'll take out Kate Ross, no matter how much protection she has."

# Fourteen

CLOSING THE SUV door, Kate started the interrogation. "What happened? What'd you discuss? What'd you find out?"

Jesse put the key in the ignition. "Slow down. We'll get to it all." He started the SUV and drove away from his home. "I'd still prefer you were at the safe house and not your apartment, Kate."

Going to a safe house would be the smartest thing to do, but she couldn't bring herself to go into hiding. She was stronger than that. Deep down, she wanted Jesse to see that too. She also wanted, no needed, to be involved.

"Why? I've got two FBI agents, you and two HIS men protecting my apartment. I can't imagine being safer."

He winced then cleared his throat. "Actually," he turned to Kate, "you have three of my men protecting your apartment."

She furrowed her eyebrows. "Where?"

"We, um," he broke off, shifting uncomfortably, "have a sharpshooter across the street."

"What? Where? There's nothing but occupied apartments across the street."

"There's a rooftop."

"Ow."

He pulled in a quick breath, stopped the car, and turned to Kate who held her injured hand. "Are you okay?" he asked in a worried but soothing voice as he reached over and placed his palm softly on her thigh.

The warmth of his hand filtered through her, slowly climbing up her thigh. "Yes, I was stupid. It's nothing to worry about."

He squeezed her thigh and removed his hand. So close. "Be more careful next time."

"You really don't need the third guy."

"Kate, let me worry about that. Now, do you want to know what we talked about or not?"

Nice divert. The information did need to come before anything else. Her life, and the life of everyone who could be hurt while protecting her, was at stake. "Of course I do. I didn't get a chance to discuss it with AJ."

"Dev and his team knocked two men off the list. They're down to three—Shane Walker, Carlos Mendez, and Joey Brown. Do you remember these men?"

"Yeah, I remember them. Did any of them receive large payments around the time of the murders?"

Shaking his head, he answered, "No. He did catch one guy with high deposits around the time of two of the murders, but he's not on the list. He was on the original FBI list. Richard Freeman. It all checked out with his business receipts though."

A shudder rippled through her. "I didn't like the man when AJ and I interviewed him. Not in the way I disliked the other three scumbags. Richard just kept staring at me. I don't think he looked at AJ once." She shrugged. "It's a shame I couldn't arrest him for being creepy."

Checking the rearview mirror before turning to her briefly and shaking his head. "The men couldn't find any faults in his alibis so he's not your man."

She bristled. Yes, she was grateful HIS was investigating for her so they could find this killer before he had a chance to kill again, but she was also human, having the men go back through her cases searching for faults left her mixed with "find it to make sure we get it right" and "do you really think I can't do my job?" She hoped they treated hers the same as they did the ones of his they were reviewing.

"They should finish with the other three soon. Shane has their interest. He's living beyond his means, and his shaky alibi turned up floating in the Thames."

"*Humph*. Well, that's a sign of potential guilt right there."

He exited off the interstate. "We'll see."

Shifting, she turned toward him, slid her leg up and rested her knee on the edge of the seat. "I want to do the interviews. This is killing me sitting back and letting someone else do the work."

Jesse reached over and took her hand in his. "I know. But, you can't be involved in the interviews. Think about it. If one of them is the killer, putting you in front of him could be deadly. We're trying to keep you alive, not serve you up on a silver platter."

That brought guilt flashing forward again, flooding her mind and body. "I still can't believe it. I really liked Joy." She'd had such a great future ahead of her, and some maniac had wiped it away. He probably considered her acceptable collateral damage.

Two people had died for her. In both cases she'd been at fault.

She hadn't listened to her partner, and he'd tried to protect her. With Joy, Kate had given her the poison, encouraged her to have as much as she wanted. That could have easily been her sister and Jesse too.

The bastard needed to pay and pay big.

Jesse lifted their joined hands and kissed the back of hers. "I'm sorry, sweetheart."

Kate swallowed past the lump in her throat. She hated to admit that she appreciated his attempt to comfort her.

"We will be very careful going forward," he said softly.

"We will… but I still want to see my sister and a friend of mine at the hospital."

"Kate." He sighed.

"No, Jesse," she said hurriedly, "I'm going to see Jason on his birthday."

Squeezing her hand, he sat up a bit straighter. "Who's Jason?"

Was that jealousy she heard in his voice? She held back a snicker.

"Jason is a boy with leukemia that I visit at the hospital. He'll be thirteen this year, and he doesn't have a family any longer. I want to spend his birthday with him so he has someone besides a doctor or nurse." She would not miss it. They had to find a way. She'd purchased him a signed football by his favorite quarterback hoping it would be a good luck charm for him.

Jesse quickly considered it and nodded. "We'll make it work."

"Thank you."

Looking around the apartment, Kate swam in pain. The place was clean, as it had been before anything had happened, but it was still in her mind. Everything else faded away and it was all she could focus on—Joy's death.

Ready to turn in for the night, she turned and Jesse engulfed her in his arms and peered deep into her eyes. "Damn, Kate. I want to give you a kiss to curl your toes, to weaken your knees enough I have to carry you to bed. I can see you want it too, but I see the pain you carry. I can't take advantage of you, no matter how much it's killing me."

Kate didn't care what he said. She reached her hand behind his neck and pulled him down for a kiss. Resistance met her attempt. Confused, she released him and noticed her cheeks were wet.

He leaned his forehead against hers. "I can't wait to get you naked, Kate, so I can worship your body, but tonight's not that night."

Guilt again. This time, it was because she was aroused. Her body heated as her breast felt swollen and a throb pulsated between her thighs. She knew she should feel only guilt considering all that had happened to Joy.

He wiped tears from her face. "Would you like me to hold you until you fall asleep?"

Did she? The slow jerk of her heart at his asking endeared him to her more. *Yes.* The comfort would be welcome. She didn't want to be alone with grief over Joy. "I'd really like that."

He led her to her room and prepared the bed while she changed into a large T-shirt and shorts. She nervously climbed into bed and watched him strip to his boxer shorts. His body was magnificent. She couldn't help but stare, noting his rigid cock. She licked her lips and the arousal that had begun to dim while they'd settled in and had returned full force.

"Not tonight, sweetheart. You've had a hell of a day. Let me just hold you." He climbed in beside her and drew her into his arms. She laid her head on his shoulder and relaxed. Thoughts of Joy dying because of her vanished as she fell asleep with his hand running through her hair.

———

"GOOD morning, sunshine."

Entering the kitchen, Kate accepted the delicious smelling cup of coffee Jesse offered. Dottie rushed to her from his side. Her dog usually waited by, if not on the bed, until she woke each morning. Her spotted pet had already fallen for Jesse, following him around, responding to his commands.

He'd showered, shaved, and had breakfast cooking. He was not the same man she'd seen in previous mornings.

Looking at him through narrowed eyes, a butterfly fluttered in her stomach. "Who are you, and what have you done with the grumpy man I'm used to in the mornings?" She'd woken alone and wondered how long he'd unselfishly stayed with her.

He chuckled and turned to the counter. "I do hate mornings, but this morning I woke up refreshed and decided to get a head start."

Kate blew on the steam before taking a sip of coffee, then moaned after it slid down her throat.

An egg cracked open on the floor, snapping her out of her morning caffeine bliss and the haze that enveloped her with the first sip.

"Damn. Clumsy."

Opening her eyes, she laughed and waved him off. "I'll get it. Get a head start on what?"

He cracked eggs in a bowl and picked up a whisk. "Just the day, sweetheart. Have a seat. The newspaper is on the table. Breakfast will be ready shortly."

Sliding into a chair at the table, she relished the euphoria of someone taking care of her for a change. Especially Jesse.

Then reality struck on the front page of the newspaper. The poisoning couldn't be ignored, or the fact that a multi-millionaire FBI agent was the actual target, had been leaked.

"I unplugged the phone, so you won't have to deal with reporters today. And no one is getting by my men without your consent."

She took a deep, shaky breath. "Thanks."

The domestic version of Jesse set plates of scrambled eggs, bacon, and toast on the table. She really needed a grocery store run but she'd keep food levels low if that was what it took for him to do this for her. To set her heart aflutter.

Settled into breakfast, she asked what had been bothering her. "Don't you find it odd that he sent poisoned chocolates to try to kill me?"

Jesse nodded, then swallowed around a large mouthful of food. "AJ and I talked about that. The killer couldn't be sure you'd eat them. Plus, not that men don't use it, poison is usually a woman's drug of choice. Not what we'd expect from a high profile killer."

She stopped with the fork at her mouth. A woman. *Oh God.* She took her bite and chewed it slowly. Was it possible that Elizabeth went through with her threat? No. She may have talked tough, but Kate didn't see her as the killer type. Yet, people surprised the hell out of her all the time.

The Facilitator hadn't attached a note this time. But if he had, he'd know that she wouldn't have eaten them. What if they weren't from him? What if Elizabeth was Joy's killer?

How would Jesse react to her suspicion of Elizabeth? Only one way to find out. "Jesse, you should know that Elizabeth threatened me. She said she'd do anything to have you."

He tilted his head and pulled his eyebrows in, a look of deep thought on his face, then shook his head. "She has been known to be jealous. As for attempting to kill you with the chocolates, I don't think she'd have done it that way because there was a chance I would've eaten the candy. And, I'm damn sure she couldn't be the Facilitator. She's not that put together to control herself to kill people methodically, keep quiet about it. No, she's just running her mouth out of jealousy." He shoved his fork in his eggs.

He knew Elizabeth better than she did. Still, she'd talk with AJ and have her checked out. She didn't want to think about it all. They'd discussed it yesterday and were nowhere closer. "What are we doing today?"

"Whatever you want to do, as long as it's indoors. If you can't think of anything, I have a suggestion or two." He raised and lowered his eyebrows a few times in a suggestive manner yet there was a fun twinkle in his eyes.

A surprised laugh erupted from her. "I need to do some cleaning."

He set his cup down. "I'll help."

Cleaning allowed her to clear her mind and think about the important things in her life. She needed to put serious thought into her future. Even if her hand healed properly and she could remain a field agent, should she? Or, should she leave the FBI and work with Ariana at Ross Communication?

Being a field agent had been more satisfying than she had imagined it would be. She liked her partner, and the camaraderie of her fellow agents. Bringing criminals to justice was extremely fulfilling.

Was her place truly at her sister's side though? She knew a little about the operation because she'd worked there in the summers throughout college. With Ariana teaching her, she could swiftly learn everything she needed to know.

The choice between what she wanted to do and what she probably should do tormented her. Was there a right answer?

She finished cleaning, making her decision. It felt right. She didn't wish to upset her sister, but she belonged at the FBI.

---

AFTER dinner, Jesse led Kate to the living room continuing dinner conversation and the bottle of wine. She chanced it and sat on the couch, but not close to him. Tempting as it was, there was still something holding her back, and she couldn't figure out what it was.

"Tell me about your adoption."

Something inside her urged her to open up to him, share it all. But, most people didn't know what to say, especially people from large families like his, and she didn't want the inevitable awkwardness or pity after she finished her story. Not from him.

"We talked about my parents before—Nancy and Tom Miles." She swallowed around the knot in her throat, holding back tears. Even though she couldn't remember her parents or the shooting, it still distressed Kate that she'd lost them before she'd had a chance to know them.

"Because I had no living relatives who could care for me, foster parents were arranged for me to live with when I was released from the hospital. My parents' accountant called the Ross family knowing they wouldn't squander my inheritance."

"You were lucky you had a good advocate with the right contacts. I've heard stories of children being lost in the system. Being moved from home to home, some of them in abusive situations."

She shuddered when she thought about those poor children who had no control over their situation. She wanted to be a foster parent, then maybe adopt, but her job prevented her from committing. She couldn't think of giving a child a home, and then ripping it away from them if she died in the line of duty. And that was always a possibility.

Reaching out her glass for him to pour more wine, she smiled at the softness in Jesse tonight. Her quivering nerves could be from the wine, but she couldn't lie to herself like that. It was him.

"Yes, I was very lucky. The Rosses treated me the same as they did Ariana. When I was six, they adopted me. They, of course, saved my inheritance for me. They paid for my college themselves. When I graduated college, they bought me a car and turned over my inheritance from my parents."

"I heard you became a millionaire at the death of Jay and Kelly Ross. That you and Ariana were left everything. They didn't leave anything to any other relatives." He set his glass down on the coffee table and petted Dottie who had placed her head on his lap.

"Yes, the inheritance was split between us. I know Mom and Dad loved me like I was their own, but I feel guilty about them leaving me half of everything. I expected most of everything would be left to Ariana. I haven't touched the money. If I need anything, I'll dig deeper into my birth parents' inheritance. My share of the Ross inheritance will go to Ariana when I die or her children. She's the one who works hard at growing the business. She's their true daughter. She deserves it."

Ariana hadn't agreed with Kate on how her will had been written, she'd argued that their parents would roll over in their graves if they knew Kate wouldn't accept what they had given her and was so willing to give it away to someone other than her own children even if it was her sister's. It was then that she shared with Ariana her inability to have children. After a good cry-fest, her sister understood, but more importantly, she understood why Kate hadn't found the right person to marry yet. Plus the fact she hadn't fallen in love.

"You shouldn't feel guilty about their leaving you an equal share as Ariana. In their mind, you were their real daughter too."

Kate sighed. "I know what you're saying is true, but it still doesn't dissolve the guilt I feel."

Kate wondered what made her share the depth of her feelings about being left the inheritance with Jesse. She hadn't shared this emotional conflict with anyone, not even her close friends. Sharing with him felt right. Things with him were getting more complicated.

---

LATER, they watched a romantic comedy, and Jesse wondered what Kate thought during the pseudo sex scenes. His mind filled with thoughts of her tasty lips. Thinking of his mouth on hers and trailing them down her silky neck had blood rushing to his groin. He didn't want to shift to get comfortable and scare her. Tonight had to be the night. He couldn't wait any longer. They'd waited too long already.

After the movie and the news, they stood to go to bed. She didn't stop him when his arms slid around her and drew her close. He slanted his lips over hers, savoring her taste, the heat of her mouth, and the stroke of her velvety tongue. She clung to him as he deepened the kiss, devouring her mouth with the pent-up need flowing through him.

Her arms encircled his neck, and she pulled herself closer. Anticipation rode him, strengthening his determination to have her tonight.

His lips trailed down her neck. "I want to take you to bed, Kate." Reaching around, he grabbed her ass and pulled her closer so she could feel his desire for her.

Jesse's mouth returned to hers as he palmed her breast. She moaned and arched her body into him. Breaking the hungry kiss, he took several deep breaths to slow his racing pulse, then he held her hand to lead her up the stairs. Kate was finally going to be his.

Only, she didn't move. Instead, she slowly shook her head and breathlessly whispered, "No. I can't do this, Jesse. I can't just do sex."

"What if it's not just sex, Kate? What if it's more?"

Her eyes looked hopeful. "Is it?"

Running his fingers through his hair with frustration, he answered, "Hell, I don't know." What the fuck was wrong with him? He knew it meant something. Why couldn't he admit it?

"Then I can't do this."

Jesse looked in her eyes and saw a fire blazing. One that he'd ignited. There was no denying she wanted him. "I want you to look me in the eye and tell me you don't want me."

Again, she hesitated. "It doesn't matter."

Furious, he raised his eyebrows. "Hell yeah it matters. Tell me you don't want me, Kate."

Her body trembled either from lust or nervousness or both. "I don't want you, Jesse." She quickly looked away.

"Liar."

He dropped her hand and told her good night. Walking up the stairs, he prepared himself for an ice-cold shower. He'd never imagined he'd still be sleeping in the guest room. He'd never had to work at getting a woman into his bed. But, Kate wasn't just any woman he wanted in his bed. She was special. But he needed to figure out in what way she was special to him.

# Fifteen

AJ AND DOTTIE awaited Kate when she walked down the stairs in the morning. She'd been nervous about seeing Jesse, but his not being there wasn't what she'd expected. And, it hurt that he'd avoid her. "Good morning, AJ. What are you doing here?"

He walked to the kitchen with her. "Reagan was sick this morning so Jesse went to see her, and he wanted you to have company until Matt arrived. Since I live close by, I get the pleasure." He flashed his killer smile as if that would make everything better. Usually it did, but this morning, not really.

"Is she bad?"

He shook his head. "Nah, just a little tummy ache, but she wanted to see him."

Her heart squeezed at what the angst he must feel with his daughter sick and him here. Then, warmth seeped through her hands surrounding the large coffee cup because of its heat and that Jesse cared enough to have someone here so she didn't wake up with one of his men. "You don't have to be here. There are enough men outside that I'm fine inside all by myself."

They strolled into the living room and sat on the sofa. "Do

you really think I need someone with me?"

Dropping on the couch, AJ leaned his head back and stretched it. "Of course not. He called and since I had case stuff for you, I didn't argue."

"Thank you, AJ." She almost jumped up and hugged him. "Not being in the action has made me miserable and feeling useless."

He chuckled, his light tone lifting her mood. "Have no fear. Your partner has arrived to save the day."

"I have someone for you to check out. Do you know Elizabeth who hangs around Jesse?"

AJ closed his eyes and shook his head. "I do. The woman thinks she's in love with Jesse. Big pain in the ass. What about her?"

"She threatened me. It's probably nothing, but since we're not certain who was behind the chocolate, I thought you should check her out. Jesse brushed it off."

AJ rubbed his hand over his face. "I agree with Jesse, but I'll still check her out."

"That's all I ask. Now where are things?"

They talked on it and their other cases until Matt arrived and AJ departed. The afternoon passed slowly. Even with Matt in the apartment, it felt empty without Jesse. His presence or lack thereof, mattered to her.

What was she going to do? Last night she'd almost caved. His kisses had been close to overpowering. She'd surprised herself when she'd found the strength to tell him *no* when her body had been screaming *yes*.

He'd asked her what if it was more. For a moment, she

thought that she'd meant something to him. Then he'd said he didn't know.

She groaned. As a lost cause, she would lose this battle in more ways than one. It was only a matter of when.

---

JESSE returned with a gruff attitude so Kate stayed out of his way. The tension between them was almost unbearable. Matt tried to converse with Jesse, gave up and left.

The two of them prepared and ate dinner without muttering an unnecessary word. She only knew one way to fix things, and she still wasn't sure it was the right thing for her.

When Kate heard Jesse talking to his daughter, she decided to slip away for a well-needed, lengthy, bubble bath. Turning on the hot water and dumping in the lavender scent and then lighting the lavender candles on the counter sent a relaxing scent floating through the air.

Before settling in for a good soak, she blew bubbles in the air. Kate's laughter bounced around the room while Dottie chased the drifting bubbles until she tired, then she circled and plopped down on the rug by the bathtub.

Leaning back, Kate hastily clipped her hair on her head to keep it dry. Soft music wafted from her iPod speaker system. She closed her eyes and couldn't fight it as her mind flooded with visions of Jesse and what could be. Her and Jesse in bed. Her, Jesse, and Reagan as a family. Her eyes popped open wide at that thought. She had no idea how she'd be as a mother, but she wouldn't mind being one to Jesse's daughter, especially if it brought him along.

The fact that they would never happen didn't stop her from fantasizing about them as a family. She could easily fall in love with both of them. Heck, she was probably already half in love with Jesse. *Whoa.*

From beside the bathtub, her cell phone rang.

"Hello, Mary."

"Kate, I need you," Mary whispered.

Kate sat up straight, water sloshed over the side of the bathtub, and Dottie jumped up and barked.

"What's wrong, Mary?"

"Dan was here. I think I'm really hurt."

*Son of a bitch.* "I'm on my way. Don't open the door to Dan if he comes back." She should've arrested him the other day no matter what Mary had said.

"I won't. Thank you, Kate."

She got out of the tub, pulled the drain, wrapped herself in a large bath towel, dried off and dressed in record time.

Jesse was talking on the phone and didn't pay her any mind. She sat down and put on her tennis shoes. She didn't want to bring anyone else into this, but she wasn't foolish enough to go out alone.

"Where the hell do you think you're going?" Jesse asked as he slid his phone in his front pants pocket.

"Something's wrong. Mary needs me, and we're going to see her."

"You're not going without me." His gruff voice made her wonder what the call had been about.

She mentally shook her head. Mary needed her. Her curiosity had no place right now. "I said *we*. Now, hurry up. *We* need to leave." She tapped her foot impatiently.

Jesse put on his shoes, placed his hand on her back and ushered her out the door. On the drive to Mary's, Kate fretted. After checking to make sure they weren't being followed, he reached over and took her hand in his. She held on tight.

Mary had only called Kate once before to go to the hospital, and it had been bad. The situation had to stop. Her insides were tying up in knots worrying over her friend.

"What's this big emergency? Is that asshole there?" Jesse asked gruffly.

The concern in his tone warmed Kate. She swallowed past the lump forming in her throat. "Dan paid Mary a visit. She says she's hurt."

"Son of a bitch."

"Those were my thoughts exactly."

They had to park a good distance from Mary's house and didn't wait for Kate's protective details. They jogged, and Jesse held her hand the entire time.

At the sight of the broken door, they pulled their weapons. Jesse nodded at Kate and she opened the door. "Mary, it's me, Kate."

Jesse went in first and immediately halted. Kate peered around him at Mary and gaped. A sharp pain lanced her heart. Dan had done a number on her friend. Kate wanted to pull her into a hug and wished she could make it all better. Wished she'd been there for her friend sooner.

"He's not here," Mary said in a broken voice.

They put away their weapons.

"Mary, let me look at you." With shaking hands, Kate

reached under her chin and turned her head to see more of Mary's face. The saliva abandoned her mouth, leaving it drier than any desert, and her hands shook during the inspection.

"I called you because I think I have a broken rib. I'm shaking so badly that I can't drive myself to the hospital." Mary's weak voice broke, filling with something that sounded like regret.

"Of course, we'll take you. Do you have any other injuries?" *God, please don't let it be anything more than the black-and-blue face.*

"No, that's it."

Mary winced taking a breath, and Kate wanted to kill Dan. "Let's go then."

On the drive to the emergency room, Kate realized Jesse hadn't said anything to either of them since they'd arrived at Mary's home. He'd conferred with his men while she'd spoken with Mary at the apartment. He looked like he wanted to kill someone. She almost snorted aloud. Dan seemed to have that effect on people.

Sorrow washed through Kate when she walked into the familiar emergency room. The one she'd sat to learn Joy had died. She pushed it aside as best she could. Mary needed her. She had to focus on something. Hugging her friend, she softly told her, "It doesn't look like a long wait."

The diagnosis of bruised ribs and not broken ones brought relief to Kate, and she guessed to Mary also. She'd prefer her friend had no pain or injury, but if she had to choose, Kate was happy it was the lesser of the two.

Mary was insistent she return to her home, so Jesse drove Mary home. Based on his grip, Kate expected the steering wheel to crack. The same thing went for his teeth with how tightly he'd clamped his jaw. They'd yet to discuss Mary's attack, yet she knew he had serious opinions and emotions about it. She'd seen his anger, but she'd also witnessed his concern when he'd looked at Mary.

Kate's concern for her friend's health, her injuries, had turned to molten anger. Afraid she'd say something she'd regret, she remained silent, which added tension on the ride home.

They walked Mary to her door, which had been hastily repaired, and Jesse finally broke his silence. "I'm leaving a man outside your door in case Dan comes back."

Kate's heart melted a little at his gesture.

"I'll be okay. You don't need to do that."

"It's done. Mary, this is Les. Les, this is Mary."

Mary stared at the tall, broad-shouldered man wearing a weapon on his hip and a cowboy hat.

He removed his hat with his left hand, held it over his chest and held out his right hand. "Nice to meet you, ma'am," he said with a true southern drawl.

Looking to Kate first, she turned and welcomed him. "Nice to meet you, too."

"I'll be right outside, ma'am. Make sure to lock the door and don't open it to anyone but me." He looked over at Jesse, then turned back to her and tilted his head in Kate and Jesse's direction. "Or one of them."

Mary stood transfixed, nodding.

"Okay, let's go." Jesse ushered Kate out of the apartment.

When they returned to his SUV, he banged his hands on the steering wheel three times, saying "Son of a bitch" with each hit.

"That bastard has gone too far. Will she finally press charges?"

"I'll talk to her tomorrow about it. I didn't think tonight was the right time."

"It's time for that asshole to know that I meant what I said," he muttered.

She suspected it would be the last time Dan would ever bother Mary.

When they arrived at Kate's apartment, Jesse told her good night and went upstairs without even trying to seduce her into bed. She should be happy he'd backed off, but she wasn't. She didn't like the loss it created in her heart.

Around midnight she woke to the sound of AJ entering the apartment and Jesse leaving. Was it Reagan? Was she okay?

IT rained the day of Joy's funeral. That didn't stop the large showing of the young woman's family and friends.

Jesse stood by Kate's side wearing a fitted black suit and black raincoat. He held a black umbrella over the both of them. She peered down and her gaze followed the droplets of water running off his black shoes. She suddenly hated black.

There he went and confused her again by clasping her hand after avoiding her just the day prior.

She looked from their intertwined hands back up at the casket. The heavy weight of guilt lay on her shoulders, and the outrage at the unknown killer racked her body. Tears slowly found their way down her cheeks. *My fault,* she repeated in her mind.

Joy had been such a great person, full of laughter, and she'd always had a kind word to say. Dottie had loved her. While Kate didn't want to die, she never wanted anyone to die in her place.

*I'm sorry, Joy.*

The devastation surrounding Joy's parents was palpable. Kate had no idea how she could face them. Kate scanned the crowd and noticed Doug, Joy's boyfriend, with red-rimmed eyes. He and Joy had fought the night before she'd died. They hadn't had time to make up. She could only imagine how torn up he must be knowing the last words to her were in anger.

Lost in thought, she barely heard the preacher give the final prayer.

Most of the mourners visited the Ryans after the service. She hated socializing after a funeral. Was it supposed to be subdued and sorrowful for the deceased? Or joyful, remembering their life?

"Mrs. Ryan, I'm so sorry." Kate held Joy's mother's hand, not knowing what else to say. "Sorry I killed your daughter" didn't seem to be the right thing.

She smiled at Kate. "Joy loved you and Dottie. She said you were the best boss she'd ever had."

An invisible hand reached in and wrapped its hand around her heart, opening and closing tightly.

Mrs. Ryan squeezed Kate's hand. "Don't you go blaming yourself for this, sugar. It wasn't your fault."

Unshed tears blurred her vision. Damn the asshole who'd taken Joy. "We're going to find out who did this. I'm not going to rest until they're behind bars."

*Or dead.*

JESSE held Kate's hand as they walked to the SUV. Joy's death had ravaged her emotionally. He knew she blamed herself, but the blame should really lie with him. He was the reason all of this started.

He maneuvered the SUV out of its tight parking spot.

"Dammit! She's dead because of me. I want that son of a bitch."

"Kate, Mrs. Ryan is right. It's not your fault. If anything, it's mine."

Covering her face with trembling hands, she gave a vent to the agony of her loss. "It *is* my fault, Jesse. Those chocolates were meant for me. *Me*. I gave them to her."

Nothing he could say would change her mind. He could only comfort and support her. Reaching for her hand, something that began to feel natural, he told her, "I'm here for you."

She briefly met his gaze, then looked away without saying a word.

Back in her apartment, he watched her quietly stand in the center of the living room looking pensive, not disturbed or angry as he'd expected. After she'd vowed justice on Joy's killer, she'd withdrawn, and he had no idea if it was sorrow or anger that she felt. Knowing her, it was probably both, plus a large heap of guilt. He had no idea how to snap her out of whatever this was.

After a few minutes of her staring into the fireplace, she turned to him. "I need you to make love to me." She didn't stutter or waver. Instead, determination filled her words, as well as a surprising vulnerability he'd never seen before.

The need for comfort in her eyes pulled him to her. He wanted his touch to remove all traces of pain. It may be fleeting, but he would banish her guilt with pleasure.

"Are you sure?" His question was tentative. It wasn't how Jesse'd imagined their first time, but he'd happily oblige if it brought her back to him.

"Yes."

"I don't want you to have regrets in the morning."

A soft smile touched her lips, and a flash of heat lit her eyes. "I will have none. I need you, Jesse."

*She needed him.* Her words released the knot of doubt in his stomach. He reached out a hand.

Not wanting to rush, he undressed her slowly before undressing himself. She was as perfect as he thought she'd be. He couldn't wait to love every inch of her lush body. She wanted to feel alive. He would definitely help her with that.

Gazes locked, he led her to the bed, guiding her down beside him. He kissed her gently then was surprised when she took over the kiss with a fierce hunger. His hands roamed her body as he trailed kisses down her throat. As Jesse savored her silky neck, her body jerked with wrenching sobs. He looked up, pushed some hair off her face and then pulled her into his arms.

He should've known her request was a mistake. She was too vulnerable.

"I'm sorry. I don't usually cry."

"Shh. It's okay."

"Hold me. Please don't leave me. Not tonight."

Knowing how much it cost her, crying in front of him and asking him to stay, Jesse had no intention of leaving. He couldn't let her go. "I'm not going anywhere."

He held her tight against him thinking about the change in his feelings toward her. He'd told her the truth. He wasn't going anywhere, and he didn't mean just for the night.

# Sixteen

KATE JERKED AWAKE. She dressed quickly, and, not knowing what to think, wandered restlessly around the room. For two nights Jesse had held her while she'd slept, comforting her without attempting to seduce her. Lying in his arms, her problems had faded away. Falling asleep with her head on his chest, her hand over his heart and his hand running through her hair had felt natural, like she'd belonged there.

She had no idea if he'd stayed throughout the night, because like before, she'd woken in her bed alone. She shook her head, still in disbelief at her initial request. She'd never asked a man to make love to her before. She didn't even have the excuse that she'd been drunk. At the time, her mind had been clear, determined and focused, even though she'd been aware she'd hit a low on her current emotional roller-coaster ride.

All she'd wanted was for his kiss and his touch to take away everything... the pain... the guilt... if only briefly. Unfortunately, she'd temporarily forgotten sleeping with Jesse would be so much more than just sex to her. Kate closed her eyes. Thank God, he'd only comforted her.

Sighing, she knew standing in front of the mirror in her bathroom wasn't going to cut it. It was time to quit being a coward and face him. It wasn't every day she asked a man for sex and then cried.

A rap sounded on the door and she jumped, her heart hammering.

"Kate, are you dressed?"

The foolish thought of not answering crossed her mind but flitted back out. She inhaled deeply and released a long exhale, and opened the door. "I was just coming down. I wanted to thank you for taking care of me." Her gaze focused on his chin, since she was unable to look him in the eyes.

"Well, get ready to leave. You wanted to be in on this. AJ has the delivery guy."

Her eyes snapped to his. The caring displayed in them awed her. *What if it's more?* She mentally shook her head. "I need to put on my shoes. Did someone walk Dottie this morning?"

"Yeah. Ken did."

On the drive to the FBI offices, Jesse spent most of the time on the phone with Reagan, who surprised Kate when she'd asked to speak with her.

"Are you coming to girls' night?"

"I sure am. I'm looking forward to it."

"Uncle Brad and Uncle Matt *says* they're coming. I don't want them there. Only girls."

A wide smile spread on Kate's face. "Your Aunt Emily and I will make sure they don't crash your party."

Jesse turned to her and raised his eyebrows with laughing eyes, and an amused grin split his face.

"I knew you'd take care of them, Miss Kate."

Her heart singing with delight, she looked forward to spending an evening with Reagan.

As they parked the SUV at the FBI office, Jesse's cell rang. "Stay in the car until I finish this call, Kate."

He answered his call. "Hamilton."

She cut her eyes at him, they were at her office, the "alphabet building." Was he kidding? She looked at him again, ready to ask him just that when he hung up the phone. "Let's watch AJ work his magic."

Smiling, she exited the car. She'd seen AJ work that magic plenty of times. He was damn good at getting someone to confess. It would be nice if she could be in on the interview, but she wouldn't push her luck. For once, she'd sit back and be a good girl. This was too important.

On the drive back to her apartment, her mind trailed away to what happened.

An individual in a dark alley wearing sunglasses, a ball cap, and a hoodie had paid the delivery guy. All the delivery guy could remember was that he was small for a man. That could fit all three of their suspects, plus a large portion of the population of Baltimore. They needed Ed, the driver during the shooting.

At first, she'd been upset when AJ had invited Jesse into the interview, but then she'd seen him work. When AJ hadn't been able to get the information from the delivery guy, which surprised the hell out of her, Jesse had tried a different approach. By the time he was done, he had the perp helping because he was solving the crime with them.

She wasn't sure if the idiot realized what he'd done or not, but who cared. She gained a new respect for how Jesse had handled things. Calm… professional… yet cutthroat. Yep, damn sexy.

The more she got to know this man, the more her insides turned to jelly at the prospect of what could be between them. She smiled. *I'm letting go to see what we can make together.*

"Jesse, I need to go shopping. We're entertaining."

# Seventeen

KATE AND HER friends held a group dinner once a month at her apartment since she insisted on cooking for everyone. Jesse hadn't won a single argument about her friends not visiting. They'd all been cleared, and she'd refused to back down. He had to admit, he really just wanted to keep her to himself. Secretly, he was glad AJ couldn't make it. He didn't care if that meant he was being selfish.

Having her in his arms again made him realize that he wanted her to be a part of his life. His and Reagan's.

It'd been so long since he'd been in a relationship; he didn't know where to start, how to show her he wanted more than sex. His holding her at night and being there for her should've told her she meant something to him. She had to know.

Knowing when he had her in his bed he'd be making love to her instead of just having sex, should've worried him. He hadn't made love to a woman since his wife, but he reveled in the thought. He needed her tight body beneath him while he kissed every inch of her, not just tasting but loving.

Thinking of her naked body stirred him. He wanted her, but

he knew she needed him as a friend, someone to comfort her. He could wait. She was worth it.

That night started with her friends. It intrigued him that she had theme nights for meals each day of the week. She explained how she did the same for her friends' monthly dinners so they could enjoy different cuisines that always included one new recipe she bravely tried out on them.

That night was Mexican food night, and she'd explained she would be trying a new recipe for something called sopaipillas with chocolate sauce.

He'd enjoyed shopping with her, watching her attempt to remember what she'd written on the shopping list she'd left at the apartment. Sure he could've had someone go into her apartment and read it to them, but it'd been more fun watching her. Plus, the irritation on the security details at their constant backtracking in the store made it all worthwhile.

After they unloaded the groceries, Kate tossed him a frilly apron to wear, then sent him to the chopping block to dice onion for the soup. Thankfully, he managed to cut them without crying. The last thing he needed was to give her ammunition to make fun of him.

Preparing the ingredients for the soup together had been pleasurable. He'd been comfortable and at ease beside her. It would definitely be enjoyable every month.

She poured the items they'd cut into a large pot and covered it over a low fire. Next, she placed the chicken in a pan to cook for enchiladas. He'd never seen someone so efficient in the kitchen, especially with her current limitation. She hummed to herself while she cooked, not seeming at all stressed about the large meal she had to prepare or the fact she would be trying something new.

Once the chicken finished cooking, she instructed him in the proper technique to make enchiladas before he put them in the oven.

But, when she handed him the ingredients to cut to make pico de gala and guacamole, he had to call bullshit. "You know they make this stuff already so you don't have to go to this much trouble." Then under his breath, he added, "At least I won't have to."

She must've heard him because she chuckled and caught herself. Serious again, she smiled. "Fresh is always better."

He enjoyed their playful banter while they prepared the group dinner. They settled into a comfortable domesticity, and it lightened his heart. He didn't miss the smoldering looks she sent his way when she thought he wasn't looking either.

He'd waited long enough. Jesse stepped behind her, and his arms encircled her waist, relieved that after she initially stiffened, she relaxed and leaned her head on his shoulder.

He kissed her temple. "This has been nice, Kate. Really nice."

"Yes, it has."

He pulled her close against his erection. "Feeling you sidle up next to me as we prepared the food and watching your sexy ass shake when you stirred the pot has done this to me. Get them out of here quickly." He spun her around and the raw desire in her eyes burned bright.

"Tonight, this is happening, Kate. *We're* happening. I need to touch every inch of your body, be buried deep inside you and feel you clench around me when you come. And Kate," he whispered, "you will come."

Her breath hitched and the shiver that ran through her rippled back to him.

"Tonight, Kate."

She nervously wet her lips, and it drove him crazy.

Leaning down, drawn to her lips, he stopped short.

"Rylee's on her way up. Be prepared, she has alcohol," the laughing voice said in his earpiece.

He suddenly wanted to growl, grab her and run away from it all. Closing his eyes and attempting to steady his breathing, he bit out, "Dammit. Your guests are arriving."

Someone knocked on the door.

Breathlessly, she said, "That would be Rylee. She's here to help me set up."

"It's her. Tonight, Kate." He unwound his arms from her, moved to the door and opened it.

"Agent Hawkins, you're early, for once," Jesse said.

Rylee, known for being the last to arrive anywhere, cocked her head and smiled. "I like the apron. Are we playing Suzy Homemaker tonight, Jesse?"

He narrowed his eyes and quickly untied the forgotten apron. "Smartass."

Laughing, she walked around him into the apartment. "Hi, Kate." Rylee held up a bottle. "I knew you'd do margaritas tonight. I thought we'd try a strawberry margarita mix."

Kate wiped her hand on her apron before accepting the bottle. "I've always wanted to try them in strawberry."

"Are you women going to get drunk on me?" Damn. He needed Kate sober.

"Doubtful, but it doesn't mean we won't be having a good time."

Kate's wicked smile set his blood to pumping and had him wondering who the *we* was she referred to—her and her friends or the two of them. He went with the two of them and wanted to rush Rylee out and bolt the door closed. The hell with dinner.

She continued, "Josh drives Mary to the dinners, and he doesn't drink much." Raising her eyebrows in an almost suggestive manner, she continued, "Rylee stays the night since her place is so far away."

His head snapped to a smirking Rylee. *No. Way. In. Hell.* Not tonight. He'd pull her aside later. Get her a cab if he needed to. Hell, he'd pay for a hotel room for her at the Ritz. Kate was his tonight. His alone.

Jesse's cell phone rang. "Excuse me." He walked out of the kitchen.

"Jesse, we need to talk."

"Hold on, Dev." He turned back to Kate, covered the mouthpiece and asked, "Got room for one more?"

She nodded. "Of course."

He removed his hand from the mouthpiece on his phone. "Come on over. Don't ask why. Just bring a bottle of Mexican wine."

---

IN the kitchen, Rylee pulled out the blender and poured in the margarita ingredients. "So, how's it going between you two? You've been holed up here for quite a few days. Anything... you know... happening?"

Kate felt the heat rise to her face. She remembered the conversation they'd had. "Nothing's happening."

"I seriously doubt that." She stopped any response from Kate by starting the blender.

While the drinks blended, Rylee opened a bag of tortilla chips and put them in a bowl. Kate took them to the living room, making a return trip with the condiments.

Jesse was sprawled on the couch with his legs stretched out before him, ankles crossed, channel surfing. She'd enjoyed preparing to entertain with him, even though he technically wasn't a host. It felt like playing house.

"Jesse, do you want a margarita?" Rylee asked.

"No, thanks, I'll have a beer." He stood, walked to the refrigerator and pulled out a beer.

Rylee chuckled. "Is it a Mexican beer?"

"What do you think, smartass? Kate picked it out for tonight."

"Quit calling me that, and I'd call you whipped." Rylee laughed and held up her glass in a toast.

"You'd best bite your tongue, squirt."

Rylee stuck her tongue out at him.

Kate laughed, feeling jovial and envious at the same time. Rylee and Jesse had a fun relationship. He treated her like a kid sister. While she and Ariana had fun as children, she couldn't remember ever sticking her tongue out at her sister. Nor had she seen Rylee do that with Mary and Josh. *Speaking of which, where are th*—The doorbell rang, cutting off her thought. "That'll be Josh and Mary. I'll get it." Kate moved toward the door.

Jesse cut her off. "You will not. We've been over this. You don't open the door."

"But you already know who it is, and I bet it's Josh and

Mary." She really had to remember to ask for an earpiece.

"It is, but"—he walked to the door—"just to be safe, I'll get it."

Waiting until he ushered Josh and Mary in, she had an idea form. When he looked at her, she stuck her tongue out at him. It felt good, freeing.

"I figured you'd have margaritas ready, so I brought wine for dinner." Josh handed her a bottle of a Mexican vineyard cabernet sauvignon.

Before she could thank him, Rylee's cell phone rang and she groaned. "I've gotta take this." She walked away from the group into the small office area.

Josh frowned at Rylee's departing back and then turned to Jesse. "I see you chose to participate or were forced to drink Mexican beer? I think I'll join you." After grabbing a beer, the men moved to the couch.

Focused on Jesse's rear and then his getting comfortable on her sofa, she started when Rylee returned with a frown. "I'm sorry, but I have to go. I'll be gone for a while, Kate."

Kate's smile disappeared, a small pang bounced in her heart. The undercover assignment. She'd learned a little about it and worried about Rylee on this one. "I hate you having to leave."

"Me too, but you know how it is." Rylee shrugged.

"No, I meant on the assignment. Just promise to be smart and stay safe."

"Of course."

Kate embraced her friend and attempted to lead her to the door. Jesse must've witnessed her moving in that direction and jumped up. "I'll show her out."

"Good-bye, Rylee," she said.

"Bye, Kate. I'll see you when I get back." She looked behind her. "Bye, Mary."

"Bye," Mary piped up.

Watching Rylee leave, concern swamped Kate. She turned and caught Mary's eye. She would worry about Rylee, but she wouldn't allow it to put a damper on her evening with friends… and then with Jesse. She gulped and excitement skittered over her body. Needing to ground herself, she turned and returned to the kitchen with Mary. "How're you feeling?" she asked her friend.

"I'm better."

Kate smiled. "I'm glad to hear it."

"I decided to press charges after all."

Kate fought jumping for joy. "Mary, I'm so proud of you. What made you finally change your mind?"

"He messed with my friends. I should've done it right after he touched Josh. It was past time I did something. I was being chicken. As long as you and Josh are there with me, I'll be okay."

Before Kate could respond, she heard a knock on the door. A moment later, Devon arrived, carrying a bottle of a Mexican chardonnay that he offered to Kate. "This is for my party crashing." He smiled with that angelic smile that probably had women dropping their panties. He was a handsome man. Not as handsome as Jesse but handsome all the same.

"Thanks, Devon. You didn't need to do this, but we appreciate it. Let me introduce you to everyone." After the quick introductions, he and Jesse disappeared into her office area, talking quietly before she announced food was ready. She made a mental note to ensure she was privy to their conversation at the end of the evening.

"Dinner's served."

They sat around the table, passing around platters of food. Jesse sat at the end opposite Kate and dished out the enchiladas. It didn't give her the opportunity for a chance brush of the hand or leaned in close whisper. It *did* allow her to catch him watching her... and him to catch her gazing at him.

Josh started the conversation. "So, I hear you helped fix this, Jesse."

"Damn, Rylee," he breathed, but his voice projected across the table.

Kate laughed and brought her napkin to her mouth so she could swallow her food. She captured his gaze and it was so intense... so mesmerizing that she'd almost stood and walked to him before she reclaimed her wits. There was a great deal of promise in those eyes. So much so that she had to shift in her seat to help ease the building ache inside her.

"Kate, what's the recipe you're testing on us?" Mary asked, apparently oblivious to the current Kate knew had to be zipping back and forth between her and Jesse.

"Uh, the dessert." She began again, more firmly, "Sopaipillas with chocolate sauce."

Mary turned to Jesse. "Did you help with that too?"

He laughed and winked, playfully, at Mary. "No. She wouldn't let me even touch the recipe. She insisted she had to do it all herself."

"That's our Kate," Josh stated.

Kate, while excited for the coming evening, knew joy with

her friends having fun with Jesse. Conversation flowed easily and they finished an enjoyable dinner, refreshed their drinks and went into the living room.

"Thank you for dinner." Devon's smile was infectious. "It was nice of you to include me."

"Kate, as always, you outdid yourself." Josh tilted his beer bottle to her.

Mary rubbed her stomach. "Kate, and Jesse, it was delicious. I like that new dessert, Kate. You're amazing in the kitchen."

"Thank you," Kate and Jesse said simultaneously and snapped their eyes to the other. Goose bumps coursed over her skin. *Tonight.* That was what he'd said.

"I'd say that I'd help do the dishes, but I know you won't let me." Mary set her drink on the coffee table.

"You're right. I'll take care of it. That's what the dishwasher is for. You're here to relax and have fun. How's it going at work, Mary?"

"Same ole, same ole. A man called into the university and wanted to know how much he had to pay to get his doctorate. When I quoted him the price, he said that was too high for him. He asked how much it would be to buy the piece of paper saying he had his doctorate."

Josh raised his eyebrows. "He didn't! You're a prestigious school. How could someone think they could just buy their degree from you like some diploma mill?"

"They try it all the time. There are even some who say because they paid for their program, they should get the degree whether they finished the work or not. People are wacko."

They laughed.

"Mary, I don't believe I've ever heard you use the word wacko."

"Well, today, Kate, the word fits."

A broad smile crossed Mary's lips when she finished speaking and Kate couldn't have fought the emotion bubbling in her chest if she'd tried. Mary was happy. While there remained a shadow in her eyes, it had already lifted to the point where Mary appeared almost serene in her comfort. It had been years since Kate had seen her friend truly relaxed.

"Last month, it was mine, so, this month are we going to tell all of Kate's most embarrassing moments, or is Devon going to regale us with Jesse's embarrassing secrets?" Josh smiled.

Kate didn't hesitate. "I go for Devon telling the stories."

Jesse's evil glare didn't faze her.

"I dare my brother to tell stories about me."

Devon laughed. "You don't scare me. You stopped scaring me when I turned fifteen."

"We're all ears." Josh moved forward on the couch.

Clearing his throat, Devon looked deep in thought before he spoke. "Well let's just say that Jesse was a daredevil. When he was six, he thought himself Superman."

Jesse rolled his head back and groaned. "Not this story."

Laughing, Devon continued, "Well, he wore his cape everywhere. He had Superman pajamas and underwear, which he wore on the outside of his pajama pants."

Jesse didn't hide his displeasure at their laughter.

"He decided he had superpowers, and one of those powers was to fly. He climbed up the old oak tree beside the house and took a nosedive out of it. He broke his arm but still insisted he could fly, that some Kryptonite must've been nearby."

Jesse's scowl grew. "It wasn't funny at the time."

"He swore we were trying to take away his powers."

"I still believe you put Kryptonite near there." Jesse burst out laughing as soon as he finished the statement.

The others in the room joined in, Kate picturing a young Jesse wearing Superman pajamas.

Sobering, but wearing a mischievous grin, Devon tapped a finger on his chin. "Let's see. Oh, the twins were pranksters. Well, still are, but one day they decided to get back at Jesse for him not letting them go to their friend's party when Dad was out of town and put him in charge. As soon as Jesse left his room each morning, they poured water on his bed. They did it every morning for a week and told our dad that Jesse had been wetting the bed. Now, Jesse was seventeen at the time. Dad believed the twins after the maid confirmed his sheets were wet every morning. Dad wanted to take him to a specialist so he wouldn't wet the bed any longer at his age."

Jesse shook his head. "That was embarrassing. I was pissed he believed those little brats."

"It was a simple payback that turned into a much better revenge than they'd imagined."

Kate laughed at the boy and teenager, almost man, that he'd been and what he'd dealt with growing up. Each story endeared him more in her heart. Jesse was a wonderful person who made her heart thump like crazy.

After a few more stories, Josh stood. "I love the stories, but I think it's time we leave."

Kate's nerves went on alert at what the night promised after everyone left her and Jesse alone. Then, she remembered Devon and pushed down her anticipation until they found out what he knew. "I'm so glad you made it tonight," she found herself saying.

"I had a good time. Sorry it was mostly at your expense, Jesse."

"Glad I could oblige you."

Mary stood. "Thanks, Kate. I had fun tonight."

Kate walked them to the door and gave each of them a hug before they left. She walked back into the living room.

"Now, boys, what's going on?"

# *Eighteen*

ONLY A RELUCTANT messenger delivered bad news in person. Whatever Devon had to say, Kate could deal with it. HIS had the best investigators and protection specialists working the case. She wasn't sure when her loyalty to solving the case shifted from the FBI to HIS, but she didn't feel regretful. She trusted Jesse and his team with her life.

She put her hand on her hip and narrowed her eyes at Devon. "Spill it."

He looked anxiously at Jesse who nodded, presumably giving him permission to talk in front of her. She'd tackle that action later. This involved her. She wouldn't allow them to keep secrets from her.

"We've cleared our last three suspects. Joe had a lead on Ed, the driver, but when he got there, it was too late. Ed had already moved on."

"Dammit!" Jesse's expression tightened. He punched his right fist in his left hand.

Deflated, Kate dropped on the couch. They had nothing. This maniac had the upper hand. He could be anywhere, be anyone. "What about other cases of Jesse's? Did you find anything there?"

Jesse sat beside her, picking up her hand in his.

Looking at their linked hands, Devon dropped on the chair, smirked and shook his head. "Nothing yet."

"What about the money? Have you followed it?"

"Without a starting or ending place, amount or dates, there's nothing to follow. I've dipped in a few places, but nothing yet. Don't get me wrong, I'm still searching. AJ just gave me the names of people they suspected hired the Facilitator. It's possible I can find something that can lead us to him. If it's there, I'll find it."

"What if we use me as bait to draw him out?" She could end this, even if it meant she had to bear the heartache of losing Jesse because his job had ended.

"No!"

She started at the force of their response. "Why not? I'm a trained FBI agent. I can do whatever needs to be done."

"We don't know what we're up against. I won't let you risk it."

She angled herself toward him, her brow cocked. "Won't *let* me? Jesse Hamilton, you don't own me. If I want to be bait, I *will* be bait."

"Kate, let's listen to all that Devon has to tell us."

She narrowed her eyes. "Okay." She refocused her attention. "Go ahead, Devon."

He looked at her then Jesse, a bewildered look on his face. He looked back at Kate. "Steve is on the street looking for information. He's posing as someone who needs to hire the Facilitator."

"The FBI didn't have any luck trying to hire him. Why do you think your guys will be able to?"

A grin spread wide on his face. "We're not the FBI. Don't worry how we'll do it. Know we'll find him."

She trusted they'd find him. She still had to believe they'd find him before someone else was hurt. She had so many people surrounding her at all times, and the thought of something happening to any of them troubled her. This had to be resolved and soon. "I trust you."

---

AS soon as the door closed behind Devon, Jesse pulled her against him. "I've wanted to do this all night." Unable to restrain himself, he swooped down and captured her lips with his, his tongue stroking hers, drinking in the sweet taste he'd craved. He explored until she melted against him.

Jesse eased back and placed small kisses at the corner of her lips. Kate moaned softly, and the sound traveled right to his groin. His cock hardened in rush of raw and powerful desire. He'd wanted her for so damn long underneath him, and finally, she'd be in his bed.

"Do you want another beer?" she asked nervously.

Jesse stopped and studied her. Fighting his body's desire, he could be a bit more patient. They had all night. "Let's have some wine."

Handing her the glass of wine he'd poured, her breath hitched when his hand skimmed hers. "To us," he toasted.

She touched her glass to his but said nothing.

They silently observed each other over the rim of their glasses as they drank, the air thickening around them. Unable to hold back any longer, he set his down, took hers and slowly placed it on the counter.

Hoping to place her at ease, Jesse leaned down and gently brushed her lips with his once then twice before covering her mouth with a soft, gentle kiss. Forcing himself to go slow, he fisted his hands at his sides to keep them off her, letting just their lips touch. His mouth moved over hers, devouring its softness. He traced the fullness of her lips with his tongue, teasing them apart, entering and exploring with slow, seductive strokes.

Her taste intoxicated him.

Lifting his head, Jesse gazed into her eyes, watching the green overtake the blue in a display of passion. Groaning, he crushed her to him and smothered her lips with his, kissing her with a desperation he couldn't control.

After tonight, she'd know she was his.

Her arms slid to rest on his shoulders, gripping tightly, anchoring her to him.

Slowly, his hands roamed her tight body, one stopping on her lush hip the other moving around the front of her, sliding up her ribcage to her breast.

Her gasp only enticed him more, lit a fever in his body.

Holding her soft breast in his hand, his thumb toyed with her nipple until he felt a stiff point through her shirt. His groan echoed in the room. Knowing that making love to her in a slow, loving fashion had just turned damn near impossible hit him full force.

The kiss ended, and he stepped back, holding out his hand in an invitation. When she didn't hesitate to take it, he released a heavy breath. Taking his first step on the stairs, he heard Dottie get up to follow. "No, girl. Not this time."

The dog whined but returned to her bed.

Two steps into the room, he spun around, unable to restrain himself, and he crushed Kate hard against him, fisting his hand in her silky hair. His mouth swooped down to capture hers in a deep, scorching kiss that she returned with reckless abandon. Their tongues were relentless, battling for control, for domination.

He kissed his way down her exposed throat, nipping and kissing until a shiver overtook her body, and a low, breathless moan escaped her.

Impatiently, Kate reached for the hem of his shirt, but he brushed her away, quickly undressing them, reluctantly discarding the sexy, matching pink, lace bra and panties she wore.

Stepping back, his gaze slowly moved over her amazing body, drinking in his fill of her, stopping first on her curly, dark pubic hair then moving up and resting on her plump breasts, and then pausing on her wet, swollen lips before finally returning to her passion-filled eyes.

"Do you have any idea how beautiful you are, Kate?" Her soft, feminine side made his heart expand with deep emotion. His urge to protect her had never been stronger.

Pink blossomed on her cheeks. "You're the beautiful one."

Her hand touched his chest, sending a jolt of raw heat to his already hard cock. Her touch intensified his deep-seated hunger for her. He'd planned to take things slow and feast on her sweetness, but feared the desperation inside him would take control, breaking through his restraint and rushing him, making him take her hard and fast.

Demanding more, Jesse's lips captured hers until she whimpered with pleasure. His hand slid to her breast, kneading, plumping, He ducked his head licking and sucking her nipple with possessiveness.

She sagged against him. Their naked bodies touched, pushing him near the edge.

His mouth left her breast, and he growled, "Bed." Not a moment too soon did they tumble onto the soft mattress.

Reclaiming her lips, he thrust his tongue deep and wasted no time roaming his hands over her body. He needed to touch and taste her everywhere. His mouth greedily followed his hands, and he took her breast in his mouth once more, suckling and teasing her nipple until she provocatively arched her body to him.

He slowly kissed his way down her soft body, making lazy circles on her flat stomach, enjoying the shiver that ran through her body. He met her eyes as he moved lower, inhaling the scent of her arousal and savoring it, fighting the thin line of control.

Nudging her trembling thighs apart, he positioned himself between them. His hands caressed the soft skin of her thighs then moved up and opened the slick folds of her pussy, wet and ready for him. A groan erupted from deep within his chest before he leaned down to flick his tongue over her nub.

She jumped, arching her back as he flicked his tongue over her clit again before drawing the swollen bud into his mouth, suckling and tugging on her with his lips.

Responding to his touch, her fingernails dug into his shoulders as his tongue probed her slick entrance followed by a finger. His cock jerked when she clamped tightly on it.

"Jesse," she whimpered, her hands attempting to pull him up

to her, "I want you inside me."

He wanted her to come first. His tongue and fingers worked together as he watched her lose herself in ecstasy. She'd never looked as sexy, with her eyes squeezed shut, her head thrown back, her breathing coming in pants, and her face flushed. Yes. She was so close.

Her hips moved involuntarily toward his mouth and his tongue. Her pussy clenching tightly on the two fingers he moved inside her. She clenched the sheet, and she cried out, "Oh God, Jesse."

He kept his rhythm steady throughout her orgasm, watching her ride wave after wave as he extended the pleasure as long as he could, feeling his cock leak precum. He had to get inside her. Soon.

He kissed his way back up her flushed body and took her mouth, her taste still on his tongue before he rolled off the bed for protection. When he leveled himself above her, settled comfortably between her thighs, his mouth hovered above hers. "Are you sure, Kate?"

Trembling with excitement, she reached her arms around his neck and pulled him down to an sensual kiss that deepened his arousal. *Damn.* He took that as a yes.

Positioning himself at her slick entrance, his body shook with the urgent need to be inside her. He looked in her eyes filled with heat and tested her, entering her with the tip of his sex and then pulling back out. He gritted his teeth and sweat broke out on his forehead. She was tight, and her orgasm had her wet and ready for him. Going slow became an even greater challenge.

"Please, Jesse." She drew up her knees and spread her thighs open more to him, grabbing his ass, pulling him closer.

That was all he needed. Fuck slow. He entered in one swift thrust.

She cried out and he froze.

"Are you okay?" *Please don't let me have hurt her.*

Kate moved restlessly against him. "Yes, I'm okay." Wrapping her legs around his hips, she pulled him deeper inside her.

Fuck that was enough to make him come.

To calm himself, he buried his face in her neck and inhaled. She felt so tight, so hot and so wet around him. It was sheer ecstasy. He wanted to lose himself in her. "God, you feel good." *Right.*

Kate continued to move under him, pushing him closer to the edge. Jesse's control snapped and his blood raged in his body. Their lovemaking turned frenzied, wild and passionate. Hungrily, their mouths found each other as he stroked in and out of her fast and hard, her little moans driving him in an uncontrollable pace.

His balls grew tight, tension building in his groin, waiting to explode. He adjusted his rhythm so that with each deep thrust, his cock rubbed against her swollen clit. Together they found a tempo that bound their bodies together.

"Let go, sweetheart. Let go."

Kate's breathing changed. Her body tensed, and she clutched onto him as if he were her lifeline, crying out his name as she climaxed, her inner muscles clenching hard around him.

He threw his head back, closed his eyes and his breathing suspended while a powerful orgasm overtook him.

Collapsing on top of Kate, Jesse knew their coming together had been more than sex. They'd connected on a whole different plane. One without barriers.

He rolled off her, left the bed to clean up and returned to lie down beside her, pulling her into his arms. He kissed the top of her head while his hand rubbed up and down her soft arm. She was where she belonged.

The depth of his feelings for her should have scared him. He'd refused to let himself ever feel like this, risk the heartache again. But, he knew she *was* the woman for him.

"THAT was wonderful," he croaked.

"Mm," was all she could say as she played with the dark, curly hair on his defined chest. Resting her hand over his heart, she felt the beating returning to normal. It calmed her, reassured her. She felt safe, warm and loved in his arms.

"Did you want the rest of your wine?"

She lifted her head off his chest and looked into his eyes. Disappointment tried to weave its way into her. She shouldn't care he didn't want to lie with her after such unbelievable sex, but she reminded herself that was what it was—sex. She cared, but she knew that was all it was and had agreed to that. One day it might change.

"That sounds good."

Jesse gave her a quick kiss and left the bed. Pulling on his jeans, he gave her another quick kiss before leaving the room. "Be right back, sweetheart."

Remaining in the bed, a broad smile broke out on Kate's face.

That had been the most exquisite sex she'd ever experienced. Her orgasms—yes, plural—had been so powerful she'd almost passed out. The experience had been exceptional not only because Jesse was such a fantastic, unselfish lover, but because she could no longer deny her deep feelings for him. He'd ingrained himself inside her without so much as trying. She was glad she'd taken this step with him. They'd never move forward if she hadn't. She groaned.

Jesse didn't do relationships, pure and simple, but he'd treated her like they were in a relationship. He'd been there for her, acting like someone who cared, someone whose feelings were involved. She couldn't dismiss her concern that he'd walk away when the job was done, without any regrets.

He'd made it clear he wasn't looking for a relationship. Now that he'd had her in bed, what would happen? While she knew he wouldn't leave her not when her life was in danger, she honestly didn't know what would happen next, and she couldn't bring herself to ask because she didn't want to hear that he was done with her. A crushing pain settled in her chest at the thought of losing him while protecting her. It wasn't the first time she'd thought it, but it was the first her emotions were so deep into him. Nothing could happen to him, Reagan needed him. *She* needed him.

It hit her with the force of hurricane strength winds. She was falling in love with him. And like many coastal inhabitants, Kate wasn't prepared. They were barely ready for a relationship though. That was what she wanted. She didn't want to walk away like she'd planned. That realization made her blissful and dispirited at the same time.

As a father, she wondered if he'd want more children. Her not being able to have any could impact his decision on whether to take that big of a chance on her.

A new determination filled her. She had to win him, had to make him see her as someone other than just another woman in his bed. Kate didn't even know if he'd want her back in his bed again. She wasn't going to wait and see what he did. Kate had never been the aggressor in a relationship before, but if she needed to be, she would. If she couldn't win Jesse by the time this case was solved, when the killer was caught, then she'd walk away, broken heart and all. She just hoped that didn't happen.

Settling back against the pillows, she pulled the covers over her breasts and crossed her arms across her chest. She loved this family. It was where she belonged. She'd start by winning Jesse's heart. She'd have to have it completely before she could tell him the truth about future children. If he loved her enough, it wouldn't matter.

When Jesse didn't return, she left the bed, pulled on his shirt and went downstairs. Before she reached the bottom of the stairs, she heard him talking.

Walking in to the room, Kate wished she'd stayed upstairs. Ken stood in the living room holding a young boy. She wanted to disappear into thin air when they all turned and looked at her. She was standing there in only Jesse's shirt for goodness' sake.

Her embarrassment quickly vanished when she saw Jesse's expression. Something was seriously wrong.

"What is it?"

"We received another note. Pack a bag. We're leaving."

# Nineteen

KATE FROZE AND stared at Jesse with wide eyes and raised eyebrows. She needed a minute to process what he'd said. "What?"

"We received another note. This time he hired this kid to slide it under your door. We're moving right now. Now, go pack a bag."

Her eyes drifted to the piece of paper he held with a tissue and then to the kid. The terrified child couldn't have been more than nine with short, red hair and a face full of freckles. His wide, green eyes darted around the room looking for an escape from Ken.

Dottie sat in front of the boy whining, tail thumping against the floor, waiting for him to pet her.

She stepped forward. "Hello, I'm Kate and that's Dottie. You may pet her if you want." She used a soft, calming voice, or at least she hoped it sounded like that to the child who turned to look at her. "What's your name?"

He hunched his shoulders before answering. "Peter. Can I really pet her?"

Kneeling down, Kate smiled and nodded. "Go ahead."

Peter tentatively reached out and placed his hand on Dottie's head. When she rubbed against it, then licked it, the little boy giggled. That was the sound that should be coming out of a nine-year-old, not the frightened whisper of his name.

Kate narrowed her eyes at Jesse. She didn't need to say a word to him.

Jesse rubbed the nape of his neck with his free hand. "Kate, we've already questioned the boy. He can't help us."

She shot Peter a reassuring smile. "Perhaps Peter needs to be getting home. I imagine your parents are worried about you, right?"

Peter nodded.

"Where are your parents?" Jesse asked.

When Peter just stared at her, she looked at Ken. "Will you take him home?"

Ken raised his eyebrows then looked at Jesse who nodded. He knelt down and spoke softly with the boy.

Kate winked at a smiling Peter, who eagerly followed Ken from the apartment.

Jesse raised his eyebrows. "Satisfied?"

Standing, she smiled. "Very. Now, tell me what's going on?"

"Just what I said. The bastard sent another note."

The distress in his voice registered with her. "What does it say?"

Just a few minutes ago, she'd forgotten all about the death threat against her. She'd been so lost in loving Jesse. Lost in his arms, his touch and his kiss. Lost in love.

"Don't worry about it. Now, go pack." He turned from her,

dismissing her to follow his order. "Ken, get ready for our departure. I'm calling in the entire team to HQ. Move the girls also. I want the full force on all of them, and I want my daughter with me."

He turned back to Kate, seeming surprised to see her. "Why are you still standing there? Go pack a bag."

Incensed, she crossed her arms over her chest. "What does it say?" The note had to be about her, otherwise Jesse would've told her what it said. And it had upset him, so it couldn't be good. She prepared herself for the worst.

Jesse heaved a heavy sigh. "It simply says, 'She's going to die.'"

She absorbed the information. A cold shiver rumbled through her. It wasn't new to them that the Facilitator wanted her dead to punish Jesse, but the note emphasized his determination for her to die. "We already knew that. Why leave? He can't get to us here. I have the best protection there is."

"I can't risk this psycho won't change his target and go after my sister or my niece or heaven forbid, Reagan, since he can't get to you. I want Reagan with me, Kate, and I want her feeling secure in her own bedroom. Besides, you know it's safer at my house. With the security systems we have in place, and the entire team protecting us, he won't even get close."

His home was the safest place for all of them. She'd been in awe when AJ had given her a rundown on all of the security features at Jesse's house. She doubted even the FBI's best could get around his system.

It had to be torture for him, leaving his daughter's safety to his brothers. He used his laptop to video-chat with her more than he did actual work on it. The sacrifice he'd been making for her safety had to end. She couldn't keep him from Reagan just to prove a point that he didn't control her, didn't tell her where to go. "Okay, but Dottie goes too."

"Of course she does."

Kate turned and raced up the stairs with Dottie at her heels. She quickly changed and packed a suitcase, paying no attention to what she packed. She had no idea how long she'd be staying there or where she'd sleep. Would he put her in his room? Surely not in front of Reagan. That put a crimp in her plan to win his love.

On the short journey from her apartment to Jesse's SUV, she'd been closely guarded by Jesse, HIS, and FBI, with Neftali, the team sharpshooter, watching the area for potential dangers. Jesse remained on the phone the entire drive to his house, talking with his brothers, ensuring Reagan, Emily, and Amber were safely on their way, and the men were in place. They were attempting to move the two-year-old and five-year-old girls without waking them, hoping to prevent them from being scared of the late night move.

Finally arriving, she breathed a sigh of relief. They exited the car and Jesse carried their bags into his home. "This way."

Dottie sniffed the furniture while she followed Jesse upstairs to a large bedroom she knew to be his and watched as he deposited both of their bags on his bed.

"Um, Jesse, shouldn't I be staying in a guest room?" It was the last thing she wanted, more than happy to be sharing his bed with him, but she worried about Reagan?

Jesse lowered his brow. "No." He walked to her and played

with a strand of hair that had fallen forward over her shoulder. "You belong here."

If only he meant forever. She swallowed and fought back the heat he created just by being near her. "What about Reagan?"

"What about her?"

He looked deep into her eyes and reached up to lightly stroke her cheek with the back of his hand. She closed her eyes, savoring the pleasant sensations his touch evoked.

Remembering their conversation was difficult but necessary. "Reagan. She shouldn't see me in your bed. It's not proper."

He leaned down to kiss her but stopped right before touching her lips and spoke. "She'll have to get used to it." He reached around her and pulled her hard against him, his mouth captured hers in a sizzling kiss, burning her all the way to her toes.

Conversation topic lost, she succumbed to the pleasure seeping through her body as his tongue slipped into her mouth. Her mind knew only his kiss. He grasped her buttocks and pulled her tightly against him. The feel of his erection growing against her belly fanned warmth between her thighs.

"Daddy, Daddy."

Jesse released Kate, stepped back and bent down to catch Reagan as she raced into the room, jumping into his arms. He lifted her, pulled her close and kissed her cheek. "Hey, pumpkin. Why are you awake?"

She pulled back and looked at him. "Uncle Brad tried to move me and *woked* me up. He told me I'd see you. I couldn't go back to sleep. I missed you, Daddy." She put her small hands on each side of his face and gave him a kiss, then giggled when Jesse made loud, smacking noises.

"I missed you, too. Say hello to Miss Kate."

She turned in his arms, a bright smile on her angelic face. "Hi, Miss Kate. Are you having a sleepover too, like Aunt Em and Amber?"

"She is, pumpkin. Remember I need to protect her. Now, it's time to go back to bed." He looked at Kate. "I'll be right back."

"Good night, Reagan." She wished she could be part of tucking Jesse's daughter in for the night, reading her bedtime stories until she couldn't keep her little eyes open any longer.

"Night, Miss Kate."

Jesse walked out of the room, his daughter in his arms.

Kate looked around the bedroom and the four-poster king-size bed. The beautiful mahogany frame had been carved with precision, tangled vines and leaves wrapped around the corner posts. The headboard and footboard stood high with the same design tangled across them. The mirror to a long dresser also matched the design, the vines and leaves surrounding its oval shape. The set was exquisite.

She walked over and picked up the photo on Jesse's bedside table. Despair tried to seep its way in but she fought it.

Jesse walked into the room and stopped. He moved forward with an outstretched arm. "That was my wife, Jen, with Reagan when Reagan was one month old."

Kate handed him the picture. "She's beautiful."

He looked at the photo, tenderness in his eyes. "Yes, she was."

Looking back at Kate, he said, "The guys are here, so I need to go. You can settle in. I won't wake you when I come to bed, but tomorrow we'll finish what we started a few minutes ago."

"Dammit, Jesse, I should be at this meeting. We've discussed this. Don't leave me out."

"Kate, I'm not trying to leave you out. We're going to discuss security, that's all. There's no need for you to be a part of that. Get some rest."

She studied him. "Okay, Jesse. If I find out you discussed this case without me, you're going to regret it." She had no idea what she'd do, but she'd think of something if the time came. She had to trust him.

He laughed at her. *Laughed.* She envisioned wringing his neck. Before she could say anything else, he leaned down and stole a quick kiss, then turned to leave the room, taking the photo of his late wife with him.

"I ought to sneak down there and listen," she muttered to herself. Then she looked at the comfy-looking bed and decided sleep was a better idea. She knew enough about security that she didn't need to listen to them hash out their schedules.

As she searched in her bag for something to sleep in, she thought about the opportunity she had. Both Jesse and Reagan were under the same roof.

As she put on a T-shirt and shorts, she remembered the next day was Jason's birthday. She should've mentioned it to Jesse. She'd love for the two of them to meet. Jason could use a male figure in his life, and Jason was important to her. She wouldn't let Jesse stop her from seeing him.

She climbed into the massive bed, choosing the side opposite where Jen's picture had been. The plan to stay awake failed. She was asleep within minutes.

"YOU put Kate in your room." Brad's anger seeped into his voice.

"Yeah. So what if I did?" Jesse narrowed his eyes at his brother. He wasn't some little schoolboy. He was a grown man. So what if he put her in his room?

"You're fucking her, aren't you?"

He crossed his arms across his broad chest. He was well on his way to pissed. "Be very careful, Brad."

"You're too personally involved with her to provide protection," Matt injected into the conversation.

Jesse stared at his brothers. They had never ganged up on him before. "Fuck you. I can protect her. What we do has no bearing on this."

Brad pointed his index finger at Jesse. "You're the one who told us never to get involved. Besides, it's part of the basic rules for protection. Everyone knows that. You're putting her at risk."

Jesse stared at Brad. The golden rule of protection didn't apply to him and Kate. *His* Kate. Putting her life in jeopardy was the last thing he would do. There was no question that he would give his life for hers. He gritted his teeth in anger.

"I hope you know what you're doing. Not only for her protection but also for Reagan. She's going to see you two together and hasn't seen you with anyone before. She may get the wrong idea."

Jesse startled them with his response. "No, Devon. She'll get the right idea." Before his brothers could form a retort, he said, "AJ's here. Let's get started."

What would happen to his daughter if she bonded with Kate and Kate didn't want to stay? She'd finally given in and slept with him. That had to mean something, didn't it? He couldn't contemplate her leaving.

AJ strolled up to his brothers and glanced around the group. "Something I need to know about?"

"Yeah, Jesse's fucking your partner." Brad smirked and crossed his arms over his chest.

"Asshole," Jesse seethed.

Jesse didn't want to have this conversation with AJ. Instead, he needed to ensure the women and girls were safe. Having them all under one roof was a huge relief to him.

"What? It's true. You can't hide it when you have her sleeping in your bed."

Jesse wanted to punch Brad in his big mouth. He wouldn't leave it alone. He knew how AJ would react.

"Is this true, Jesse?" AJ asked calmly.

He cleared his throat. This had gone on long enough. "Don't start throwing punches again, AJ. It's none of your business."

"Bullshit. You're using her. I warned you about hurting her." AJ's hands fisted at his sides, ready for a fight.

"Back off, AJ. I'm not going to hurt her. She's *mine*."

Brad, Devon, and Matt looked at each other and smiled. AJ wore a disbelieving frown and swore.

"Now, we have a killer to catch." Jesse walked away from them. "All right men, let's get going. Ken, you have a team outside already?"

"We're covered. We put the FBI detail inside. Out of the way." The men looked at AJ and chuckled. "Does this mean we're still on to give Ambassador Hahn a couple of men the next two days?"

Shit. He'd been so focused on keeping Kate and Reagan safe he'd forgotten about that assignment. "Can you make it work?

You have me, Brad, and Matt to add to the mix for here."

Ken nodded. "We can cover the house and the detail. We'll only need Brad and Matt when Emily takes Amber to the doctor."

Even though he'd agreed to the ambassador's protection ten months earlier, he'd cancel it in a heartbeat if it impacted the protection of his family.

"I'll keep Kate here, so there won't be any problems. Now, I'm sure you've all heard of the new note. We're giving it to AJ for prints, but we're not holding our breath. You've done an excellent job protecting them to this point. Finally having them in one place should make this easier for you, but don't relax assuming our system will catch someone. We have the best there is to offer, but no system is failsafe."

Devon and Brad, the two designers of the system, made noises close to a grunt.

"We'll limit the women to the house, except for Amber's doctor appointment, and she'd best be heavily guarded since she has to go. Now, I'd prefer the kids weren't out in the yard, so don't let Reagan sweet talk you into taking her out to play." He looked at the headshakes around the room. "He's going to try again. Be ready, everyone." He turned to his brother. "Dev?"

Devon cleared his throat. "I hate to say this, but we need more time. Joe picked up Ed's trail again, so hopefully, we'll have him soon. No hits on hiring out the Facilitator."

They discussed what had happened and their plans. When the meeting was close to ending, Jesse reminded them, "Ed's our key. Find him."

The men dispersed and Jesse turned to Devon and said,

"Something is really bothering me. I've got someone I want you to check out and dig and dig. There's something there that we're missing."

Devon surprised Jesse after he'd disclosed the name of the person he wanted checked out. Devon had already started to do some digging on the person himself.

Jesse walked into his bedroom, stopped and smiled at the glorious sight of Kate curled up in his bed. He never thought he'd have another woman there after his wife had died. Never thought there would be any place in his heart for any other woman.

His brothers had made a great point about Reagan. He had to consider her feelings. He didn't think she was old enough to understand. She hadn't seen him with a woman. He'd never brought one home, specifically because of her.

Undressing, Jesse slid into bed, pulling Kate to him. She didn't wake but cuddled up with him. He relaxed with her safely in his arms. He'd find a way to explain to his daughter why she was in his bed. And, although Kate didn't know it yet, she was moving in with them when this was over. She was going to be a part of their lives. Sure it was soon, but he knew what he wanted, and he didn't believe in wasting time. His wife's life being cut short taught him that.

He dropped off to sleep worrying about his daughter's reaction to Kate sleeping in his bed, her reaction to Kate being there all of the time, her reaction to his touching and kissing Kate in front of her and, worst of all, her reaction if Kate died because he screwed up again.

# Twenty

KATE WOKE WITH a heavy arm over her waist and Jesse's hard penis poking her in the buttocks. Hoping she wasn't dreaming, she slowly opened her eyes and found herself looking into a pair of small, golden-brown eyes.

Reagan stood beside the bed, holding a worn teddy bear and a scrunched-up look on her face. "Was you scared? My daddy lets me sleep in his bed when I gets really, really scared. I'm a big girl now so I tries to sleep in my bed."

Kate wasn't sure how to respond, fearing saying the wrong thing. She didn't know what Jesse planned to tell Reagan about her being in his bed. She was so very thankful she wasn't naked. That really would've been hard to explain.

Jesse lifted his head and looked over Kate at Reagan. "Morning, pumpkin. What are you doing in here?" Under the covers, he teased Kate by slowly rubbing his groin against her.

"Was you helping Miss Kate not be scared, Daddy?" Reagan climbed on the bed and sat beside Kate, her wide eyes looking at her father.

"Something like that. Why don't you go downstairs and see what Mrs. Kessler is doing?"

Reagan hopped off the bed. "Okay, Daddy. Miss Kate, are you coming? Mrs. Kessler makes scared all better."

"Sure," she answered hesitantly.

Kate rolled out of Jesse's arms to follow Reagan downstairs. She ran her fingers through her hair in an attempt to look presentable. Her T-shirt and shorts would have to be sufficient since the little girl waited at the door.

Reagan took her hand and tugged. "I'll show you the way."

Kate looked back at Jesse, whose face appeared concerned with a frown marring it. Her heart sank. He didn't want her getting close to his daughter. Damn.

They found Emily and Amber in the kitchen with an older, gray-haired woman cooking eggs on the stove.

Emily turned to them. "Good morning, Reagan. Amber's been waiting for you. Kate, I'd like you to meet Mrs. Kessler. She helps Jesse take care of Reagan."

Kate smiled and held out her hand. "Nice to meet you, Mrs. Kessler."

The woman surprised her by hugging her instead of shaking her hand. "Lord, it's about time. Please call me Lorraine. I can't get any of this bunch to do it."

Kate looked at Emily who shrugged.

"Okay, Lorraine. What can I do to help with breakfast?" Kate asked.

She felt awkward standing there looking as if she'd just rolled out of bed. Maybe Reagan wouldn't notice if she snuck back upstairs and changed.

"Nothing, nothing. I'm expecting all the boys this morning, so you'd best grab a plate before there's nothing left."

She turned to a child's laughter. Dottie licked Reagan's face. "I love your dog, Miss Kate."

Kate walked over and knelt down beside them. "First, call me Kate. Second, Reagan, this is Dottie. Dottie, this is Reagan. Say hello, Dottie."

Her dog raised her paw to shake. More giggles from Jesse's daughter floated through the room.

Amber yelled, "Dog, Mama, dog."

Emily caught her daughter as she tried to climb out of her booster seat. "Not right now, Amber. After you eat."

Jesse sauntered into the kitchen. "Good morning, Mrs. Kessler. How is my favorite cook today?" He kissed the girls on the top of their heads, kissed Mrs. Kessler and Emily on the cheek, and Kate on the lips.

Kate froze. She hadn't expected any affection from him in front of his family, in front of Reagan again.

"Right as rain." Mrs. Kessler turned back to the stove, humming a tune Kate had never heard.

"Daddy, Daddy, guess what? Dottie shooked my hand. Watch. Do it again, Kate. Make her do it again."

After learning the command, Reagan repeated it over and over. Dottie sat, extending her paw each time and occasionally leaned forward to lick the little girl's face.

"Let's wash your hands, young lady, and get to the table." Jesse reached down for his daughter who gave Dottie a big hug first.

As the group settled at the table, Devon, Matt, and Brad filed into the kitchen, each stopping to drop a kiss on Mrs. Kessler's, their sister's and nieces' cheeks.

"Uncle Dev, Uncle Dev." Reagan almost bounced out of her chair. "Guess what?"

Devon smiled at her enthusiasm. "What, kiddo?"

"Dottie shaked my hand, and Daddy kissed Kate on the lips."

Kate stiffened, but saw nothing but smiles from the family.

"How about I kiss you on the lips, my little pumpkin?" Jesse reached over, tipped Reagan's chin up and gave her a kiss on the lips. "Now I've kissed both of my girls on the lips this morning."

"Guess what, Kate?" Before Kate could answer, Reagan continued. "You're Daddy's girl, too. We get to have all kinds of fun as Daddy's girls. Mrs. Kessler says Daddy spoils me. Now, he can spoil you, too."

Again Kate was at a loss for words. First, the kiss, and then the declaration to his family that she was *his* girl. She glanced around the room. Emily and Devon shared a knowing smile. Matt played with Amber. And Brad watched them intently.

Mrs. Kessler put plates of food on the table, ignoring the dynamics occurring in the room. Kate looked at Jesse, who wore a huge grin. He winked at her then turned to Emily.

"Em, Brad and Matt are going with you and Amber tomorrow."

Emily nodded. "Are you planning to end this soon?"

"We don't fail, Em. You know that."

Emily made a face at Matt for his remark. "I know you don't. I'm ready for life to be normal again. I want to go back to class." She added more dry cereal to Amber's plate since most of what she'd already given the little girl was on the floor.

Kate watched the closeness the family displayed along with the patience and love the brothers showed the children.

Thinking of children reminded her about Jason. Kate looked at Jesse. "I need to go to the children's hospital today. It's Jason's birthday."

Matt furrowed his eyebrows and looked at her curiously. "The children's hospital?"

Kate beamed. "My sister and I volunteer there, and Jason Monroe is a child who recently lost his parents."

Smiling, Matt said, "Well, it's a small world. I know Jason. His father was in my unit. I visit him as often as I can since he has no one left. He's mentioned someone named Kate. I didn't put it together."

"The same here. He's mentioned someone named Matt, but I thought it was a nurse. You should know he idolizes you, Matt."

"Jesse, can we go?"

He smiled. "It's all arranged."

"What?" Floored, she took a moment to recover and make sure she'd heard him right because she was ready to jump up and launch herself into his arms. "How did you know?"

"It's my job to know everything. We're a bit tight on a detail since we have men tied up with an ambassador, but Brad and Matt are going." He winked at her. "I didn't tell Matt either what we'd be doing."

The twins nodded. Kate could've sworn Brad hid a knowing smirk behind his piece of toast.

She'd never dreamed such a wonderful man hid behind that gruff exterior she'd first met. "Okay. Wow. Thank you. We have to go by my apartment and pick up his present." She hadn't thought to bring it along. She'd been focused on the note.

"Brad can go pick it up. I won't have you going back there right now."

She took a deep breath to keep calm. If they were going to be together, she'd have to work on his telling her what she was and wasn't going to do. She gritted her teeth. "Fine."

---

THEY stationed the FBI detail outside the door and led the procession of Hamilton brothers into Jason's hospital room. Jesse could see the love Kate had for the kid, and the love the kid had for her.

"Kate, Matt," Jason gushed, crawling from the bed to give her a hug. "Look, I can get out of bed now. The doctors said I'm doing well."

They'd insisted they talk with his doctor before they came to see him. Jesse had watched the relief appear on Matt and Kate's faces when the doctor told them Jason was responding well to his treatment.

"Happy birthday." She held him tight before reluctantly releasing him.

"Happy birthday, Jason." Matt slapped him on the shoulder with one hand and shook his hand with the other.

Puffing out his chest, he said, "I'm thirteen now. An adult."

They chuckled. "Not quite. Jason, meet Matt's brothers, Jesse and Brad."

They shook hands, wishing him a happy birthday.

"What's that, Kate?" He pointed to the wrapped present she held.

Chuckling, she held it out to him. "This is for you."

He accepted the gift and greedily tore the paper. "Wow. It's a football, and it's signed. Thanks, Kate." He reached out and hugged her again. "Is that for me, too?" He looked at the gift Matt held under his arm.

"Sure is, buddy." He tore into the wrapping paper. "Look, Kate. Football cards."

"There's a card for every active NFL quarterback. They'd all signed their card for you," Matt said.

Jason sifted through them, shouting a couple of the names out loud and displaying their cards for all to see. When he'd appeared to shuffle through them all, he sat them down, very carefully. "I can't wait to show the other kids. Thank you, Matt."

A look of surprise flooded his face when Jason gave him a hug.

"Thank you for coming, sir. Are those for me?" Jason asked Jesse jumping from using manners to a boy's eagerness for gifts.

Seeing the joy on the boy's face, Jesse was glad that he'd sent Matt to pick up gifts from him and Brad.

Jason opened the football target from Jesse to perfect his aim and a playbook from Brad. After all the gifts were open, he went back through each one, treating each as a treasured gift. "Thanks, everybody."

"It gets better." Kate walked out the door to the nurse's station and returned with an ice cream cake. "We can't burn candles in here, so you have to make a wish and pretend."

Jesse watched her interact with Jason. It was hard not to love the kid. He knew she worried about his Leukemia, but she kept it well hidden when the two of them were together. She'd be a great mother to his daughter.

Yes, he wanted her to be Reagan's mother.

Because it was his birthday, the staff allowed Jason to throw the football in the hallway with Matt.

"You've got form," Matt said as he tossed the ball back to Jason.

"But, I can't throw far."

"That's easily remedied once you're out of here and can build up your strength," Jesse added, standing in the doorway near Jason. He wanted to kick himself after that. Where would the kid go? No matter where he went, Jesse would find a way to help him be ready for the try-outs the kid kept boasting about.

Jason tired out, and they returned to the room. Kate read him a story before they left. She explained to him she might not be able to visit for a little while. He said he understood, but his disappointment was obvious. Jesse would have to find some way to let her visit with him.

"Thank you, Jesse." Kate made an attempt at a smile as they left.

He reached over and took her hand in his. "You're welcome. He's a great kid."

She sighed. "I feel so bad for him. Once he gets better, he goes into foster care. It'll crush him if his foster parents don't support his playing football. That's his dream."

"I know lots of people. I'll think about someone who can take him in, like the Rosses did for you." He knew a couple who would put Kate's mind at ease.

"That'd be great. What are you going to tell Reagan about us being in the same bed?"

Ah, the real source of her anxiety. He checked the rearview

mirror again before responding, "I'm going to tell her the truth. You're mine." He squeezed her hand.

When she didn't respond, he looked over at her. "That's okay, isn't it?" A sliver of doubt crept up his spine. One minute he'd take them two steps forward then she'd take them one step back. Since they'd slept together, he hoped they didn't move back again. She had to know how he felt about her.

"You're her father. You know what's best."

Her answer didn't satisfy him. "You are mine, aren't you?"

She bit her bottom lip, then nodded. "For as long as you'll have me."

That was more like it.

Jesse checked the rearview mirror again, knowing his brothers were somewhere behind them keeping an eye out for anyone tailing them. It had been a spontaneous trip, but he didn't rule out someone staking out his place, waiting for them to leave.

Jesse breathed a sigh of relief when his brothers pulled their SUV behind him in the driveway. They hadn't been followed. His girls were safe.

His focus couldn't leave their security, but he had a family to build.

# Twenty-One

KATE STEPPED OUT of the shower and wrapped herself in a large bath towel. As she rubbed lavender lotion on her body, Jesse walked into the bathroom, and his eyes roamed over her. She tingled under his gaze as if his hands had followed his eyes, touching and caressing her body.

Jesse moved close and leaned his forehead to hers. "God, you're beautiful. I want you to wait for me on the bed. Just like you are."

Either he pulled her towel down or it slipped. The reason no longer mattered when he reached up and rubbed his thumb over her nipple. It formed a stiff peak, making Kate catch her breath.

"After a quick shower, I'll be in there to explore every inch of your sexy body. Of course, I'll need to rest along the way." He raised his eyebrows seductively. "But, I'll ensure those places receive my special attention."

Kate reached out and wrapped her hand around the large bulge in his pants.

"No, Jesse. I'll wait for you like this, but I'll be the one doing the exploring and giving the special attention, especially right here."

SHEILA KELL

She squeezed him and was rewarded with a throaty groan. "Don't take too long in the shower." Kate slipped past Jesse, surprised he didn't stop her since she'd teased his large cock to fully erect.

Butterflies floated in her stomach. Kneeling on the bed, she faced the bathroom and focused. This had to be perfect. Taking control from the beginning was necessary because once Jesse touched her, she'd get lost in a sensual haze and want nothing but him inside her.

She closed her eyes as her body came alive as she recalled every kiss and every touch of his hands, fingers, and tongue. A moan escaped her lips.

"Is that moan for me?"

She opened her eyes, and her breath caught. Jesse stood in the doorway, naked, a half smile on his freshly shaven face and his erection standing against his belly. Good Lord, sex oozed from the man.

His gaze raked intimately over her. Her nipples hardened and her pulse raced.

He stalked toward her, stopping an arm's length away, making no move to touch her. "So you're in control. Are you going to tease me? Make me beg? Make me cry out for mercy?" The low, gravelly tone in his voice made her smile.

Trembling with need, she reached out to touch him, to indulge in the feel of his warm, smooth skin over taut muscles. The exploration began. She glided her hands over every place her eyes roved. Stopping on his bulging right bicep, she traced a tattoo. She'd forgotten to ask about it before and the question would still wait because it wasn't the time for chitchat.

She glided her hands across his soft skin to the sculpted muscles of his shoulders. Her heart thudded so loud she thought he'd hear. She knew how wonderful his hard body felt against hers. Waiting to have him inside her was harder then she thought it would be, but Kate was determined to go slowly and savor every moment.

Continuing the sensual journey, she slid her hands down his shoulders to his expansive chest, where his heart beat fast beneath her hands. She teased his dark nipples with her thumbs while her fingers played in the short, curly hair. Kate longed to lick them, have her tongue tease them like he did to her.

Jesse groaned but showed great restraint by standing still. His only noticeable show of fighting to remain in control was his hands fisted at his sides. The excitement playing around inside her danced around with how she affected him.

Breathing hard, she continued. Her next stop was his clearly defined, hard abdomen that grew rigid under her touch. His sharp intake of breath broke the silence.

She locked gazes with him and heat shot through her. He hadn't even touched her, yet she felt the moisture between her thighs.

"Prepare to beg," she whispered. "Lie down on the bed for me and keep your hands to yourself."

He obeyed and issued a deep, guttural groan when she straddled him. He reached up to touch her breasts, but she knocked his hands away.

"Not yet. You got to do this last time, so it's only fair I get to do it this time."

The way his hands wrapped in the sheet, anchoring him as he

relinquished all control to her was an erotic gesture. It amped up her red-hot need for him.

"I'm all yours."

She placed her hands on his chest and leaned down to kiss him. It was a light, teasing kiss that sent electric shocks through her system. Lost in the moment, she slowly deepened the kiss, his lips parting and welcoming her tongue. He didn't hold back, but let her lead the kiss, making her melt from the inside out.

She lifted her mouth from his to gulp in air. His groans echoed through the room as she pressed unhurried kisses on his neck then used her mouth and her hands to touch, tease, and taunt him as she made her way down his body to his stiff groin.

Locking gazes, she took him in her hand and brushed her lips across the base of his cock then slowly licked up his length, swirling her tongue to taste his precum.

Another groan erupted from Jesse's chest. "You're killing me, sweetheart."

Kate smiled as his body stiffened when her tongue glided over his balls and all the way up again, licking the vein on his cock from base to crown, circling the engorged head before sliding her warm, wet mouth over his erection.

His hands tightened in the sheets, his breath came in jerky puffs and his hips thrust up, begging for her to take him again. "Deeper, Kate. Take me deep."

Wanting to satisfy him, she sucked him in deep and hard using her fisted hand and mouth in unison, pumping up and down his shaft. The shaft that she wanted inside of her, like she was taking him with her mouth. The fiery ache burned inside of her, needing to be taken care of soon or she'd incinerate.

His body jerked when she used her injured hand to lightly graze his balls, feeling them draw tight.

He reached down and pulled her up. "Enough."

She smiled seductively, knowing how close she'd brought him, then crawled up and straddled him.

"Condom."

She left the bed and returned with a condom and rolled it on him, then positioned his cock between her thighs, guiding him into her heat, and sliding all the way down. She didn't move but savored the feel of him inside her.

"Damn, you're wet. It's time for me to touch you now."

She didn't object when he reached up and grasped her breasts. She arched into his hands and let him caress them and tease her nipples. "Lean down."

Mindlessly obeying, she leaned forward and moaned as he took one of her breasts in his mouth. She needed to move, to take away the ache and release the growing bliss. He reached down, grasped her hips and began to guide her up and down in a slow, sensual rhythm.

"Ride me, Kate," he growled between tantalizing bites on her nipple.

His deep, husky voice rippled through her. Setting their rhythm, she freed her breast and took his mouth with hers. One of his hands left her hip and tangled in her hair. Grabbing the back of her head, he angled her head to deepen the kiss, and their tongues did an intricate dance.

Anticipation licked through her as a fever lit her body. She sat up, put her hands on his chest and adjusting their rhythm. Intense pleasure mixed with the ache inside of her drawing tight into a fiery knot waiting to be released.

"I've never seen a sexier sight." He pinched and tugged at her nipples, tormenting her, shooting fire-bolts to her belly.

She couldn't repress the moan or the involuntary tightening around his cock.

The groan vibrating deep from within his chest sounded almost like a wounded animal, the pain of holding back for her sake evident. He grabbed her hips. "Fuck." He moved her up and down faster.

Feeling his urgency in the new rhythm, she didn't fight the spiraling sensation when he reached between them and rubbed her swollen clit, circling, keeping a constant friction that had her climbing to the ragged edge.

She fisted her hand in her mouth to keep from crying out. Then she fell, free-falling into seemingly endless wave after wave of tiny fiery explosions, leaving her floating like a feather from cloud to cloud, drifting slowly back to earth in a state of bliss, collapsing on top of Jesse, limp, sated.

In a single fluid motion, he quickly flipped them over, grabbed her ass and drove into her, thrusting hard and fast, groaning harshly as he finally claimed his own release. He slumped forward, his flushed, sweaty body to hers.

She smiled. It couldn't get better than this.

JESSE lifted himself off Kate and went into the bathroom to clean up. Their lovemaking had been different, more passionate, more intense. She cared for him, probably as deeply as he cared for her. He should say something. "That was incredible," he said as he walked into the bedroom. A smile fell on his face at the sight of a sound asleep Kate. He reached out and pushed the hair from her face. She was beautiful.

Leaning down, Jesse kissed her forehead before moving to his side of the bed. He slid next to her and held her against him, her back to his front. She fit perfectly. She was meant to be there.

His daughter liked her. A lot. After tonight, he didn't worry about her breaking Reagan's heart. She was staying.

Only one thing could ruin it all, and he'd make sure that didn't happen.

JESSE jerked awake at the sound of a female voice calling his name, dragging him from the metallic smell and sticky feeling that had ripped his heart out. Visions of the crime scene with crimson pools of blood that surrounded his wife ricocheted his failure and loss throughout him.

His first thought was that Jen was calling him, telling him it was only a nightmare, that he hadn't failed, but he then recognized the voice. It was Kate. His Kate.

"Jesse, you okay? You were having a nightmare." Her hand rested on his chest, right above his pounding heart. Her eyes were flooded with concern.

How long had she been trying to wake him, witnessing him in his own hell?

"It was nothing." He threw his arm across his eyes and tried to calm his racing pulse and his erratic breathing.

"It helps if you talk about it," she said gently.

He climbed out of bed, pulled on his boxer shorts and paced the room. *Should I tell her? She might not trust me to protect her.*

*Might expect me to make the wrong choice and not be there when she needs me.*

A muscle clenched in his jaw, and he fisted his hands at his sides while he fought the battle raging inside him. He knew she cared about him but could what they have withstand this? They'd yet to discuss any feelings or what came next for them. His failure to protect the one he should have could be too much. Jesse didn't want to lose her, didn't want her to send him away. He was in too deep.

He stopped and turned to her. Of course, he needed to tell her, but when he opened his mouth to speak, he found it suddenly impossible. The heavy weight of the guilt he wore constricted his lungs. Closing his eyes, he fought to regain control.

Then the nightmare flashed before his eyes. It had been five fucking years, but it still felt like yesterday. He'd told her no, let her go inside herself and then taken a call instead of finding out what held her up in the store. He should have been there. He should have saved her.

"I was married." The rawness of his voice surprised him.

She stared at him for what seemed like forever before she spoke softly, "I know."

He cleared his throat, pushing the lump through his closing throat. "We were married for four years. Two months after Reagan was born, she died in a convenience store robbery." He fought to continue, fearing her reaction. "It's my fault she was there by herself. I should've been there to save her." The tone of his voice captured his tortured soul.

She remained silent, allowing him the time to collect himself and explain.

A muscle clenched in his jaw as he paced again. He couldn't look at her, didn't want to see the accusation that would appear in her eyes. "We stopped to get gas…" He then told her the story. Turmoil roiled through him as he ripped open the wounds, blood flowing from them, tearing apart what remained of his empty and damaged soul.

Stopping, he looked at her. "I won't go through that again. I'll protect you, Kate. You can trust that I won't make that same mistake.

"If it hadn't been for my family, Reagan and I would still be lost and grieving. I couldn't function after I lost Jen. Em was young, but she stepped up and took care of my daughter for me. I was a mess. Not only had I lost the woman I loved, but could have saved her. I knew something was wrong. She was taking too long.

"My brothers finally helped me snap out of it and focus on Reagan. She became my everything. I feel responsible for letting her mother die. It was my fault. I'll never fail again, Kate. I'll keep you safe."

He'd told her everything and waited for her reaction. He hadn't wanted to share his story with her because he couldn't face what would inevitably happen next. She'd send him away.

"Jesse, it wasn't your fault."

"Of course it was. She was my wife. I was supposed to protect her," he said more sharply than he'd meant.

"Wife or not, you can't believe that. You may think you need to protect everyone, but you're only human. I think you're putting the blame on yourself because you wished you'd have kept her from going inside in the first place. But, I imagine she'd have done it if she wanted to." She crawled off the bed and wound her arms around him, hugging him tightly. She pulled back and looked up at him. Instead of accusation for failing his wife as he'd expected, around the tears sliding down her face, he saw compassion and what he hoped was love. He didn't deserve her.

He wrapped his arms around her and accepted the comfort she offered, comfort that warmed him and touched his naked soul.

He had lived too long with the consequences of his actions. At least that was what he'd thought. She was right and he should've seen it before. Oh, his family had probably told him, but it took this wonderful woman for the point to stick. He could never get his wife back. The pain of his loss, and his responsibility for it, had eaten a hole in him.

Tightening his hold on Kate, he knew he couldn't let go. He wouldn't fail again.

# Twenty-Two

KATE WOKE TO a hand stroking her breast, making slow circles around her taut nipple. Excitement traveled through her naked body, heating her throughout. Visions of Jesse waking her in the middle of the night danced before her closed eyes. He'd taken her from behind in a quick, hard fuck that she hoped cast out his demons. Afterward, he'd held her tight, tenderly kissing her temple before falling back asleep.

He pinched her nipple and a soft moan escaped her lips. She sighed in pleasure and opened her eyes to the bright morning sun streaming through the windows, warming and brightening the room. Then, a pair of lust-filled eyes came into view.

"It's about time, sweetheart." Jesse leaned down and licked her nipple.

She involuntarily jerked at the new sensation of his hot tongue sliding over her. Panicking, she grabbed his head and pulled him away. "What about Reagan?" She didn't want his daughter walking in on them in the middle of a morning of wild monkey sex.

"I locked the door." He returned his attention to her breast.

Kate arched up to him, craving the pleasure she knew he would deliver.

Before all coherent thought left her, the date popped into her head and her breath caught. With a bit of maneuvering, she slipped from under him and jumped out of the bed. "Crap, I'm not going to be ready in time." She rushed to the walk-in closet where Jesse had opened up a space for her clothes.

"In time for what?"

She peeked her head out of the closet as Jesse rolled onto his back and put his hands behind his head. The sheet dropped down to his waist, forming a tent over his erection. Her body thrummed, and she almost dropped the bra she'd just selected.

Standing stock still, she tried to decide her priorities. She stared at where Jesse's dick stood at attention, ready for her to slide down onto him. She took a deep, cleansing breath and slowly exhaled. She couldn't take this diversion, no matter how much her body yearned for Jesse. She'd already had to back out on spa day; she couldn't not show for this. Hell, it was here. "For Ariana's visit. Remember?" She batted her eyelashes, saucily. "The visit my amazing boyfriend allowed since the spa was not doable."

He smiled slyly and cocked an eyebrow. "Your boyfriend? How very juvenile."

She sauntered close, a little sway in her step, and bent down and gave him a quick kiss on the lips. "My boyfriend or the term?"

He playfully swatted her bottom.

She squealed and bolted. To her utter satisfaction, he gave chase, cornering her in the closet.

"Let me show you what this boyfriend wants." He wrapped his hands around each ass cheek and pulled her tight against the hard length of him. Then he kissed her soundly, once again challenging her resolve. But nothing made it better than hearing him refer to himself as her boyfriend.

With her legs a little weak from the best morning kiss she'd ever experienced, and the high of Jesse's fun, she leaned into him, resting her head on his shoulder until she could hold herself upright without assistance.

Sighing, she reluctantly pushed on his chest to separate them. "Leave me be so I can shower and dress. She'll be here for coffee." She turned to the closet and reached for a yellow, flowered shirt. "And, before you think it, I'm showering alone." She selected a pair of jeans and underwear, then retreated to the bathroom. Behind the closed door, she spun around with a happy dance at how things were going with Jesse.

---

"YOU managed to get out of going to the spa." Ariana raised her hand to stop the protest ready to spout from Kate's mouth. "I'm not saying you did it on purpose or anything. It just happened during our scheduled time. Let's see, over the time we've scheduled to go you've been undercover, on a stakeout, sick with pneumonia and now this. You don't do it halfway, Kate," she said with a smile.

Realizing the statements were meant to bring levity and not criticism, Kate laughed even though her sister had a point. The strangest things occurred to her near their spa trip. The time was supposed to be a relaxing day they spent together. It seemed all that happened was Kate begged out. Maybe they needed to come up with something else to do, but coffee would work for the present. She blew on her cup, steam wafting past her face, then she drank what Jesse had made for them.

"What's going on with you and your bodyguard?" Ariana raised a perfectly shaped eyebrow and smiled. "You looked a little cozy when I arrived."

Kate smiled at the memory. They had been with his hands on her lower back, sliding up her arms. She shuddered, still warm to her core with want of him.

Lost in thoughts of what she'd do to Jesse later, she'd almost forgotten Ariana's question. Then, Jesse's words came back to her. *You're mine now.* "We're in some sort of relationship."

Ariana shook her head. "Which I gather is code for you're finally sleeping with him."

Her cheeks warmed. "Yeah, we're sleeping together." Although, she wouldn't really call it sleeping. She almost snickered out loud.

"It's about time you got back on the horse." Ariana took a sip of coffee and looked at her sister thoughtfully. "So, what's this 'some sort of relationship' mean?"

Kate cleared her throat and drew her brows in low. "Well, I can tell he cares for me. He calls me his. He has me sleeping in his room."

Ariana choked on a sip of her beverage. She coughed into a napkin and waved her to continue.

"I only wonder what it will be like when he doesn't have to have me living here once this is over. Stupid, I know, but it's there in the back of my mind."

Ariana studied her sister, her mouth slowly dropped into a frown. "Oh, no. You fell in love with him, didn't you?"

Kate lowered her gaze to the red coffee cup in her hand. "I did. I didn't mean to. It just happened."

"What are you going to do then?"

She looked back up at her sister. "I'm going to keep loving him, because I'm not sorry it did. And, I'll keep up hope he'll fall in love with me someday." Her heart still fluttered with his calling himself her boyfriend. It was trivial in their situation, but to her, it told of him liking her more than just for a quick romp.

"Kate, you're a lovable person. I wouldn't be surprised if he wasn't already in love with you by the way he watches you."

*In love with me? No. Not yet. Care for me? Yes.* "I doubt it."

Her sister flashed her a disbelieving smile. "Just be patient." Ariana stood and took her cup to the sink. "I wish I could stay longer, but business calls."

Kate emptied her cup and they walked through the house. At the front doorway, they encountered Jesse and Ken chatting. The men stopped when the women came close.

"You didn't stay long. Did my woman run you off?"

Kate almost leapt for joy at Jesse's words.

Ariana looked back at Kate with a knowing smile. "I need to get back. You do live out of the way."

"I'm walking her to her car. I'll be right back." Kate grinned at Jesse.

The two walked toward Ariana's Mercedes. Out of habit, Kate scanned the area. "Let's talk about what we're doing to help the Humane Society at the Fall Festival."

"Are we just donating this year?"

Her sister laughed. "Pay attention to me for one second. The other men are looking around like crazy."

Chagrined, Kate focused on the conversation with her sister. "What did you want to do?"

"Well, we're donating. I didn't know if you wanted us to spend part of a day helping at the booth again. I know how much you love it."

Kate had never missed the Fall Festival in Fells Point and didn't like the idea of missing it this year, but she might, if things weren't settled. Because if there was still danger, she wouldn't consider attending. "Sign us up." She'd worry about another volunteer covering her time later if they hadn't captured the Facilitator.

Dottie bounded over and rubbed against Kate, leaving white hair on her navy outfit.

Kate reached out and pulled Dottie, by the collar, to her side. "I'm sorry."

"I learned a long time ago to be prepared for that girl. I have a lint brush in my car." She squatted, very ladylike, and called to the dog. "Let her come here."

Watching Dottie lick foundation and powder off her sister's meticulously made up face, made her fretful. Ariana was always nice to her dog, but Kate hated it when Dottie's hair got on someone's clothes—anyone's clothes. "I can get the lint roller for you."

A giggle escaped her sister. It wasn't often she let the child in her slip out. "If you want." She shrugged. "It's in the center console."

She turned toward the car again. After ten steps, she heard

Jesse bellow, "Kate Ross, you'd best not get in that car and try to leave."

Spinning around quickly, ready to give him a piece of her mind for thinking such a thing, she almost tripped on her feet. "I'm just—"

An explosion rocked behind her. Jesse's frightened eyes as he raced to her were the last things she saw before darkness enveloped her.

# Twenty-Three

KATE STRUGGLED TO open her eyes as nausea took hold and decided it best to keep them closed. She took a few deep breaths, but the queasiness didn't subside. Someone needed to turn off the jackhammer to stop the pain in her head. She'd heard how debilitating migraines could be. Maybe she had one.

She heard voices. Jesse's was the first that registered. He sounded frantic. Something had happened.

"Is she going to be okay?" he asked with a hitch in his voice.

"That's for the doctor to decide." It came from a voice she'd not heard before.

"She's more than likely got a concussion. We'll know more once we get her to the hospital." Another unidentified voice.

Her body jerked and her heart pounded when someone gripped her arm. Cool material wrapped around her skin and grew tighter. She gasped, a semblance of realization penetrating her foggy brain. She'd been hurt. There'd been an explosion. More than that, Jesse had been asking about her.

Kate slowly opened her eyes as clouds floated out of the sun's path and brightness invaded, intensifying her headache. She closed her eyes again, welcoming the darkness.

"She's waking now. Ms. Ross, I'm Tim, and this is Parker. We're going to take good care of you."

"I don't need to go to the hospital." Her voice shook. Chancing it, she opened her eyes again, thankful the cloud cover had returned. She looked around for Jesse. She'd heard his voice, knew he was close by.

"Kate, thank God. How do you feel?" Fear filled his eyes while distress colored his voice. She'd never seen him like this, vulnerable, afraid, not his confident, in control self.

"I've got a hell of a headache." Headache was a small word for what she felt. Her head had never been this agonizingly painful.

He took her hand and brushed the stray strands of hair from her face with the other. His shaking didn't go unnoticed.

"Do you hurt anywhere else?" Tim asked.

She looked at the EMT and tried to smile. It hurt too much to smile, to move facial muscles. Hell, it hurt to blink, and the bright light returning didn't help.

"My head feels like it's going to explode. And I'm a bit nauseous. That's all."

"Let's hope that's all there is after the nasty experience you've had."

"What happened?" She remembered an explosion, thought it came from her sister's car, but wasn't quite sure.

Jesse squeezed her hand. "We're not sure. Yet." He clamped his jaw tight and a muscle twitched in his jaw. "Hell, they could've set a delay time detonation or they could've pushed the button from some-fucking-where out of our sight."

She swallowed at the memory, the simple movement making her head throb even more. "I know if he'd been near that your men would've seen him." A thought struck her. "Ariana?" Her chest tightened while she waited for him to answer.

"Don't worry. Just some cuts and scratches. Before you ask, Dottie is okay also. She's at the vet getting a few stitches. Ken is with her. Sweetheart, you were the only one knocked unconscious." The shake eased from his fingers as he brushed his thumb over her skin. He remained wide-eyed, staring down at her, refusing to leave her side so the EMTs worked around him.

Worry for Jesse thrummed through her. She didn't like the vulnerability so transparent on his pained features. "I'm all right now. You can let me up." She struggled to sit up, aiming to reassure him, but a wave of dizziness overtook her. It left her with no alternative but to fall back onto the gurney, her head protesting the movement.

"No. You're going to the hospital to be checked out." Jesse squeezed her hand.

"I don't need to go to the hospital. Really, it's just a…." Her words trailed off. There was no denying him this. Plenty of people had been knocked unconscious and didn't require an ER trip, but she knew that Jesse in many ways needed the reassurance more than she did. "Okay, I'll go," she whispered. "But, I hope you'll be by my side.". When a small smile lifted his lips, lightness settled in her chest.

He nodded, opened his mouth to speak and closed it. He nodded again, short, as if deciding to do something. Kate wanted to say something to ease whatever had him struggling so, but she didn't know what to say.

Kate's heartbeat skipped when Jesse leaned close to her, a finger caressed her cheek in an uneven line. Maybe around scrapes.

"I'm sorry, Kate," he said with a voice so choked up she had a concern that he'd been injured. "I don't know what happened... and you could've died—you and your sister." He dropped his forehead to hers and she witnessed the pain in his tear-filled eyes. She had to do something for this wonderful man who would probably change places with her.

"Jesse," she started as she reached up a hand to the side of his face. "There's nothing to forgive."

Eyes closed, maybe in an effort to stave off his tears, he touched his lips lightly to hers. He gifted her a smile that melted her insides.

"Wait." She snaked out her arm and latched onto his forearm. "Reagan? I know she wasn't outside, but is she okay?"

His eyes flashed with worry and love. "She's fine." Jesse stepped back when the EMTs lifted and pushed the gurney into the back of the ambulance. "I'm riding to the hospital with her."

Tim shrugged, realizing he had no choice. "Jump in, but stay out of my way."

---

"MISS Ross, your cat scan is fine." The emergency room doctor scribbled something on her chart. Kate wasn't sure he'd introduced himself. If he had, she'd forgotten his name. He looked forgettable, average height, average brown hair, average features and average body. He'd have made a great spy being able to slip in and out of places without much notice.

"Can I go home now?" She'd agreed to come, but she was

ready to go home… Jesse's home. It did seem like home to her. It had all the people she cared for in one spot.

The tortured look on Jesse's face told her he felt that he'd failed her. Yet, no one had done a thing wrong.

"You have a severe concussion, and we're keeping you overnight for observation."

"Really, I don't need to stay overnight. My head feels better." Nausea had remained with her but had blessedly eased a little, but she couldn't shake her severe headache. She wanted to deal with it quietly if she could leave the hospital. The past few weeks had left her with too many visits to this hospital and she was getting sick of it; she needed to leave.

Her anger with this shooter turned poisoner turned bomber intensified.

"Kate, you'll stay."

She turned her head toward Jesse too fast and winced at the pain. "Are you sure everyone else was okay?"

"Everyone is fine. Ariana said she'd have to wear pant suits for a while to cover the bruises and cuts on her calves, but that's it." He tried to give her a reassuring smile, but failed.

AJ would have new FBI agents assigned to her, if not already. They might have to park out on the road well away from Jesse's house, because after this fiasco, he probably wouldn't allow FBI, with the exception of her and AJ, on his property. This was going to be a battle of wills between brothers because both were going to want her in their safe house.

No one cared what she had to say even though she was the one they were protecting. Well, she had a big voice, and they were going to listen.

The doctor gave an order to the nurse then turned his attention to Kate. "I'm leaving you something to help with the nausea and the headache. I'll see you in the morning." He and the nurse turned and left the room.

Jesse approached the bed and took her in his arms. His hug was gentle, tentative, like he held glass. "I thought that I'd lost you." His hoarse, tortured voice was barely above a whisper. "I thought I'd lost you."

His continued display of emotion touched her heart and broke it at the same time. She hated to see him in so much pain. "I'm all right."

"You could've been killed."

"You could've been too." She shuddered at the thought.

He released her and reached for her face, avoiding the bruise on her cheek. With her face in his hands, he leaned down and kissed her, softly... tenderly... and lovingly. She wanted more and tried to deepen the kiss, but he wouldn't allow it.

"We're going to find this bastard, so you can be safe again. I can't understand how you don't hate me for bringing this to your doorstep." His voice had been choked full of conviction and sincerity.

She'd forgotten everything had started with him. "I couldn't hate you, Jesse." *In fact, I love you.*

"I'm going to make sure he doesn't hurt you again."

"If Reagan's still okay, will you stay with me?"

He looked into her eyes and took hold of her hand. "You couldn't drag me away."

Ariana knocked on the half-open door. "Kate, are you all right?" She eyed their joined hands.

"Hi, Ariana. I'm fine. Just a bump on the head. I want to go home, but no one will listen to me." Kate tilted her head toward Jesse, causing a wash of pain and immediate regret of the action.

"I'll give you two some privacy." He left the room and closed the door behind him.

Her sister sat in the chair beside the bed and scooted it closer. "Kate, I'm so sorry. I didn't know. I mean, good grief, I was driving a car with a bomb and I brought it near you."

Kate reached out and took Ariana's hand and almost flinched at the sight of tears from her stalwart sister. "If you hadn't, you wouldn't be here now." The investigator in her reared its ugly head, not caring that thinking hurt her head. "Where were you before you came to the house?"

A heavily burdened sigh left Ariana. "I'm talking with the men to see what they can find out. I spoke with your man while you were in for tests." She tilted her head. "He's torn up about this, and he told me not to bother you with it while you were here."

Ignoring the last part of the comment as Jesse dealt with the situation, she dropped her shoulders in resignation. "He blames himself." She needed to find out what was going on inside his head. She couldn't let him blame himself for the explosion.

"Kate, I told you that he cares for you."

"I know he cares, but I want him to love me."

She adjusted the controls on her bed to sit up, struggling to find a comfortable position. Kate felt self-conscious in the hospital gown. She reached up to run her fingers through her wavy hair, trying to control it somewhat and make herself presentable.

"You could tell him that you love him. You are living in his house." She raised her eyebrows in challenge.

"It's not a conversation I'm willing to have with him yet. Not a chance I'm willing to take."

"The two of you are made for each other. It'll work out. Give it time."

Time. She had no idea how much time it would take for Jesse to fall in love with her. "I forgot to ask, how badly were you injured today?"

"Nothing serious. I was treated on the spot. You gave us quite a scare when you didn't wake up. I thought Jesse was going to strangle the cute ambulance driver for taking so long to get there."

"I can't believe he made me come to the hospital." Okay, she'd acquiesced, but it sounded better blaming him. It was just a knock on the head. Now, they won't let me go home." Whatever the doctor had given her had begun working. Her headache still pained her, but at least she could tolerate it now. She felt herself start to float. Before long, she'd be in a drug-induced euphoric state.

"It won't hurt you to spend the night here."

"The bed is uncomfortable, and the food is going to be terrible. It's not like a night at the Ritz." She shouldn't be whining. She should be thanking God that she was alive, but she just wanted to go home.

Ariana laughed. "You have to take what you can get."

"Well, I bet you could've negotiated a way to be released already."

"Probably."

They laughed. When her head throbbed harder, Kate stopped laughing, but seeing Ariana laugh after she felt responsible since she'd driven in the car....

A special news alert of the bombing flashed on the wall-mounted TV. It didn't appear they made it onto Jesse's property. Of course they hadn't. She would bet her badge that HIS was one pissed off group of men.

The journalist talked about Kate, connecting the shooting, Joy's death and now the bombing. She turned off the TV. "Is it bad?"

"Your boyfriend and his handsome, broad-chested brothers chased the reporters out of the hospital. I doubt you'll have to worry about them." Ariana chuckled, looking as if she was privy to a private joke.

Kate relaxed at the news. Maybe it was the medicine that had her relaxing. She sighed. "How's it going at Ross?"

"Things are good. We've settled everything on the new station."

"What are you going to do now?" She readjusted her bed, wondering if the couch would be more comfortable and if she could make it there without falling flat on her face.

"We're going to look at more syndicated talk shows. The talk radio listening audience has grown faster than expected. We have an opportunity to gain more listeners if we add a few more hosts and shows. Lee's been chomping at the bit to do this, so I'm going to give him full reign to make it happen."

"I'd love to hear about them when you put them together. You know that I love talk radio." She had to get more involved with Ross in case her career in the FBI was over. She should be involved more even if her career was safe. She owed it to Ariana and their parents.

"Of course. I wouldn't exclude you." Ariana frowned. "So,

what's going on with the bombing? I mean, I know we're not supposed to talk about it, but do you think they know who did it?"

Kate attempted a shrug, but all her muscles didn't cooperate so she lifted one shoulder high and one not too high. "We haven't talked about it, but I'd say it's the same guy who shot at us and tried to poison me. We still don't know who he is. HIS hasn't had any luck finding the driver from the shooting. Once they have him, they'll get the killer, and this will be over. I mean, I'd hate to think more than one person was trying to kill me."

Ariana winced. "I am sorry."

"No, sis. Don't you sweat it. That was just generally speaking."

"I still can't believe someone wants to kill you."

"It's a nightmare. Jesse says I should hate him for getting me mixed up in this, but I can't." If she hadn't been mistaken for someone he loved, she never would've let herself get this close to him, never let herself fall in love with him.

"I'm angry at him for getting you tangled up in this. I don't care how much you love him. Because of him, we were almost blown up today, and your life has been in danger."

"We were almost blown up because there's a madman out there who has decided to target me." She'd have to stay away from her sister in the near future to keep her safe. The day's events had been too close to losing her, the only family she had left.

Ariana stood and took Kate's left hand in hers. "The only thing that matters now is that he takes care of you. Just make sure to let me know you're safe." She squeezed Kate's hand and left the room.

Jesse entered carrying a large bouquet of fall flowers, sunflowers accompanied by peach roses, white lilies and purple flowers she couldn't identify, in a lovely green vase.

"Everything all right? Did you have a good visit? Ariana didn't look happy when she left."

Kate smiled at his thoughtfulness. She couldn't remember the last time she'd received flowers and hated she'd almost been blown up to receive them this time. "Thank you for the flowers. I had a good visit with her. She's upset about the bombing."

He sat the flowers on her bedside table. "That's understandable." He pulled her hand to his lips. "How are you feeling?"

The feel of his lips on her sent a tingling sensation through her limp muscles. "I'm all better now. I really think I should be able to leave."

He chuckled. "You are a persistent little thing. You're staying right here until the doctor says different."

She made a face at him and was rewarded with a hearty laugh.

"Now," he said then sat on the bed, "the doctor said no strenuous activity, but he didn't say no playing." Jesse pushed the button to move her bed down before climbing in beside her.

"I hate to start off our relationship with this," she said and a small smile played on her lips, "but I have a headache."

# Twenty-Four

THE FACILITATOR POUNDED his fist on his desk. *Son of a bitch!* He'd failed. Again. He'd waited so long to try again. He seethed at the fact that she remained lucky. The bomb should've worked. He'd built it himself. Having shady contacts had its benefits.

He'd followed the sister, with the bomb on the woman's car for days without her knowledge. Settled at the max distance, thankfully off Jesse's property that had been teaming with men, with the remote detonating device and had pushed the button too fucking early.

He had a job to do, and he always completed his jobs.

There was no more time. He needed to finish this.

He smiled with satisfaction in knowing Jesse Hamilton hid out with his women because of him. Jesse never should have let someone inside his compound. Chuckling, he enjoyed that. Jesse had given him the opportunity to kill her.

The Facilitator needed to take care of loose ends. He didn't trust Ed to keep his mouth shut should the FBI capture him. Someone hunted Ed and had almost found him. It had to be that relentless HIS group.

He sat down on his couch with a cold drink in his hand, yet didn't feel the condensation from the glass wetting his hand or the comfort of the burgundy leather sofa. Leaning back, he crossed an ankle over his knee. Things were not going according to plan. He'd never had this much trouble taking someone out. But, it had never been personal before either.

He'd ignored the divorce papers and tried to reconcile with his wife again. She'd refused to see him, letting him know she had a new life that didn't have room for him. Anger like he'd never known had overtaken him.

Mind drifting back to Kate, he knew he needed a foolproof plan to kill her since his past attempts shouldn't have failed. Jesse had ruined everything—as was becoming his unwelcome habit—by saving her each time. Only one solution arose... he had to separate her from him.

Standing, he stepped to the bar to refill his glass with his sixteen-hundred-dollar bottle of Glen Garioch forty-six-year-old Scotch. He'd lost count of the number of glasses he'd refilled. He stopped in front of the full-length mirror and frowned. Since losing his wife, he'd let himself go. He'd lost weight and had a haunted look about him. Sleep didn't come easily for him, nor did eating. All he could think about was Mona and how Jesse had destroyed his life.

He wasn't sure what his new plan would be. He wanted to walk up to them and shoot Miss Kate Ross with Jesse standing by. But, he wasn't going to jail. He couldn't risk being seen killing her. Jesse may never know who killed the woman he loved, but he would still suffer.

He would not fail again.

And, as always, he'd had an alibi for the next time he struck.

# Twenty-Five

"YOU HAVE TO put more pressure on your informants and find this bastard, AJ. This last attempt was too close. It's a miracle no one was killed in the explosion." Jesse's quiet voice was laced with anger. The two men stood outside Kate's hospital room while she slept.

Jesse didn't need AJ's help, but since Kate's life was at stake, he would take anything he could get. HIS pushed harder than he'd ever seen them. They usually remained emotionally detached in order to be at their best. But, they'd come to know and like Kate, a lovable and friendly person. The men treated her like family, HIS family. And she was or would be.

"Jesse, we're pushing hard. One of our own is at risk. It's not like we're fucking around."

They'd been damn lucky no one had been killed or seriously injured. Jesse swallowed the lump in his throat. Kate had been too close to the car. He should've made her stay inside. Walking her sister to the car should've been his job.

"I know you're doing all you can. It's frustrating knowing someone out there is after Kate and none of us can find him."

Jesse's every muscle remained tense, on edge.

"We're going to catch him."

"But, will we catch him in time?" Jesse had never felt helpless in an investigation. He'd never been this personally involved in one either. "I want the information on that bomb as soon as you can get it to me, AJ. If it's going to take too long for the FBI to process, I'll pay to have it processed at the fastest lab you can find." Money didn't matter to him where Kate's safety was involved. "This might finally be our break. There's bound to be a signature there. Something to lead us to him."

HIS hadn't waited for the FBI to find clues to the bombing. They'd begun digging through the wreckage and had been scouring the land surrounding his property. He needed an update even though he'd spoken with Devon less than an hour prior. He had told him that Joe followed another lead to Ed. And the men on the street dug in deeper.

The bastard couldn't stay hidden forever.

"What do you think about the sister bringing in the bomb?"

"I don't know what to think yet. I can't imagine she did it because she was also close and she didn't make Kate go to the car." He swallowed past the lump growing in his throat. "But, you know I won't rule anything out."

AJ nodded.

Staring down the desolate hospital hallway where visiting hours had long ago ended, AJ cleared his throat before he spoke, "I'm worried about something."

Jesse released a disbelieving chuckle. "Only one thing?"

AJ looked at his brother with a concentrated frown on his face. "His threats have been directed at Kate, but you could've been there also. Plus Ariana."

"I think he's desperate. He keeps failing, and we haven't given him a shot at Kate alone. He may not have felt he had any other option."

This bomb changed everything. The HIS net tightened and while Kate wasn't happy with the restrictions, he had to admit that she'd been great since he'd limited her movements. Jesse had failed and had let her walk right into the face of a bomb. His brothers would tell him if his emotional involvement impacted his judgment. Jesse would never let that happen though. He was the best person to protect Kate. There would be no arguing about it.

"Which makes him high risk. Are you going to take her to the safe house now?"

Jesse turned away in frustration. The stuffy smell of sickness hung in the air, the dimly lit corridor quiet.

"No." He turned back to AJ. "We're going to my house, and she's staying put." Putting up a hand to forestall the argument, he continued, "Right now my men have that place tighter than Fort Knox. No one except my family and team will come onto my property until this is resolved." He'd keep her there even if he had to tie her down. That brought a visual of her tight naked body on his bed, her dark, brown hair spread out on his pillow, her arms bound above her head automatically pushing out her creamy breasts. His cock twitched thinking about sinking deep inside her. He needed a swift kick in the ass. She lay in a hospital bed, had a killer after her, and he was thinking about fucking her.

Before they said good night, Jesse told his brother, "Don't

forget to take your team with you." He ground out his words, "I meant it when I said family and team."

Jesse's baby brother sighed. "I can't do that, Jesse, and you know it. She's FBI. You've only had this leeway because Arthur likes you. Don't push it or she'll be with the FBI… without you."

A grunt served as his response and a good-bye to his brother. Jesse glared at the FBI agents, then nodded at Danny and Mike, his trusted men, before he entered Kate's room. Sound asleep, she looked peaceful, no hint of worry about a madman trying to kill her and almost succeeding.

He plopped in the chair beside Kate's bed. It had been too close. He should've seen her sister to the car.

The asshole had been damned smart to use Ariana's car.

Sighing, Jesse leaned forward, put his elbows on his thighs and covered his face with his hands. He loved her. There was no question about it. Almost losing her today made him realize his true feelings for her. He swore he would never love again, but he couldn't help but love her. *His* Kate. A stubborn, frustrating, independent, kind and compassionate woman, all wrapped into one beautiful package.

She'd impressed him with how she'd excelled as an FBI agent. Partnered with AJ, they had closed more cases than anyone else at their field office. HIS could use an asset like her—if he could get her to leave the FBI and join them. Hell, Kate might be as devoted to the agency as his brother. They'd tried to recruit him to join HIS when they'd created it, but he'd refused. Still refused.

Humbled by her benevolence toward the children at John's Hopkins, Jesse had witnessed maternal instincts from Kate and knew she'd make a great mother for his daughter. Reagan loved her and had asked him if she was going to be her new mommy. He hadn't known what to say. At the time, he'd planned to have Kate move in with him. How did you explain to a five-year-old that you planned to shack up?

Kate had stolen his heart and turned his world upside down, and he wasn't sure what to do at this point. She didn't love him. Sure, she cared about him, liked having him in her bed, but she held something of herself back. Until he figured out what it was holding her back from loving him, he couldn't tell her that he loved her. He wouldn't put his heart out there to be squashed. If she wasn't ready to hear it, she'd send him packing.

There was only one thing to do. Make her fall in love with him. Learn to trust him. Be his wife.

At the thought of his wife, Jesse's chest ached. He would never stop loving Jen, but what he felt for Kate was different. Not more or less, just a love for a woman who was strong and brave, and who held his heart.

His chest tightened. Falling in love with her placed him in a similar situation he'd lived through before. The pain of his wife's death and his not saving her had torn him up for years. Hell, it still did. Talking with Kate had helped him deal with what was inside him, but the memory still existed.

He put his chin in the palms of his hands and looked up at his sleeping woman. He had her to protect. But unlike with Jen, he knew a killer was after Kate. He had his chance at redemption. This time he would save the woman he loved.

He stood and leaned over the bed, lightly kissing Kate on the forehead. He whispered, "I love you, Kate." Jesse stiffened when she moaned and turned on her side. When her eyes didn't open, he relaxed and moved to the couch and tried to get comfortable. He trusted the men outside the room with her life, but he still wouldn't leave her side.

———————————

LOOKING up from her plate of uneaten scrambled eggs when Brad and Matt entered her hospital room, Kate couldn't hide her disappointment that neither were the doctor. Jesse wouldn't leave her room to find the doctor, but promised he'd sent someone to locate him.

"Good morning." She forced a smile that, unfortunately, tugged at the headache that had been made bearable with her morning medicine, but hadn't disappeared.

"Mornin', Kate." Matt smiled brightly. "How're you feeling?"

"Here." Brad dropped an overnight bag on the bed. "Em put it together for you. Thought you might need some clothes and shit."

Her pasted smile turned into a painfully, joyous smile. She had clothes to wear, clothes that weren't torn, dirty or gaping in the back. Thank goodness they had a sister who kept them in line.

"Turn around," she commanded. She didn't want the gown to open, flashing them on her walk across the room.

The twins rolled their eyes but complied.

Jesse didn't turn, but wolf whistled when she removed her hand from the back of her gown to open the bathroom door.

Inside the room, she leaned against the closed door to steady herself. She still had some dizziness, but she was determined to leave the damn hospital.

She looked at herself in the mirror and cringed. Her waves of hair on her right side had frizzed out while the waves on her left side had flattened from sleep. Reaching up, she lightly touched the scratches and bruises that decorated her right cheek. A shiver swirled down her spine. Had she not looked back to tell Jesse she wasn't leaving, it would've been the front of her face that received the brunt of the explosion, maybe even her eyes.

This time the killer had gone too far. He could've killed Ariana.

She should've stayed inside the house. Then again, if she had, Ariana would've been in her car when the explosion occurred. Sighing, she turned to the bag. It couldn't be changed. They'd assumed all was well. Shame on them.

She pulled the clothes from the bag and changed out of her hospital gown. The gown whispering over her skin reminded her of a whisper she thought she'd heard in a dream the previous night. In her slumber Jesse had told her he loved her. If only it hadn't been a dream. She had faith that she'd hear those words one day soon.

Dressed and ready to tackle the Hamilton brothers, she opened the bathroom door and was surprised to see Dr. Harris standing in the room. He saw Kate and smiled, relief in his expression.

"Good morning, Ms. Ross."

"Good morning, Dr. Harris. What are you doing here?"

His smile widened. "I was informed that you were here and decided I'd check your hand. Have you had any problems with it?"

"It's fine." She held out her injured hand realizing she hadn't given it a second thought lately.

Jesse waved off his brothers and remained close to her. His legs braced apart and his arms crossed over his massive chest while the doctor examined her hand. Jesse had to be the reason Dr. Harris arrived when he had.

"Let's get those stitches out. Shall we?"

Those words made Kate want to kiss the doctor. Remaining still while the sutures were snipped out, she listened intently as the doctor explained the exercises he expected her to complete several times a day until she could follow up with a physical therapist. She would do whatever it took to regain the strength in her right hand, so she could be an agent again.

That thought didn't sound as tantalizing as it had before. Being on the other side of an investigation and having AJ bring them nothing more than HIS found, left a bad taste in her mouth.

Jesse told her that her partner had visited while she'd slept. They'd had a discussion about the FBI agents and she guessed AJ had won even though no one wanted the men there, and they seemed to know it.

Sitting on the bed waiting for the doctor needed to discharge her, she noted the grim expressions the twins wore. "What's wrong?" They were keeping something from her. Again.

Matt rubbed his hand on the back of his neck. "With all that's been going on, we, um, forgot Dev's birthday."

"Hell." Jesse ran his fingers through his short hair leaving a few strands standing. "It's today isn't it? Did you get him anything?"

They both shook their heads.

Kate looked at the men, distress written all over their faces. She smiled. "I can help, but first I have a question. Did I overhear Jesse right?" She hoped the appropriate amount of chagrin showed since she'd just told on herself for eavesdropping. "Didn't you say that Devon doesn't go out in the field?"

The men looked down and shuffled their feet, discomfort seeping off them. Only Jesse appeared brave enough to face the question. "It's not important at the moment. We have other issues."

She bit on her lower lip. Choosing not to pursue it at the moment so she could leave, she smiled and said, "Well then, let's at least have a party."

"Em and Mrs. Kessler are already on the party."

"Then you two are off to buy gifts while Jesse takes me back to help… and to be safe." She smiled brightly.

The twins groaned and muttered, "Shopping."

Jesse leaned over and kissed her lightly on the lips. "Thank you."

# Twenty-Six

KATE DIDN'T ARGUE with Jesse when they returned to his home and he guided her to his bed. Waves of dizziness still rocked through her when she moved. Taking the medicine her ER doctor prescribed, she lay in Jesse's arms, savoring his gentle and reassuring hold.

She'd slept through lunch and woke alone. Slowly standing, relief reached from her head to her toes when she hadn't had to fight off dizziness. The headache was another matter. Taking the non-drowsy pill from the doctor, she ventured downstairs.

After washing down the turkey sandwich Mrs. Kessler required her to eat with the glass of milk set in front of her, she followed Emily's directions and pulled the needed serving platters and bowls from the cupboard.

Kate was awed at the cake Mrs. Kessler had made from scratch and decorated. It looked like a professional one people paid a fortune for, decorated with a computer, three monitors and a keyboard that looked like Devon's setup on it. The men were lucky to have someone who loved them so much.

Emily finished chopping, and they put together the snack

trays of vegetables and fresh fruit. Although Reagan and Amber ate some fruit and vegetables, she had Kate make peanut butter sandwiches and cut them into small triangles with no crust. Emily also made the girls a crackers and cheese tray.

Plates of food for the men stationed outside protecting them, were set aside to be delivered once pieces of cake could be added.

"How old is Devon?" Kate didn't know Jesse's age, hadn't thought to ask, but she knew he was two years older than Devon.

"Thirty-one. How old are you?""

"Twenty-six."

"Hmm."

When Emily didn't say more, Kate had to bite her tongue nearly enough to prevent blood being drawn to ask what she meant.

"I think we're ready to bring it all out to them," Emily told her.

They each carried a tray, leaving the cake on the table, and strolled into the living room. Kate stopped. A tidal wave of warmth flowed through her at the scene greeting her. Amber giggled as AJ tossed her up then caught her. Reagan had the other men focused on a story she told them about her and Dottie, who lay at her feet.

Kate didn't remember times like this with Jay Ross. He'd been a serious man who'd worked all the time, whether in the office or at home. As a little girl, she'd craved his attention and didn't understand what she'd done wrong. Ariana would comfort her when she'd cried because he hadn't attended her events, like her first grade play where she'd played a tree.

She'd feared he hadn't wanted her because she wasn't his daughter like Ariana.

Somewhere along the way, Kelly had straightened Jay out, and he'd worked less. As a teenager, she'd had his full attention. Unfortunately, those were the years she could've done without it. He hadn't approved of her tight, short clothing. Hadn't approved of her wearing makeup. And, most certainly hadn't approved of any boy she'd brought home.

He'd told her when she'd graduated high school that he'd finally had to accept she was grown and no longer his little girl. The little girl he'd missed growing up. The little girl he'd loved.

She loved them. Loved that they'd taken her in. Helped her heal. They hadn't needed to adopt her. She knew it and appreciated every moment she'd had with them. Their sudden death had devastated her.

"Are you going to just stand there staring, or are you bringing that tray in here?" Jesse had Reagan on his hip, her small arms wrapped tightly around his neck.

Kate's smile was instantaneous. This would be her family. It wouldn't be only her and Ariana any longer.

"You didn't have to do this for my birthday."

"Of course we had to." Emily set a tray on the coffee table. "You're my brother. And I like making fun of you getting old."

Devon ruffled his sister's hair. "Thanks a lot, kiddo."

Interrupting a reaction from Emily, the men scheduled to work the upcoming security shift arrived early to wish Devon a happy birthday and partake in birthday cake. She understood why Mrs. Kessler made such a large cake.

Jesse set his daughter on her feet then reached out and pulled Kate close. "What are you doing? You don't belong on the sidelines. Your place is here. Beside me."

She melted into his side. Her heart fluttered with delight at how good things were. Real good.

He leaned down to her ear and whispered, where only she could hear, "I'm already getting hard thinking about what I'm going to do to you tonight, Kate. I can't wait to taste you, watch you as you make that climb, then come on my tongue."

His touch and those few words wooed her into that damn sensual haze. Her pulse raced, her breathing slipping into an erratic pace. Her breasts ached to be touched as heat pooled between her thighs. All so damn swiftly. She reached her hands up to touch his chest.

Before she made contact, his phone rang. "Don't move. I'm not done with you yet." He growled into the phone, "Hello."

Kate widened her eyes and her heartbeat tripped. She'd forgotten they were in the middle of a party, with his daughter in attendance. He'd had her so worked up, she'd been ready to reach up and pull his head down for a hard kiss. Demanding he make good on his promise. She closed her eyes. By God, he'd turned her into a nympho.

Jesse stiffened and listened intently to the caller. He sighed in relief. "Great job, Joe. AJ will meet you at the field office, then get your ass back here." He turned to the group standing around eating cake and joking.

"Listen up," Jesse said loudly enough to be heard over the noise in the room. "Joe caught Ed."

Excitement rippled through the room. The party atmosphere vanished. The men put their plates down and their bodies returned to the "don't fuck with me" persona she was used to from them.

"He's bringing him back for the FBI. AJ, meet him at the field office. You can have him."

AJ nodded, but remained silent, unmoving.

"Joe got him to give up the shooter. We're after Richard Freeman."

Multiple men said, "Son of a bitch."

Kate believed it. She despised the man. Could see him as a killer. The way he'd watched her when she and AJ had interviewed him as the Facilitator made sense.

"You were right," Devon said to Jesse. "I dug deep on him like you asked but couldn't find anything that pointed to him. I've got one thing I haven't been able to access."

A surprised look appeared across the men's faces. From what she'd learned, Devon could access anything from his computer. She really wanted to know what he'd done for the CIA.

"A few minutes ago, I got an idea that I want to try as soon as we finish here."

"Men, war room." Jesse turned to Kate and Emily. "Excuse us, ladies."

Kate put her hands on her hips and blocked his path. "No. Not this time. You are *not* leaving me out. I will be a part of this. He's tried to kill me three times. I owe him."

He studied her. She thought she'd have to push past him and rush into the room before he could stop her. He wiped his hand over his face and slowly nodded. "Okay. You can be in on the planning, but you are *not* taking part in capturing him. Is that clear?"

She wanted to be the one to capture him, put the cuffs on him. She deserved to have the right. But, she still didn't have a strong firing hand. She'd be stupid to participate. But, that didn't mean she couldn't be there, watching. "Okay."

AJ approached Jesse. "It's our job to capture him and you know it. My leeway only extends so far."

"Look, AJ. This has been too personal. We'll bring him to you. I promise in one piece."

"Dammit, Jesse! Why can't you let me do my job without interfering?"

"Do your job then. Make sure Ed isn't holding anything back. Joe is bringing him to you." Jesse wouldn't back down on HIS capturing Richard. She felt the same way.

Her partner balled his hands into tight fists to rein in his anger. "All right. Don't screw this up." He turned and stalked out.

"Daddy, Daddy." Reagan tugged on his shirt. "Are you going to catch the bad guy?"

He dropped to one knee beside her and rubbed his hand on her cheek. "We are, pumpkin."

"What about Kate? Will she stay with us after you make her safe?"

Kate held her breath, waiting for his reply. If he wanted her to stay, she would. But, if he didn't... well, she didn't want to think about that. Especially since everything was about to be over.

"We'll talk about this later. Go with Aunt Em until we're done."

His daughter cocked her head to the right, a scrunched-up face concentrated on her father as if she could read his mind. She straightened her head and smiled. "Okay, Daddy."

He kissed her. "I love you, Reagan."

"I love you, too, Daddy." She skipped to Emily.

"Let's get this bastard." Jesse took Kate's hand and led her to the war room.

———————

JESSE looked up from the floor plan Devon had quickly pulled from somewhere online. "Any questions?" he asked the men in the room.

He'd outlined their plan to capture Richard, livid that his brothers "suggested" he stayed behind to guard the women. Even though they were right and he had the most at stake there, it didn't make it any easier for him to accept. This bastard had tried to kill the woman he loved.

So, he took their "suggestion" and reluctantly agreed to stay behind with the team protecting the women and children. Protecting his family.

The team suited up, putting on bullet-proof vests, extra weapons and clips, and tested their communication systems. Seeing his team prepare, knowing they were about to take out the threat to Kate, had relief surging through his system. She would finally be safe.

Devon turned from the computer he'd been cursing at during the meeting. "Son of a bitch," he shouted.

The room stilled and everyone turned to Devon. The hair on the back of Jesse's neck stood up on end.

"He's got a fucking twin. They were separated at birth and their adoption records hidden by a pro. Someone accessed them a couple years ago, and there's a trail of someone searching for

Richard's long lost brother, Carl."

"So that's how he always had an airtight alibi. They're in this together." Jesse's heart pounded at how they could've screwed up and risked Kate's life, again, but quickly focused, regrouped. "Okay, team. That changes things a bit." He turned back to Devon. "Find out all you can about Carl. We especially need to know where he lives."

"Already on it," Devon said in mid-spin back to his computer system.

"We have to fucking hold back until we find them both. We can't afford to capture the one we think is Richard and leave the actual killer still out there."

Ken spoke up, "We'll watch Richard's house so he can't get away."

Jesse nodded just as his cell phone rang. "Yeah, AJ." He wasn't in the mood to argue with AJ over this again.

"I'm going with you," AJ said.

Jesse inhaled deeply to calm himself. He didn't need this shit. "You don't trust us?"

"Of course I trust you. This isn't as FBI. I'm part of this family, and he fucked with our family. I will be in on this."

Smiling, proud that AJ put the family above all else, Jesse told him the new development, and AJ agreed to be ready when called.

After the men dispersed, Jesse pulled Kate against him, locking her in his embrace. "It's almost over." He kissed the top of her head.

The more he contemplated it, the more he felt gratitude toward his brothers for leaving him behind. He would be here to protect the women in case something went wrong. He had the utmost confidence in his team, but things could always go to hell in a handbasket at any time.

"Jesse, I'm sorry." Devon stood. "I should've caught something wasn't right sooner."

Looking over Kate's head at this brother, Jesse said, "It's okay, Dev. It happens. Not usually to you, but it happens. Does the knot on your head have anything to do with this? Do we need to go back to the hospital? Have them do another scan?"

Devon shook his head. "No. That knot is long gone."

He murmured, but Jesse heard him say, "Along with my memory."

Jesse decided it was time to stop dancing around the topic so he let Kate go and moved close to his brother. In a low voice, he spoke directly to Devon, "Don't you think it's about time you found out what happened? It's been close to a month."

Looking down, Devon shook his head. "I'm not sure I want to know."

Laying a hand on his brother's shoulder, Jesse lowered his voice so even Kate couldn't hear. "But you want to know… need to know. Find out and see if you can get your memory back."

"I'll think about it." Then, in a louder voice, to signify the end of the conversation, Devon continued about their perp. "Someone didn't want their files found. They grew up separately without knowing about their parents or each other. I think it had to do with their father. He's America's number two most wanted man."

Jesse wrapped his arms around Kate and she gasped as he squeezed her tight.

"Sounds like the apple didn't fall far from the tree. Where's the father?"

"No one knows."

# Twenty-Seven

HOT WATER RAINED on Kate's head, cascading down her body. She closed her eyes, ran her fingers through her wet hair and softly massaged her scalp. An invigorating feeling slid slowly through her body, stimulating every muscle from her head to her toes. She took in a deep breath, her lungs full, held it for a moment then sighed as she exhaled. Her headache had finally eased to a faint throbbing.

Jesse had vetoed her involvement in catching Richard and Carl. She hated it, but she'd listened to him. She trusted his men to capture Joy's killer.

Ready and patiently waiting, HIS kept a watchful eye on Richard. They weren't giving him another opportunity at her life. The team remained frustrated they hadn't been able to locate Carl to end it.

The shower door opened. Startled, Kate froze, her eyes flew open wide.

"Let me do that for you." Jesse stepped into the shower. His sensual gaze raked over her body igniting little sparks as it passed by her sensitive areas. He reached for the bottle of a lavender-scented shampoo she'd brought with her, opened it and sniffed. "I love how this makes your hair smell."

She'd never taken a shower with a man. Didn't know what to expect. Her pulse raced at the thoughts of all that she knew could be done. "I-I'm showering."

"Turn around." He poured shampoo onto his hand.

She didn't tell him she'd already washed her hair. She glanced down at his growing erection and spun around. Oh, boy. She'd definitely never had sex in the shower. The thought sent a shiver coursing through her from her head down to her toes.

"Yes, that's what you do to me, Kate."

He softly delved into her hair, soaping the entire length of the strands, gently massaging her scalp. Instead of the massage relaxing her, it sent tremors of need coursing through her body intensifying the desire that only he could quench.

"Turn around," his hungry voice demanded.

Jesse soaped his hands and when Kate reached up to wash the soap from her hair, he grasped a breast in each hand, lathering in soft, seductive strokes. She sighed in pleasure. His touch ignited a fire deep in her belly. It washed away everything but the present. The two of them loving each other.

Moving his hands down her wet belly, Jesse teased her with slow, titillating circles before moving around to her buttocks, massaging and squeezing them. Then, he dropped to his knees and washed her legs, kissing a blazing trail on her inner thighs that scorched her core.

Her erratic breathing caught when his finger brushed over her clit teasingly. "Rinse." He stood.

An urgent need to touch him bolstered her. "My turn." She

savored the feel of his soap-slick body as she washed his hard, muscled chest and abdomen. The longer she touched him, the deeper her arousal flamed. Leaving his erection for last, she quickly washed the rest of his body.

Reaching for his erection, she stroked him as his fingers reached between her thighs. Kate lost focus of what she was doing as his fingers found her nub. Every nerve ending in her body sizzled and her world tilted.

Before she realized what had happened, his arms encircled her, crushing her against him. He leaned in to kiss her, the kiss hard, demanding and brutal. His urgency matched hers.

Pleasure flashed through her, and she needed him to feed the flames that flashed through her, waiting to be built into a firestorm that only he could extinguish with his hard dick She needed him. *Now.*

He groaned, dragged his lips from hers, and sent fiery heat following his kisses down her throat to her breasts.

"God, Kate," he rasped, "when I'm around you, there isn't much I can do to keep my hands off you."

Her heart swelled. His wasn't a declaration of love, but she'd gotten to him as much as he'd gotten to her.

He clamped his mouth over her nipple and then flicked it. She'd had too much. His touch and kiss made her body scream for him to be inside her.

"Now, Jesse. Please. I can't take it anymore."

"I need a condom," he ground out as his mouth moved to her other nipple.

"No, you don't. Take me now, Jesse."

He stopped and looked in her eyes. "No?"

Kate shook her head. Why was he standing here talking when she was about to explode? "I can't get pregnant. Now take me, Jesse."

He didn't hesitate. Reaching for her, Jesse lifted her against him, his hands grabbing her ass, pushing her back to the shower wall. "Grab my shoulders and wrap your legs around me." He shifted and rubbed his cock against her entrance. "You're going to have to help."

She guided him inside. This type of urgent need had never possessed her. The type that if she didn't get what she needed, she'd combust.

"Hang on." Jesse impatiently thrust upward, and she took all of him.

Pulse racing, she leaned her head back against the wall and heard a mewling sound only to realize it was hers. It wasn't enough. "Fuck me, hard and fast, Jesse."

He drove into her, urgency in every deep stroke. Hanging on tight, Kate's fingernails dug into the tense muscles in his shoulders, and her legs wound tightly around his waist. Ecstasy was just one thrust away.

She cried out as an orgasm overtook her with the force of a tornado, spinning her out of control. Intense pleasure blew through her like powerful winds tearing through the trees.

He quickened his pace, thrusting faster and harder. She vaguely heard him groan as his body jerked, and she felt him climax inside her.

Heads on the other's shoulder, they remained in an embrace, not moving or speaking. The water spraying on them was the only sound.

Jesse slowly lifted his head and gave her a light kiss on the lips. "That was fucking awesome." He released her, and she slid down his body. When her legs didn't immediately support her, he caught her.

"That's my first time having shower sex," she told him shyly.

He raised his eyebrows and smiled. "Well, we'll have to catch you up for your years of deprivation."

Kate halted in drying herself and watched Jesse. Things had grown so comfortable and natural between them.

As Jesse dried her off, he questioned, "Kate, what did you mean by you can't get pregnant?"

She froze. Had she told him that? He'd driven her so wild that she'd have probably told him anything to get him inside her. It was too early to tell him her secret. Yeah, he'd hinted at future times with her, future shower sex, but that wasn't enough. She needed his heart. She needed it all before he knew and discarded her.

He stopped toweling her off and put his hands on her shoulders. "Look at me, Kate."

She gazed into his eyes, the ones that had hooked her at the beginning. She didn't want it to be this way. To keep him, she needed things to be different. Once he heard, he might still want her around for a plaything, but he'd never love her or marry her.

"Kate, you can tell me anything."

She had no choice. She wouldn't lie to him. "When my parents were murdered, I was also shot." She paused to take a moment to find the right words. "There was extensive damage, especially to my reproductive system. I can't have children. Ever." There, she'd said it. Put the ugly truth out there.

He leaned down and kissed her lips softly. "I'm sorry, sweetheart." He wrapped his arms around her and held her tight in a comforting embrace.

Mark had been the only man she'd told her secret who would still have a relationship with her. Of course, he'd have said anything to get his hands on her money. Other men had bolted when she'd told them. Even her money hadn't been enough enticement for a lifetime with a barren woman.

As they lay in each other's arms, moonlight spilling into the room, Kate wondered where they would go from here. Afraid of what the answer would be, she couldn't ask. The danger was almost over, and he knew she could never give him a family, never give Reagan siblings.

No matter her fear of the outcome, and if a future was possible, she wasn't a coward. She wouldn't run and hide. Her feeling too strong, her heart his, she'd wait it out and see. Even if the result destroyed her.

———

EVEN Reagan appeared to notice the tension in her father. She ate quickly, asking to leave the breakfast table as soon as possible. Jesse hadn't stayed in bed with Kate that morning. He'd hesitated and then left the room without a word.

The thought of her saying good-bye when everything was over had her heart constricting. The previous night, she'd promised herself she'd be brave, but with already telling him about her infertility, something so raw and deep, and the way he'd shut down on her from the moment she'd woken, her courage wavered.

It pained her even more if she had to say good-bye to Reagan. The little girl had planted herself firmly in Kate's heart. Potentially hurting her by Kate and Dottie leaving was the last thing she wanted to do.

Devon walked in, and Mrs. Kessler forced him to sit and eat. "I sent Brad to another location to check for Carl."

Jesse nodded but didn't speak.

Devon gave Kate a questioning look. She shrugged and reached for her coffee. She couldn't tell him it was her fault his brother was like this.

Jesse's phone rang, and he answered before the first ring ended. "Yeah?"

Kate and Devon patiently waited for him. The outcome of the team's mission could be complete, and the asshole Freeman brothers arrested.

"We'll be there." He ended the call. "Your location paid off, Dev. The boys got 'em."

Kate exhaled a sigh of relief. They were all safe. HIS had come through. Everyone could go back to his or her normal lives.

Standing, Jesse asked, "You coming, Dev?"

"No. I'll get our new potential cases together for you."

Nodding, Jesse turned to Kate. "Let's go."

She jumped from her chair so swiftly it tipped back. If he hadn't caught it, it would've fallen to the floor. "I can't wait to question them." She would make sure the bastards rotted in prison.

"You're not going near either of them." Jesse's jaw clenched.

She narrowed her eyes at him. Balling her fists, Kate fought the blind fury that he evoked when it came to her work. "I most certainly am. You seem to forget that I'm an FBI agent. It's my job to question suspects."

"We'll fucking see about that." He strode from the room.

Kate's neck ached from the whiplash that was Jesse's moods.

---

"NO, Kate," AJ firmly stated. "You can watch, but you're not participating. I'm not letting either of them near you. You're the victim. You know you can't question them."

He was right, but she still..... She sighed, reluctantly agreeing. "You're right. I'll just watch."

"Jesse, you ready?"

She straightened and seethed. "What? He gets to go? He's not even FBI. He was almost a victim too."

AJ turned to her. "Leave it, Kate."

Before she could respond, the men turned and walked away. Jesse hadn't said a word to her. No, "I'll be right back." No, "I'll be a minute." And, especially no, "I get to question Richard and Carl and you don't."

The ride to the field office had carried the same heavy weighted atmosphere as breakfast, almost suffocating her. He wouldn't even speak with her. He hadn't taken her hand like normal when he drove. She'd wanted to reach for him but couldn't. The more she thought about it, his reaction, his exclusion, her confession, the more her anger bubbled. They needed to make a clean break.

Relegated to the small observation room, she observed Jesse, AJ, and Trent enter the interrogation room with Richard. He trained his intense dark eyes on Jesse. Hatred immediately flooded them.

Her cell phone rang. "Hello."

"Hi, Kate. I wasn't sure if you were still on for today with everything that's been happening?" Ariana asked.

Shit. With everything going on, she'd completely forgotten they'd volunteered time at the Humane Society booth at the festival. She pinched the bridge of her nose with her free hand. "I'm sorry. I forgot."

"Completely understandable. If you can't come, I can go by myself. Are you even well enough? How's your head?"

Sighing, she rubbed the creases between her brows. "My head's okay, thanks. I'll be fine." She felt torn. She wanted to watch the interrogation, see Richard and Carl crumble, but she'd promised she'd relieve the other volunteers, that she'd man the booth for them, helping them collect donations. Her integrity overrode her curiosity. "I need a ride. Can you pick me up at the field office?"

"Are you back to work already? And what about the threat? I don't want you here unless it's safe."

"No, I'm not back officially yet. We captured the guy who tried to kill me." Finally, she was safe; there was no reason for her to hide, to drag a protection detail with her. She could go to the festival without fear. Pausing briefly, she wondered why relief didn't relax her shoulders. Closing her eyes to calm her buzzing brain and the anxiety that still coursed through her, Kate willed herself to get it together.

"Great. I can pick you up. I'll be there in fifteen minutes."

She gazed wistfully at the interrogation room. Kate could count on her partner to wrap this up for them.

THE Fall Festival in Fells Point topped the list of Kate's favorite things about living in the area. The loud noise, the music and the crowds moved her mind to extreme happiness.

Arriving early, she and Ariana stopped at a few booths along the way to the Humane Society tent. It felt good to be free. No longer having to look over her shoulder, or hiding out at Jesse's, was liberating. With no more need to be surrounded by bodyguards, she could relax and enjoy herself.

She caught a glimpse of Josh and Mary holding hands. About damn time. She didn't think those two would ever find each other. Josh had confessed to Kate that he loved Mary, and Mary had confessed her crush on Josh. As long as Dan had been in the picture harassing her, she wouldn't go out with anyone else for fear of what he would do. The exact thing Dan had done when Josh had defended her.

Kate smiled. At least Mary got a happy ending.

Patronizing local artists and businesses was important to Kate. At a Fells Point homemade tent, she purchased a necklace with a topaz crystal and a small hand-painted picture of a Dalmatian.

The photo reminded her of Dottie. She still had to go back to Jesse's to get her clothes and her dog. Maybe she'd have her sister take her so she could avoid him. No, she didn't know the code to the gate. She could call Devon. He'd let her in to get her things.

Her phone vibrated, and she pulled it from her jeans pocket. It was Jesse. Her mood was too good, having finally lifted, to have him ruin it. Besides, she would never hear him over the band. She put the phone back in her pocket, the call unanswered.

At the pet treat booth, the hairs on the back of Kate's neck stood at attention. A quick scan of the area and she stiffened, and her heart pounded a bit too hard when she noticed Dan browsing at a nearby booth. He wasn't bothering her or Mary. In fact, it didn't appear he knew either was there, and she didn't feel the need to point her presence out to him. She could only hope that Josh kept Mary away since Kate had lost them in the crowd.

Weighing everything, she decided that the situation warranted watching but not acting—yet, so she and Ariana continued on and stopped at a hat tent. Her phone vibrated again, and she ignored it.

The niggling in her gut had her glance over her shoulder, and Dan brazenly followed them. His smug expression pissed her off. She put on her professional, federal agent hat that kept her from striding toward him and slapping that smile off his face. She leaned toward Ariana. "I've got a problem."

"What's wrong? If you don't have cash on you, I can cover whatever you want to buy."

"It's not that. There's someone following us." Thankfully, she'd put her weapon in her purse before leaving for the field office. She hoped she wouldn't need it, but having it brought a sprig of comfort.

Ariana spun around. "Where? I thought they caught the man trying to kill you."

"Don't look. He's a different story. I'm going to say something to him. I'll be right back."

Ariana grabbed her arm and stayed her. "Are you sure?"

She could've sworn she detected fear in her sister's eyes. *Well, hell.* As an FBI special agent—nearly healed, she had a burning itch to confront the asshole. Experience had taught her that telling Dan to do something typically pushed him to dig in deeper, which could bring their encounter to physical. Still on leave, she'd been warned to avoid that type of thing. If AJ wasn't buried neck deep in paperwork, she could call him to make sure Dan didn't bother anyone.

On the other hand, as a sister and co-owner of Ross Communication, she didn't want to create a scene or put Ariana at risk in any way.

That left one logical choice—Jesse. However, she'd rather be the one punching Dan in the face. Too noisy to talk. She would get Ariana to safety first.

"Let's go to my place. We'll have to miss our booth time." Herding her sister through the crowd, she glanced over her shoulder and caught him watching them, but at a safe distance. Ire rising, she wondered if he was testing the waters to see if Jesse's men came out of the woodwork. What she wouldn't give to have Ken or Danny from the HIS team around.

On the walk to Kate's apartment, her phone vibrated again. Jesse. *Perfect! If I can hear him.* "I need to take this call. Let me step into this shop." Kate answered the phone. "Hold on a sec." She entered the store and walked to the back, trying to find any space where the music wasn't too loud for her to hear. "Hello, Jesse."

"Kate, where the hell are you?"

"Jesse, I can barely hear you. Dan's here. He's following me. I wanted to say something to him, but I'm with Ariana."

"Where the hell are you?"

"I'm at the festival. I'm on my way to my apartment."

The music level increased, and Kate couldn't make out what Jesse said.

"Jesse, I can't hear you. I'll call you later when it's quiet." She ended the call. "Is he still out there?"

"Yeah, and he looks angry. Um, why are we going to your apartment? Can't you just arrest him?"

"No, I can't arrest him. He's done nothing illegal. As for going to the apartment, I want you safely behind a locked door and if he follows us. He's not bothering Mary."

Ariana's eyebrows knitted down in question.

"Doesn't matter. Let's go. Jesse knows about him so I'd imagine his team will take care of Dan once and for all."

Her sister's eyes bulged.

"No, they won't kill him. I don't think." She forced a sly smile in an effort to relieve the tension her sister held. Kate remained tense. Until they were safe, nothing was truly funny.

She scanned the area and thought she saw Ken. She looked back at the spot, but no one was there. Wishful thinking. "Let's get moving."

# Twenty-Eight

"DAMMIT! SHE COULDN'T hear me." Jesse wanted to throw the phone, punch the dashboard, something to rid himself of his anger, his fear. He'd tried to warn her, but she hadn't heard him.

Richard happily told him he wasn't in it just for himself. For him it had been personal, a chance for revenge, but he'd actually been hired to kill Kate. She'd have been his target whether Jesse had been involved or not. Jesse had been icing on the cake.

"She's at the festival. You're driving too fucking slow, AJ. Step on it. We have to save her."

She'd left the field office without telling anyone. She'd left without him, without a protective detail. Okay, she'd probably thought the threat to her was over and didn't need a protective detail, but she'd left without him, without talking to him.

Last night had been the right time for Jesse to tell Kate that he loved her. He'd been nothing more than an idiot for not telling her. His reasoning had sounded good at the time. He'd been worried she wouldn't believe him because she'd just bared her soul. That she'd think he'd said it out of pity. And what if she'd felt obligated to reciprocate because he was protecting her? So many ifs that could've ruined it had clouded his mind that he knew he had to wait until this case was closed and she was safe. Then he could tell her.

It could be too late.

She'd opened up to him, told him what held her back from a committed relationship with him. He'd seen what it took for her to tell him, how painful it had been for her to talk about it. He feared she saw herself as less of a woman because she couldn't have children. He should've told her it didn't matter. That she was more than worthy of love, of his love. Yet, he'd kept his fucking mouth shut.

After she'd opened up to him, he'd held her, trying to comfort her, and he'd known he had to do anything and everything to make her world safe. So, he'd woken focused on catching Richard and Carl. He'd screwed things up with how he'd treated her that morning when she'd needed him the most. It was why she'd left without him; he was sure of it. She didn't think it mattered to him, that *she* didn't matter. Well, she mattered one hell of a lot.

"I'm not driving too fucking slow. Try calling her again."

He'd already pushed the call button.

---

KATE dropped her purse and pulled out her phone. She kept her weapon on her hip. She'd grown accustomed to it on her left side, under her jacket. Besides, she wanted it to protect Ariana from Dan if necessary.

She conceded that she needed help, and Jesse was the first

person to pop in her mind. She walked further into the living room. "Let me call Jesse real fast. HIS might want to take care of Dan instead of leaving him to the police."

"Hang up the phone, Kate." Ariana pulled a handgun from her purse.

Startled, Kate stepped back, her hand instinctively reached for her weapon. "Ariana put that away. We could accidentally get shot. Dan hasn't come to the door. We're safe." She furrowed her brow. "Why are you carrying the weapon in your purse?"

Ariana pointed the gun at Kate's chest.

"Ariana, what're you doing?" Kate's hand moved to her weapon. Everything felt wrong, very wrong. "Ariana, I'm not joking, put that weapon away." Her hand itched to pull the weapon, but she didn't want to pull it on her sister. She didn't understand what was happening. Or why it was happening.

"You just wouldn't die. Why won't you just die?" Ariana's eyes were wild, her face flushed, her nostrils flaring with each heavy breath. She brought her other hand up and grasped the handgun with both hands, her grip so tight her knuckles turned white.

"What do you mean? HIS caught the man who tried to kill me." Kate's heart pounded hard enough to break through her rib cage and out of her chest. Her fear level slowly crept from frightened to terrified. She had no choice.

Ariana's eyes widened when Kate's weapon was drawn and pointed it at her. "Put the weapon away, Ariana," Kate said authoritatively. It took everything in her to bite back her fear, her confusion and concern. She slowly inched closer to Ariana, praying she didn't pull the trigger. Kate risked a lot, but she couldn't bring herself to take a shot at her sister, no matter the

SHEILA KELL

fucking procedure.

"I hired Richard to kill you, but he failed. I even tried to help out by sending you poisoned chocolates, but you didn't eat them. You seem to have nine lives. You should have cats instead of that damn dog. It's true what they say, if you want it done right, you have to do it yourself. This time I will ensure you're dead."

Shock reverberated through her mind. Sick to her stomach, she didn't want to believe what she'd heard. Ariana couldn't be a murderer. She was her big sister. Yet, the gun pointed at her forced her to accept the words at face value, as heart-wrenching as they were. Christ, Ariana had admitted to killing Joy. Rage swelled inside her, but she couldn't allow it to take over.

"What are you talking about, Ariana?" Utilizing her FBI training, Kate knew she needed to keep her sister talking until she could get the weapon out of her hands or talk her down, hopefully without firing a shot. It was her sister, dammit.

"You got half! I was their daughter, and you got half. It should have all been mine. Mine. Now, it will be." Spittle flew from Ariana's mouth as she spoke.

How had she missed that Ariana felt this way? Sure, Kate had felt guilty about the money, but at the will reading her sister told her it happened the way it was supposed to happen. They loved Kate like a daughter.

A multi-millionaire in her right, Ariana didn't need her money. Bile attempted to climb up Kate's throat. Greed. The good old-fashioned greed bug had bitten her sister.

"Ariana, if you wanted the other half all you had to do was ask. I'll willingly give it to you."

"Like you would turn millions of dollars over to me just like that. You shouldn't have told me you left me everything in your will. That gave me the easy way to have it all. All that had to happen was for you to die."

If only it were a dream she could wake from where her sister hadn't gone mad and wasn't ripping apart Kate's heart with an attempt to kill her. An awareness that began at her toes and slid up her body fueled her for the fight with the woman who'd been her best friend growing up together. She pitied Ariana and what she'd become, but she also held a slice of fear since Ariana waved the weapon as she ranted.

Kate had to keep her talking. She hadn't called the police yet, nor were Jesse and HIS there to protect her. She had to handle the situation on her own. She continued to slowly close the gap between them. If Kate died, she'd go down fighting. Her heart lurched to think it would be her sister who she'd have to injure or kill to stay alive.

"Ariana, you don't have to kill me. I'll give you everything."

"I have to kill you now because you'll tell the police or your boyfriend that I tried to kill you. I can't risk it."

Taking a deep breath, Kate stopped as close to her sister as she dared. "Ariana, no I won't tell. You're my sister. I wouldn't tell anyone about this."

"Yes, you would. I took care of you growing up, but you'd turn on me. I know it." Ariana's hands shook along with her voice.

With tears blurring her vision, Kate had to do something, quickly. "We can work this out. You don't have to do this."

She didn't want to die. She didn't need the money. Her sister could have it all. She wanted to be able to have a life with Jesse and Reagan. Her life had little meaning without them. If she survived, she'd try again with him. She had to find a way to survive.

"No, you have to die, and now, I have to do it myself." She laughed in an eerie fashion that grated up Kate's spine. "And no one will know because the noise from the festival will cover up the sound of the shots."

There was plenty of truth to her statement. The festival spilled on the streets in front of her apartment. Bands played on a stage near them with loud music reverberating through her living room. They were almost shouting to hear each other. If anyone heard the gunshots, they'd probably think it had been firecrackers for the celebration. It also meant no one would hear Kate call out for help.

"I'm your sister. I love you."

Ariana brought the gun down in one hand, relaxing her grip. "No one would do all of that for someone else."

Seeing her chance, Kate lunged, knocking them both to the ground. Both weapons flew out of their hands. Kate struggled to take control of the fight. Her sister surprised her by fighting wildly, but Kate had been trained to fight. She had Ariana secured until she grabbed and squeezed, with all her strength, Kate's right hand, along the line of the scar.

Crying out in pain, Kate's automatic reflex had been to grasp her injured hand. Ariana quickly knocked her off-balance, pushed Kate over, scrambled up and picked up her weapon before Kate reached hers.

On her knees, Kate looked up at Ariana and froze. Her sister pointed the weapon at her head, at point blank range, and she had nothing to defend herself except her voice.

Her sister's eyes looked pained. Kate thought Ariana might not be able to do this, not be able to kill her. Kate hoped Ariana's conscience would remind her of how much they loved each other. She'd stopped. Any moment now.

"I love you, Ariana. Please don't do this."

Like a flash of lightning, regret lit Ariana's eyes. It lasted only a brief moment. Then determination glowed in them. "I love you, too, but I have to kill you. I need your half, Kate. The half that should've been mine to begin with. I made a bad investment and the employee pension is gone. Your half is going to save the company, save my daddy's legacy."

Kate closed her eyes, her heart thundered in her ears and her body trembling. It couldn't be the end. Not at the hands of her sister. There were so many things she'd never done, like telling Jesse she loved him.

---

JESSE'S phone rang as they turned a corner and came to a screeching halt. The roads were blocked for the festival. "Dammit. I'm getting out here. I can run the rest of the way faster than you can get us there." He climbed out of the car and sprinted away, answering his phone on the run. "Yeah."

"It's Ken. Thought you should know that Dan followed Kate at the festival. Rob and I took care of him when he headed toward her apartment. Rob is taking him to HQ to have a personal meeting with you."

With the noise, Jesse could barely make out what Ken had

said. "You followed Kate?"

"Well, yeah. You never said to stop. We knew she wouldn't like it so we were discreet. She didn't know we were there. She's safe up in her apartment with her sister."

A bit of relief flowed through Jesse. He had to get there in time. He could save her. "Get in her apartment now. Ariana hired Richard to kill Kate."

"Fuck—" was all Jesse heard before Ken ended the call.

Sprinting toward Kate's apartment, Jesse ran through back roads to avoid the crowd. The stench of refuge and urine slipping from an alley or two barely registered with him. Feet pounded the pavement behind him. A quick look over his shoulder and he realized his baby brother must've parked the car where they'd stopped in the street.

He loved that his brother cared so much for Kate. In addition to being AJ's partner, she'd be his sister-in-law as soon as Jesse could make that happen. He had to save her from her sister first.

*Please let Ken get there in time.* His gut twisted. He couldn't let another woman die because he wasn't there, again. He couldn't lose the woman he loved. With Jen, he hadn't been with her, waiting outside and then taking that damn phone call. With Kate, he'd interrogated Richard instead of talking with her, standing beside her. He could've left the interrogation to AJ and Trent. He should have. But they may not have found out Richard had been hired to kill her until it was too late.

His pulse racing and breathing heavy, he shoved through the crowd on Thames Street, ignoring the complaints from those he shoved to the side. Once he exited the sea of people and climbed her stairs, he saw her door open. Pulling his weapon, he peeked in the room.

His heart tripped. Kate was on her knees, and her sister pointed a weapon at her while Ken pointed his weapon at Ariana. She was focused on Kate and didn't notice Ken slowly inching toward her.

Jesse knew he should leave it to Ken instead of adding another variant. Ken knew how to handle this. He trusted Ken with her life, but he couldn't stand by. He muttered, "Fuck it."

He entered and trained his weapon on Ariana. "Drop it, Ariana."

AJ entered behind him. "FBI. Drop it."

*Shit.* He thought he'd lost him in the crowded street below. He definitely didn't need the word FBI scaring her, too.

Ariana's hands shook violently. "No. She's going to die. All of you get out of here."

Jesse caught Ken's eye and they instantly understood each other. Jesse signaled AJ and then he inched toward Kate while Ken continued his slow move toward her sister.

"We're not leaving, Ariana." AJ said in an attempt to grab her attention from the other men. "Why don't you tell me why you're doing this to your own sister?"

"She knows why, and that's all that matters." She noticed Jesse near Kate. "Get away from her." She waved the handgun toward him.

Surprising Ariana, Jesse stepped in front of Kate as Ken grabbed her and quickly disarmed her. She fought him like a wildcat. It took both Ken and AJ to restrain her.

Turning to Kate, he offered her a hand, expecting her to rant at him for protecting her instead of letting her fight her own battle, but instead, she jumped up and threw herself into his arms. He put his arms around her shaking body, but couldn't hold her tight enough.

Relief engulfed him. She was finally safe.

"It was about the money." She cried on his shoulder. "She wanted me dead because I got half."

He thought that might be the reason. Once Richard told them it was Ariana who'd hired him, puzzle pieces started falling into place. The biggest piece was the bomb on Ariana's car not detonating until Kate had neared. It never occurred to him that her loving sister would do this.

"I know, sweetheart. It's over now. It's finally over." He kissed the top of her head and her temple with a soft, loving kiss.

"I'm an FBI agent, but I've never been so scared in my life. She's my sister. Maybe not by blood, but she's still my sister. I couldn't shoot her."

He couldn't imagine how he would react if one of his brothers turned a weapon on him, threatening to kill him. He knew there would be ass kicking involved before he figured out how he felt about it.

"It's all over now. She, Carl, *and* Richard are in custody. And, you don't worry about Dan any longer. You're finally safe."

"You guys coming?" AJ held Ariana's arm. Ken stood in the corner, waiting.

"Do we have to go downtown right now?" she asked Jesse in a weak voice.

Her broken voice told him how badly she was affected. "Not right now, sweetheart. We can go later. Right now I want to hold you."

Jesse nodded to Ken who quietly left.

"I'll see you down there." AJ led Ariana from the apartment.

When she looked up, she accepted the possessiveness of his kiss. He lifted his mouth long enough to whisper, "I'm not leaving you," before she continued the heated kiss.

Jesse gazed into her watery eyes and wiped moisture from her red, tearstained face. His mouth went dry. He'd never seen a more beautiful sight. "Marry me, Kate."

Her look of surprise almost made him chuckle.

"W-What?" She tilted further back from him, loosening her grip.

"You heard me. I love you, Kate, and I think you love me. Let's get married, have a life together, you, me, and Reagan. And Dottie, too." God, how he loved his woman.

"You, you love me?" she asked in a soft voice.

"Is that so hard to believe? You're a lovable woman. A stubborn and hardheaded woman, yet you're compassionate. I love you and all that you are."

"But, but, I can't have children. You haven't spoken to me since I told you. You want children, and I can't give them to you."

Jesse heaved a pained sigh. "No, Kate. I wasn't avoiding you because of that. I was an ass. I was focused on catching Richard and Carl. I didn't mean for you to think it had to do with what you'd told me. I won't lie. I'd like more children, but I'd rather have you in my life. If that means no siblings for Reagan, then she'll be an only child. At some point those bone-headed brothers of mine will give her more cousins."

Heart pounding, he waited while she studied him. She had

to say yes. He'd gambled that she loved him. She had to. He couldn't accept any other answer from her, *wouldn't* accept any other answer from her. Then the most glorious thing happened. Her lips curved into the most glorious smile, brightening her tearstained face.

"I love you, Jesse Hamilton. And, yes, I'll marry you."

He picked her up and spun her around. "You've made me the happiest man in the world."

Laughing, she hiccupped and said, "Why do all men say that when women accept their proposals?"

He stopped spinning and helped her stand on wobbly legs. "Because it's true." He kissed her lightly. "Now, we've got a five-year-old to tell she's going to have a new mother."

Kate froze. "Do you think she'll mind?"

"Are you kidding me? She's already told me she wants to be the flower girl in our wedding. And, that I couldn't take her new mommy away for too long on a honeymoon." Jesse chuckled.

Kate melted into him.

Life had never been this perfect.

# Epilogue

*Three months later*

"I'M GLAD YOU stayed home for this." Kate clasped Jesse's hand tightly.

As the newest member of the HIS team, she'd been surprised there'd been no complaints about her not participating in the current overseas HIS assignment. The team seemed to expect her and Jesse to remain behind.

She'd yet to regain full strength in her hand and with everything else that happened, she'd decided to resign. It had been a difficult decision, but she knew she'd made the right choice. Jesse had been thrilled when she'd decided to join the Hamilton family business. He'd assured her they could use her exemplary investigative skills, and when her hand firmly held a weapon, or she became proficient left-handed, they'd use her security skills. She'd considered her one shot in the toe plan again.

The men teased her, calling her, "Another FBI flunky." She took it in stride, enjoying the camaraderie of the team. They'd quickly pulled her into the fold, never opposing a woman joining them. Especially a millionaire who owned a radio conglomerate, married the boss and didn't need to work.

That had been her most difficult decision. Jay would've wanted her to do the best thing for his employees, his other family, so Lee was president, running the show for her. Her dad always said the man would do great things. She fought a tear thinking about him. But, he'd been right. Together, they worked to restore the full pension. In the interim, she'd put her money—Jay's money—personally so no employee lost their benefit

It was because of Jay and Kelly Ross that she hadn't completely cut Ariana out of her life. Convicted of Joy's murder and her attempted murder of Kate, Ariana resided in prison. Jesse opposed her visiting her sister. He couldn't understand why she'd want to do it. The woman had tried to kill her. She never offered forgiveness that would probably never come.

As for Jesse understanding, she felt he'd somehow find it in him to reach out to one of his brothers had this happened, even if only for the sake of his parents.

The word parent brought a smile to her face and lightness to her heart. She was a mother. A stepmother, but close enough. She and Jesse had married in a small ceremony with Reagan as the flower girl. She was part of a large, loving family. A family who stood by her side throughout Ariana's plea deal, and Kate's subsequent career decisions. A family she loved.

Mary had stood up for her at her wedding. She'd wished Rylee could've been there, but she'd still been undercover. At the reception, Mary and Josh announced their engagement. She'd never seen her friend happier. She was Dan-free and in love with Josh.

Subtly shaking her head and smiling, Kate mused with how some things had somehow fallen into place once the Hamilton's came into her life.

Dan had mysteriously moved away after he'd stalked Kate at the festival. She knew Jesse had something to do with it. Someone had finally been able to help Mary, and she was proud it had been Jesse. She didn't care what HIS had done, as long as Dan stayed far away.

Agitated, Jesse looked at his watch. "What's taking so long?"

And Kate thought she'd be the impatient one. Both he and Devon kept glancing at their watches and at the door they waited to open.

Devon being with them while they waited delighted her. He, of course, didn't go with the team overseas. He managed things from behind his computer. One day she'd find out why he wouldn't go in the field with his brothers.

"Are you sure it's okay that I'm here? Maybe I should wait at home." Devon glanced nervously at the door again.

Jesse slapped him on the shoulder. "Yes, you should be here. You're family."

"Where's AJ? If I'm here, shouldn't he be here?"

Jesse heaved a heavy sigh and his face flooded with concern. "I found out he went undercover, deep undercover. It's serious. He may be in trouble. I'll fill you in later. Right now, I want to kill him for taking this assignment without HIS around as backup."

AJ's current assignment was secret, even from his direct superiors. He'd been selected with a few other agents to infiltrate Baltimore's largest drug organization on a mission only the FBI

Director and Deputy Director were privy to. In previous attempts, there'd always been a leak to the drug organization called Magic Shop and agents had been lost. If they wanted to be successful, this mission had to remain secret.

Knowing he'd have to hire HIS if there was trouble since he had to keep the rest of the FBI in the dark, FBI Deputy Director Jason Hall had called Jesse when AJ had failed to check in with him as scheduled. After Jesse calmed down and stopped yelling at Jason for sending AJ undercover in his own backyard, he and Kate used their contacts to locate him. They'd found him, unable to check in and unwilling to accept their offer of assistance.

"Are you recalling the team?" Kate understood the danger AJ had involved himself in. One screw-up and he'd be dead. Or as what happened with Magic Shop, he'd disappear, never to be found again.

"Not unless we have to. We made a commitment and are going to keep it. HIS stands behind its word. AJ can handle himself."

It wasn't just the brothers she'd watched wanting to protect AJ. The men, no matter how much they messed with AJ, had a fierce protective streak when it came to him. Kate was worried. Jesse hadn't felt it when they'd met with AJ, but she had. Her former partner was crossing the line—fast. Too fast. There had always been an unhappiness lurking inside of AJ she knew he fought. Pretending to be happy all the time wore on him. She'd heard a whisper earlier in the day that he'd quit the bureau and hadn't been seen. She had to verify it before she told Jesse, but that would have to occur after their current appointment.

Shit. If the rumor was true and he had turned his back on

everything, it would not only devastate the family, they could end up chasing AJ for the FBI.

The door opened and Jesse put his arm around Kate, pulling her close to his side as they waited. They'd prepared themselves for the worst but were hoping for the best.

The doctor walked out of the room. "He's in remission."

With watery eyes and weakened knees, she tossed herself into her husband's arms. He'd known how much she loved Jason. With the frequent visits where many times he included Reagan, he'd fallen in love with him, too. Even better, his daughter and Jason had become fast friends.

As a wedding present, he'd surprised her with adoption papers for Jason. She'd cried like a baby. It had been the most wonderful gift she'd ever received.

The adoption had been finalized. The same day they discovered Jason's prognosis.

Kate turned and hugged the surprised doctor. "Thank you. Thank you."

When Kate finally released the doctor, Jesse and Devon shook his hand. The doctor spoke with them for a few more minutes about Jason's progress.

They hadn't informed Jason of the adoption in case things hadn't gone as planned. First, they had to ensure no relatives were expected to crawl out of the woodwork at the last minute. The teen had told Kate he wished he could live with her, have her be his mother and Matt his uncle, and it had killed her not to tell him he would. They didn't want him to get his hopes up and have them later crushed. That happened enough with his leukemia.

When they entered Jason's room, he rushed into Kate's arms. "Did you hear, Kate? Did you hear?"

She hugged him tightly, tears sliding silently down her cheeks, her heart bursting with love for a boy who'd been like her: left in the world by accident. "I did hear. I'm so happy." When he tried to pull back, she held on. Held on to her son.

It took Jesse clearing his throat, touching her shoulder and saying, "Kate, it's time," before she reluctantly released him.

"Jason," Jesse said, "have a seat. We have to talk with you about something important."

Fear crossed Jason's face. "Did the doctor lie to me? Am I really dying?"

Her heart broke when she heard the terrified tone of his voice. "No, this is better." She smiled at him. "Please sit down."

Jason sat in the only chair in his hospital room, his back straight, and his muscles tense. He prepared himself for bad news. "Who's this?" He pointed at Devon.

"That, son, is your Uncle Devon."

*The End*

Thank you for reading *HIS DESIRE*. I hope you enjoyed it!
Keep reading for an excerpt from the second book
in the HIS series—*HIS CHOICE*

# About The Author

Sheila Kell writes smokin' hot romance and intrigue. She secretly laughs when her mother, in that stern voice, calls it, "nasty." As a self-proclaimed caffeine addict nestled in north Mississippi with three cats, she wears her pajamas most of the day and writes about the romantic men who leave women's hearts pounding with a happily ever after built on a memorable, adrenaline pumping story. When she isn't writing, she can be found visiting her family, dreaming of an editor who agrees her work is perfect, or watching cartoons.

Connect with me online:
http://www.SheilaKell.com
http://www.facebook.com/SheilaKell
http://www.twitter.com/Sheila_Kell

If you enjoyed reading HIS DESIRE, I would appreciate it if you would help others enjoy this book, too.

**Recommend it.** Please help other readers find this book by recommending it to friends, readers' groups and discussion boards.

**Review it.** Please tell other readers why you liked this book by reviewing it at your favorite retailer and /or Goodreads. Reviews make my day! After you review HIS DESIRE, please email me at Sheila@SheilaKell.com so that I may thank you personally.

Join my newsletter (http://www.SheilaKell.com/subscribe) for VIP updates, contests, upcoming appearances and news.

*Excerpt*

HIS Series Book Two
AJ & Megan

*One*

"WHO THE FUCK are you?" The tall man's bellow carried with the frigid, early evening wind. Dark brown eyes, the color of the fattening chocolate bar she'd scarfed down for lunch, glared at her.

In her occupation, if looks could kill, she'd have been dead too many times to count.

Adrenaline rushed through her, charging every nerve ending. Flashing a press card in front of his reddening face, she shouted over the sound of the music blaring from the passing car, "Megan Rogers, *Baltimore News First.*"

Transforming before her eyes, Baltimore City Councilman Richard Thomas squared his narrow shoulders and the corners of his mouth curved into his photogenic smile. "No comment," he stated into the recorder, aka her cell phone, she held before him.

The need to break his politician's façade burned deep inside her. She loathed him, and his actions that evening deepened her disgust. She'd caught him red-handed making an exchange with a known dealer. And she had the photos to prove it.

*Front page, above the fold, here I come.*

"Did you just buy drugs from an alleged Magic Shop drug dealer?" she asked bluntly.

The councilman's hard eyes narrowed into tiny slits, sending the wrong type of shiver coursing through her body.

He pointed a long, slender finger at her chest, shaking it with each word. "Look here. I don't know what you think you saw, but I did not purchase drugs. I had best not see this false accusation of yours in the newspaper," he angrily demanded.

True. She couldn't prove he'd purchased drugs. She could print the photo of the two men passing something back and forth and let the public draw their own conclusions.

Megan's ice-cold lips slowly broke into a half smile, then her heart raced when his six-three frame stepped closer. He towered over her in what she suspected was an attempt to intimidate her. She'd seen much worse in her line of work, but that didn't mean she didn't worry about the volatility of the person she was interviewing, especially when she caught them committing a crime.

Her gut told her he'd been doing something illegal. She'd followed this particular dealer, in the bitter cold for days, photographing his exchanges, hoping he'd lead her to his boss. Someone higher in Baltimore's largest drug ring, Magic Shop, must know where her brother Kevin had been taken, even if he'd died at their hands. She swallowed down the pain and fury at the thought of her brother's disappearance and centered her thoughts on the councilman.

"Then what are you doing in Washington Village speaking with Keyshawn, a suspected dealer in Magic Shop at this time of day? It's not like there's a council meeting out here. I'd think you'd avoid this area considering you once called it, and I quote, 'The Sludge of Baltimore.'"

The councilman dropped his hand, took a step back and cleared his throat. "I like to visit all areas of our fine city to help make better decisions that impact all of our citizens."

She caught herself before she rolled her eyes. Typical political BS answer.

"Now, if you'll excuse me." He turned and walked away.

The euphoria of breaking a big story surged through her veins. She fought her instinct to chase after him. She wouldn't get anything useful from him though. He'd have a great deal to say the following day when the paper published her story.

Megan's face carried a full smile.

An exclusive of this magnitude would please her editor, no, make her editor ecstatic. This scoop would allow her boss to stretch the deadline so it could appear in the morning edition. But, Megan needed to get to the newsroom soon.

She preferred to speak with Keyshawn first. She turned to

find him no longer standing where he'd been. No! She needed him. He was her key.

After Kevin had disappeared, she'd immersed herself in his investigation of Magic Shop. If his disappearance was at their hand, she knew she'd never see him again. That didn't settle well with her.

Unmasking the Magician, the Magic Shop's mysterious leader, had been her brother's goal and it had since become hers. It'd take time, but she'd do it. She would find out what happened to her brother and break the big story he'd worked so hard to bring to light.

Megan closed her eyes against the tears forming. The past few months had been pure torture. Her brother's investigation notes were nowhere to be found. She had located the names of his sources, but they'd refused to speak with her for fear of reprisal from the Magician. They believed that he'd done away with Kevin, and they valued their lives too much to continue speaking to the press, even anonymously.

Starting from square one, it'd taken her most of the last month to earn trust from her new sources. Unfortunately, neither of them were in the gang. She wasn't sure how they got it, but Raven and Tyrone provided her with excellent inside information. That was how she'd found and followed Keyshawn, the dealer who brought in the most money.

She placed her phone in her inside coat pocket and zipped it. It had to be safeguarded. It held her photos, recordings, and notes on her stories. That reminded her to back up the information as soon as possible. It had to be somewhere else, just in case.... No, she wouldn't think that. She would not disappear at their hands. She would crack their group open and finish her brother's story.

She had to move forward to do that. Knowing she'd finally have to put Keyshawn's photo in print, her days of trailing him, hoping he'd lead her to his boss, Jimmy, were over. Since she had no idea what the man looked like or where to find him, she'd have to introduce herself to the dealer and hope he cooperated. Finding his boss would take her one step closer to finding her brother or his killer and expose the drug ring.

Throughout her time in the neighborhood, she'd noticed Keyshawn had quite the rapport with the local kids. She'd found it strange they all carried the same, small drawstring bag. But, after she witnessed their sly swap with the dealer, she knew she'd found out how he resupplied. The children were called runners, aptly named because she had tried to follow one and he'd lost her. She decided to add more cardio to her workouts.

Megan couldn't imagine money would be in the bags since children ran them. Keyshawn would have to go to his boss and turn in his profits soon. Maybe she'd missed an exchange, not realizing it was that versus a drug buy.

That night would be the night of her big break in exposing the leaders in this criminal organization. The night she hoped to find a lead to her brother.

She sighed. If it'd been easy, the organization would've been destroyed long before. Vengeance was a powerful motivator though. She wouldn't give up.

The beginning of dusk and deserted streets greeted her. As one of the most dangerous streets in Baltimore, no one willingly allowed himself or herself to get caught on Johnson Street at night, unless they were dealers or buyers.

She rubbed her gloved hands up and down the sleeves of her

black, leather jacket. But it didn't help. Goose bumps still formed. Just standing there wasn't wise. She had to get moving. Though she'd worn a purple hat, scarf, and gloves, the gang's colors, to keep from standing out, it wasn't safe.

After checking the time on her Hello Kitty watch—dang Kevin and his sense of humor—she calculated how much time before she'd need to leave. Forty-five minutes should be enough time to track down Keyshawn.

Jamming her hands in her pockets, she turned in the direction he'd fled. Her destination was where he'd ended the previous day. Could she confront him around so many people? She'd have to play it by ear, preferring not to get shot.

Rushing down the sidewalk, Megan barely managed to remove her hands from her pockets in time to windmill her arms and regain her balance on the ice, before she landed on her backside. Her heartbeat raced. She needed to watch her step. No one tossed salt on the sidewalks in front of the abandoned buildings on this block.

She stepped off more carefully. Walking the familiar streets, her mind wandered. A different exchange she'd witnessed earlier in the day pushed its way to the forefront of her mind.

Two men she thought were city policemen accepted an envelope from a big, burly man she suspected was in Magic Shop. That man had scared her. He looked hard, angry and dangerous. She hadn't found the courage to follow him, though she wished she'd tried.

From the respect shown by the two men, he had to be important. Maybe he was Jimmy or another boss? Could he be the Magician? She'd photographed them and would show the photos to her sources tomorrow. Someone had to have his name.

Reviewing ideas of how she might approach that story, she didn't pay attention as she turned a corner.

"Oomph." She'd run into a wall.

The wall stepped back and a hand shot to a shoulder-holstered gun.

Danger prickled the hair on her arms, and her scream lodged in her throat.

*Oh God. Oh God. Oh God. Why had I let my mind drift, ignoring my safety?*

Once she regained her composure, as best as she could, considering the situation, she gazed up, and her heart skipped a beat. The sexiest man she'd ever seen stood before her. His tight, unshaven jaw and dark, brooding look only enhanced his appeal. She slowly turned to the short, mocha-skinned, well-built man beside him. He also held his hand on a holstered gun. Could this get any worse?

"Bitch, what the fuck are you doing here? Ain't no dealers here."

She inhaled sharply. She couldn't speak to the short man, couldn't answer him. Her heart beat rapidly, seeking its escape from her chest. The blatantly hostile look displayed on his face spelled big trouble.

Panic clawed at her. Her instincts demanded she run, but her limbs betrayed her. The dream where she was unable to scream or move had become a reality.

She turned back to the tall, sexy man. Her legs weakened as his gaze raked boldly over her body. His face remained impassive, but his eyes burned with interest. The tingling in the pit of her stomach surprised her. She gulped. This was not the time to lust after a man.

Megan couldn't take her eyes off him, her wall, even after his golden-brown eyes turned cold, hard as stone. His look rattled her, frightened her. Why shouldn't it? He was a man with a gun out in the slums late at night and looked ready to murder someone.

He stared at her but remained quiet, leaving the conversation to his scary friend.

"Get the fuck off the street before I make you."

Turning back to the short man, she swallowed, attempting to find her voice. "I'm... I'm on my way home." Her breathless response betrayed her fear.

She couldn't resist looking back at the taller man once more before leaving. She searched his eyes hoping something would break through the glacial stare. She was searching for something to make her feel safe. She shivered. Apparently that wouldn't happen. Why had she even thought that could be a possibility?

He stepped around her and walked away.

They were not wearing purple. The cold, purposeful way they moved into the night screamed for her to follow, but they walked in the opposite direction of where she'd hoped to find Keyshawn.

Observing the straightening of shoulders and respectful nods to the two men from the few people they passed, her investigative instincts fired to life. They must be important. The two men turned a corner before she moved her feet to follow. Megan hugged the walls on the opposite side of the street hoping to blend into the shadows. Her journalistic curiosity drove her. If they were important, she needed to know where they were headed. They could lead her to a boss or maybe even to Kevin.

She furrowed her brow and froze. The image of their guns

popped back into her mind. Maybe they carried them only for protection like many others. Heck, she carried one in her purse. Her intuition told her that she might be wrong though, but finding her brother trumped everything else.

The naked desire she'd witnessed flash through the man's eyes stayed with her. Instead of repulsing her, it roused her curiosity… and her intrigue, which was a dangerous combination since she had no idea who he was and knew nothing about him.

But she couldn't put it completely aside.

She almost called it a day when they stopped. Slipping into the alley across the street, she watched one of the men knock on a door before she hid from view.

Muffled voices carried with the wind toward her. Antsy, she chanced it and peeked around the corner as Keyshawn appeared at the door.

Yes! She smiled, excited that luck had followed her. She'd have missed him if she'd traveled in the direction she'd planned.

One of the men grabbed Keyshawn's bicep then pulled him down the stairs. She pressed back against the wall as they shoved him down the street. Her heart pounded loudly in her ears. Her pulse raced. What would she do if they crossed the street toward her?

Megan released the breath she held captive when they stepped in the alley across from her hiding spot. Her senses heightened. Nothing good could come from a meeting in an alley.

Her brick wall of a man stepped to the entrance of the alley, turned to the street and crossed his arms across his broad chest in a don't-mess-with-me pose.

She immediately understood why when the man who'd

accompanied him, punched Keyshawn in the stomach.

*Nooo! I can't lust after a criminal.*

Great. Once again she craved the wrong man. First, that snake of an ex-fiancé and then, the criminal. He took bad boy to a whole new level.

Taking in the scene before her, nausea hit her hard, pummeling her gut. She closed her eyes and took several deep, slow soothing breaths.

She had to concentrate on the story, not wrap her mind around one man.

Ensuring the flash on her camera phone had been turned off, she snapped photos of them in action. This meant they were enforcers for Magic Shop, or problem solvers. Keyshawn had obviously done something wrong. She wanted to know his transgression. Had he short-changed Jimmy in money or product?

Her mother would lecture her for days if she knew Megan felt Keyshawn deserved the punishment he was getting for his crimes. He ruined the streets and his product killed people. She preferred he had jail time to being beaten though.

A thought struck her and she stood straighter. That sexy criminal could be the man behind Kevin's disappearance for all she knew.

More than likely one of the two new men had been involved. She shuddered. She had more to fear from them than she'd originally thought. That bucket of ice-cold knowledge froze any lust she'd felt for the man.

Anger at them bled into every cell as she considered what might've happened to her brother. Kevin had been her hero, encouraging and coaching her as she'd worked to become an investigative journalist.

It'd worked. She'd become one, and it was all because of Kevin. But she'd lost him. Baltimore had lost his brilliance, his dedication in searching for truth and justice.

And the man she'd lusted over could be the reason her brother was missing. Rage rolled within her blood.

"Enough." Her bad boy's voice floated over to her.

The beating ended. Keyshawn lay on the ground, unmoving. The man she'd bumped into bent down and spoke to the dealer.

Suddenly realizing she'd almost left the safety of her hiding place as she'd unconsciously slipped forward to listen, Megan jolted her body to an abrupt halt and then retreated. She had to be careful to not be seen.

She flattened herself against the alley wall when they strode away. Oh how she wanted to follow them. They'd probably lead her to a boss faster than Keyshawn.

Keyshawn. She looked across the alley and wondered if he needed an ambulance. Even though he was a criminal, she couldn't leave him to die. Maybe if she helped him, he'd reciprocate.

Her opportunity passed before she could leave her hiding spot to cross the street. Two men appeared from the house and half carried, half dragged him inside.

His being on the street the next day was doubtful.

Noting the time on her watch, urgency overtook her. She had to leave in order to get her story on Councilman Thomas in on time. Her boss was only so flexible.

Without Keyshawn, her lead to anyone of importance moved to her pending file. However, she did have two new stories to investigate—the possible policemen taking a bribe and the enforcers sending a message.

She'd pick the organization apart bit by bit, if that was what it took for her to find her brother and for the Magician to reveal himself.

She nervously looked over her shoulder as she unlocked her SUV.

It was time to leave the area and her sexy enforcer behind.

*HIS CHOICE* is available now!

CPSIA information can be obtained
at www.ICGtesting.com
Printed in the USA
FSOW01n1458261117
41385FS

9 780990 916543